TARGETS OF OPPORTUNITY

*Spitfire Mavericks Thrillers
Book Seven*

D. R. Bailey

SAPERE
BOOKS

TARGETS OF OPPORTUNITY

Published by Sapere Books.

24 Trafalgar Road, Ilkley, LS29 8HH

saperebooks.com

ISBN: 978-0-85495-731-6

I would like to dedicate this book to my sister Elizabeth Bailey. She's not only a brilliant actress, director and writer, but a brilliant sister too. All my life Lizzie has been there for me in so many ways. I am eternally grateful for having known her and been fortunate enough to be her sibling.

CHAPTER ONE

Spring 1943

We were flying to the west of Thorpeness when it happened. My squadron, the Mavericks, had engaged several Focke-Wulf Fw 190s who had flown in over the English Channel, presumably from a base in Holland. Within a short space of time, the air was filled with the sound of gunfire and radio chatter from the fighter pilots. We outnumbered the Wulfs, but that didn't seem to deter them.

"Watch your back, Skipper," said Pilot Officer Jonty Butterworth as I suddenly clocked a Wulf behind me.

I rolled the Spitfire sideways as the German opened fire. Bullets zinged past the underbelly of my kite.

"That's the way to do it," said Jonty.

I pulled a tight turn and started to zig-zag. The Jerry stuck to my tail like a limpet in the most annoying fashion.

"Need some help there, Scottish?" said Pilot Officer Willie Cooper, using my nickname.

"No, of course not. I'm quite happy getting shot at," I replied sarcastically.

It was the usual banter. The three of us were good friends, and Willie and Jonty were usually my wingmen in the squadron.

The trouble with being a little too complacent is that it gets you into trouble eventually. Today was that day.

I turned again as the German fired another salvo. My hope that he might run out of ammo was not fulfilled. Once again he missed, but just by a whisker.

"Hang on, Scottish," said Willie.

"I'm trying," I told him, thinking I would perhaps try a loop-over.

As I pulled on the stick and throttled up, I realised too late that it was a mistake. The German had anticipated my move and fired again. Bullets ripped through the fuselage and hit the engine. It started smoking.

"Oh blast," I heard Jonty say, but I was too preoccupied.

The kite immediately lost power and began to dive. I hoped the German wouldn't try to finish me off as I reached to pull back the canopy.

"Bail, Skipper, bail!" shouted Jonty frantically.

"That's what I'm doing," I replied.

The wind hit me in the face as I opened the cockpit. I tried to keep the plane in a shallow dive to give myself a little more time. The roar of the wind in my ears was joined by the chatter of gunfire from the ongoing dogfights.

The ground rushed up below me at an alarming rate. There was no time to think about it. I rolled out of the cockpit and was caught by the wind. The doomed Spitfire dropped away beneath me.

I pulled the ripcord and felt a jolt as the parachute opened.

"Damn and blast it," I said under my breath.

Looking up, I saw Willie's plane make short work of the Wulf that had shot me down. I took a grim satisfaction from that. As I began to float earthwards, I saw my Spitfire crash into the ground and explode. It was a damn shame.

My thoughts drifted in those moments before I hit the ground myself. I thought of my wife, Section Officer Angelica Mackennelly. Her smiling face flashed into my mind's eye.

"Come back safe, Angus," she had said before I'd left on the sortie.

I'd told her that I would.

Looking on the bright side, at least I hadn't been shot down in enemy territory. That would have been a completely different story. My attention was forced back to the present as the ground sped towards me. As I steered the parachute towards a field and, hopefully, a flat landing, I tried to recall how to land without breaking a leg.

I hit the ground and rolled. Winded but thankfully intact, I closed my eyes for a moment, trying to catch my breath. I heard a Spitfire buzz low overhead, and then it was gone. It was probably Jonty or Willie making sure I was all right.

When I opened my eyes, I became aware of the tines of a pitchfork inches from my face.

"I've got you, you German swine… Don't move or I'll spear you, so help me God," said a young man holding tightly onto the implement. I squinted up at him to get a better look. He appeared to be in his early twenties with a thick shock of blond hair and dressed in farm overalls.

I was about to open my mouth to explain somewhat volubly that I was not German when there was a shout from across the field.

"Matthew, what in the blazes are you playing at?"

Shading my eyes, I could see another man, obviously a farmer, striding towards us.

"I've got one of them Germans, Dad! It's all right — I've got him covered," Matthew informed the newcomer.

His father grabbed the pitchfork out of his hand and flung it away in disgust.

"Dad, what are you doing? He's going to escape!" the lad protested.

The man, who looked to be in his fifties with grey hair and eyes to match, shook his head. "You bloody daft tussock,

Matthew! He's not German — he's a British pilot," he said, laughing.

He reached down and held out a hand, which I took gratefully, letting him pull me up.

"I'm sorry about that, sir," he said when I was standing. "My son … well, he's a little overenthusiastic, if you know what I mean."

"It's quite all right," I said. "An easy mistake to make." I held out my hand and he shook it. "Flight Lieutenant Angus Mackennelly from the Maverick Squadron at your service," I told him.

"Jarrod Carpenter at yours, sir, and grateful *for* your service," he replied, smiling. Then he turned to the unfortunate Matthew and scolded him further. "You hear that, Matthew? A flight lieutenant in the RAF keeping our skies safe, and here you are waving a bloody pitchfork in his face, you silly gannet."

"But Harry down the road caught a German last week…" the lad began, unwilling to give in so easily.

"Never mind that — I saw this officer shot down and jump out of his Spitfire covered in British decals," his father told him.

After a moment, Matthew gave me a sheepish grin. "Sorry about that, sir," he said.

"It's no bother, really," I replied.

Having satisfactorily settled the subject of my allegiance with his son, Jarrod turned his mind to more practical matters. "I suppose you might be wanting to get back to your unit," he said.

"Yes, I don't suppose you have a telephone?" I asked him. "I can call for some transport."

"That we do," he replied. "Not all of us have them around here, but my wife, Molly, bless her soul, she insists on all the mod cons. We'll take you back to the farmhouse; I'm sure she'll have dinner in the oven and can spare a bite or two."

"I don't want to put you to any trouble," I demurred.

Jarrod wasn't having any of it. "No trouble, sir. We don't get a lot of visitors and Molly will be glad of the company."

"Well, if you insist…"

I soon found myself sitting on the back of a farm trailer, along with Jarrod, while Matthew drove the tractor to the farmhouse. I gazed across the fields and up into the cloudless sky. The planes had all gone. I wondered what Angelica had said when she'd heard I'd had to bail. She would have known, as she listened in on the comms.

"It's a beautiful day for it anyhow," said Jarrod.

"To get shot down, you mean?"

He laughed. "Well, I wasn't quite meaning that, sir, no."

I asked him about the farm and how they were faring during the war. He had been a farmer all his life, and his son would take over the farm one day. It sounded like an idyllic life, but probably an arduous one for all that.

Matthew brought the tractor to a stop in the cobbled courtyard. On one side was a two-storey farmhouse with a thatched roof and pink pebble-dashed walls. On the other two sides were open-sided barns with some pigs and goats in pens.

Molly Carpenter bustled out at once to greet us. She was a slightly plump, dark-haired woman in her mid-forties with kind eyes.

"Hello," she said. "Have we got company?"

"Flight Lieutenant Angus Mackennelly," I said, introducing myself again. "Your husband here kindly offered to let me use your telephone."

"Aye," said Jarrod. "And stopped that young fool from skewering him with a pitchfork!"

"Oh dear," said Molly, glancing affectionately at her errant son. "Well, you'd better come in. The kettle's on and I'll make some tea. I'm sure you must be hungry after your journey…"

She kept up a stream of chatter as I followed her in through the open door of the farmhouse kitchen. It was spacious with stone flags, shelves full of crockery, and a large stove which radiated heat into the room.

I sat down at her bidding and accepted a cup of tea. Then I managed to interrupt her for long enough to call Banley Airfield and ask them to send Sergeant Bruce Gordon, my batman, to pick me up.

"You must stay for a spot of dinner," Molly said once this was accomplished.

I sipped my tea and tried to refuse. "I don't want to impose —" I began.

"Oh, nonsense. It's no imposition, is it, Jarrod?" she said, cutting me short.

"No, no, absolutely not," Jarrod averred.

"My batman will be here soon," I added, trying once more.

"Then he shall eat with us too," said Molly, brooking no opposition.

"All right," I said, realising I was fighting a losing battle against their generosity.

Without asking, she poured me another cup of tea and supplied a large slice of fruit cake. "For while you're waiting."

Matthew, who had overcome his shyness after mistaking me for a German, proceeded to bombard me with questions about the RAF. I kept him suitably entertained until we heard the sound of a jeep outside.

"That'll be my batman," I said, standing up.

However, instead of Gordon, Angelica appeared in the doorway. As soon as she saw me, she flung herself into my arms.

"Oh, Angus, I was so worried about you. Thank God you're safe," she said, oblivious to everyone else.

A discreet cough from Gordon caused us to draw apart. He was standing in the kitchen with a smile on his face. Matthew, on the other hand, was staring at us open-mouthed.

"This is my wife, Section Officer Angelica Mackennelly," I said, belatedly introducing her to the others.

"Pleased to meet you," said Molly.

"Aye, and it looks like you're pleased to meet your young fella, there," added Jarrod with a chuckle.

"Oh, leave her be," Molly told him. "It's nice to see a bit of young love in these terrible times."

Angelica blushed, but Gordon, as always, came to the rescue.

"I'm glad we found you, sir," he said smoothly. "Sorry we took a while getting here, but if you're ready to —"

"Oh no," said Molly firmly. "You're all staying for dinner — it's all arranged."

"Ah, well, in that case," said Gordon graciously, "I shall defer to your generous hospitality."

"Sit yourselves down," said Molly, becoming businesslike. "Matthew, help me get the table set for our guests."

We spent a happy hour consuming slices of roast pork, potatoes and vegetables. Molly dealt us all generous portions. I didn't like to decline, though I knew that times were tough with rationing. Farmers probably did better than most.

Having discovered that Gordon had fought in the Great War, Matthew peppered him with questions until his mother silenced him.

"Now, Matthew, these good people don't want to be bothered by all your silly questions. Give them a bit of peace."

"It's quite all right, Mrs Carpenter," said Gordon, who had weathered the inquisition with good humour.

"He wants to go to war, but we need him on the farm," explained Jarrod.

"War's not all it's cracked up to be," Gordon replied.

Jarrod nodded. "That's what I keep telling him. I was in the Great War myself."

There followed a discussion about which regiment and battles they'd been in. Angelica squeezed my hand under the table while we consumed a rather delicious apple pie and custard.

When the meal was over, Molly let us leave somewhat reluctantly. I thought we'd perhaps been something of a novelty or a distraction from daily life on the farm.

"I'm glad you're safe," said Angelica as she snuggled up to me in the back of the jeep.

"Me too," I replied with a smile.

Gordon drove us back to Amberly Manor, where we were billeted, since it was late and there was no purpose in going to the airfield. Angelica and I occupied a small suite courtesy of Lady Barbara Amberly, who owned the house. Her husband had been killed in action, leaving her a widow. She had not been in evidence for several months, having been recruited as a spy for MI6. I wasn't too unhappy about that, since Barbara and I had a history which I was sure both Angelica and I would rather forget.

As we lay together in bed, I felt Angelica's arms go around me.

"I'm quite cross with you for getting shot down, darling," she murmured, though she didn't sound cross.

"Well, I hardly did it on purpose," I told her.

"Even so, I think you should make it up to me…" Her lips curled into a familiar smile.

"Is that a fact?"

"Yes," she whispered, her lips touching mine. "It is."

The following morning, we joined Jonty and Willie for breakfast in the dining room. I accepted a plate of eggs, spam and beans on toast. Bacon had become a rarer commodity with rationing.

"What-ho, Skipper," said Jonty. "Got back safely, I see."

"Yes, indeed," I replied, sipping my tea.

"Glad to see you, Scottish. I got that Jerry for you," said Willie.

"Yes, I saw and thanks," I told him.

"Wonder what Bentley will have to say about your kite," mused Jonty as he tucked into his breakfast with his usual gusto. I had to admit I was not looking forward to reporting to Squadron Leader Richard Bentley, commanding officer of Squadron 696.

"I should imagine he'll be glad Angus got out of it alive," Angelica cut in coolly.

"Last time I brought my Spitfire back shot up, he didn't half tear me off a strip," said Jonty.

"That's because you're always doing something bloody stupid," said Willie.

"There is that, I suppose," Jonty admitted reluctantly.

Thankfully, the two of them didn't start a squabble, something they were wont to do, and we managed to finish our breakfast in relative peace.

I was pretty sure that Bentley would summon me when I got to Banley, so I was hardly surprised to discover his adjutant, Section Officer Audrey Wilmington, awaiting our arrival.

"Bentley…" she began.

"Wants to see me?" I finished for her.

She smiled. "Yes, he does."

Angelica accompanied us to Bentley's office, which was in the main building that also housed the control tower. Audrey was about the same age as Angelica, and they had become firm friends.

When we arrived at Bentley's door, Angelica kissed me lightly.

"See you later," she said.

Audrey held the door open for me to enter. Bentley was at his desk, undertaking his pipe of doom routine. This consisted of emptying out the used tobacco, scraping the bowl, tamping in a fresh batch of tobacco and then lighting it. I waited patiently until he was puffing away satisfactorily, filling the room with clouds of smoke. He finally looked up and seemed a little surprised to see me.

"Ah, Angus, just the person I wanted to see," he said, smoothing his handlebar moustache.

"Sir," I replied, saluting.

He indicated a chair, and I sat down.

"Had a spot of bother, I gather," he said, eyeing me with interest.

"As I'm sure you know, sir, I got shot down and had to bail."

"Yes, indeed, and I'm mighty glad you made it out alive," he said.

"I'm mighty glad too, sir," I said, relieved that I wasn't going to receive the Jonty treatment. Not that I had expected it, but with Bentley, you never quite knew.

"We'll have to get you another Spitfire," he said. "But in the meantime, I imagine you'll have to use one of the spares."

"Yes, sir."

He paused. "You'll continue the patrols with M Flight," he said at length. "But very shortly there'll be some new orders coming down the line."

"Oh?"

"Yes, I can't say anything now, but it will involve sorties across the Channel."

"I see."

I wasn't too enthusiastic about the idea. We'd flown sorties into Northern France before, and they were always rather fraught affairs. This was on top of escort and other secret missions that M Flight had undertaken.

I had run out of fuel on one occasion, flying over France, and had only managed to make it back to Blighty due to the efforts of the French Resistance.

"Needs must, Angus," said Bentley. "You know the drill — what those blasted Johnnies at Fighter Command want, they get."

Bentley seemed to be in a continual battle with the top brass, who alternated between sending even more pilots to the Mavericks and wanting to disband it, much to the CO's annoyance.

At the moment, our kudos with Fighter Command was riding high on the back of capturing the Ace Raider, a Focke-Wulf pilot who had been giving us a headache, attacking coastal towns. We'd also prevented the assassination of Maria Von Schmidt, the wife of a prominent nuclear scientist who was currently in America. Maria was staying with us in a house on the airfield with Olga Zielinska, an MI6 agent, acting as her bodyguard.

"Yes, sir. Well, I'll look forward to whatever it is then," I said a little acidly.

If Bentley noted my tone, he let it pass. "Yes, jolly good, and try not to get shot down again, there's a good chap. Only so many spare Spitfires to go around, plus I need you to keep leading the flight."

He smiled at me affably. I took this to be a dismissal and left the office, only to be immediately intercepted by my wife.

"What did Bentley want?" she asked me.

"I swear you were hiding around the corner," I replied.

"I can neither confirm nor deny such an allegation," she said, laughing.

She tucked her arm into mine and we walked together to the edge of the airfield. There was a particular bench we'd come to regard as our own. It looked out onto the fields, although the airfield itself was surrounded by high wire at Bentley's insistence following more than one attempt at espionage in our squadron.

I told her what Bentley had said. "He was glad I got back safely," I informed her.

"And so he should be," she replied.

"There's some new type of operation in the offing, involving going into Northern France."

"Oh," she said and was quiet for a few moments.

While Angelica was inured to my flying in combat, she didn't exactly like it. She lived with the prospect of losing me every day. Flying over France increased the risk of being shot down by a large margin.

"Well," she said eventually, "you'll just have to make sure you come back then, won't you?"

"I will, won't I?" I said with a smile.

"Or else I'll…"

"Never forgive me?" I completed the sentence, since this was her usual response.

"No," she said. "I'll be very sad indeed."

I held her close, and she sighed. I knew I would never really understand her pain, because I wasn't the one being left behind. Once in the Spitfire, all my focus was on the task that lay ahead.

At length we returned to the dispersal hut, since M Flight had another patrol to fly. The pilots were at their ease. Jonty and Willie were playing chess while Percy, Jonty's parrot, watched them with interest. The parrot had fortunately remained in his cage since Jonty had taken him up for a spin in his Spitfire and endured Bentley's wrath as a result.

"All right," I said. "Time for another jaunt around East Anglia."

I picked six pilots to fly with me, including Willie and Jonty. They were some of my usual crew: Pilot Officer Dylan Davies, Pilot Officer Arjun Sharma, Pilot Officer Jean Tarbon and Flying Officer Olek Bartnick. Dylan was from Wales, Arjun from India, Jean from Canada and Olek from Poland. One could say we were a diverse bunch.

"You can lead another patrol later," I told Flying Officer Tomas Jezek, who was Czechoslovakian and a good friend. We'd undertaken some spy-catching capers together. I trusted him to ably lead a flight, and he'd done so many times before.

"Sure, Scottish," he said with a smile. "More time for me to have some English tea."

This was one of his favourite beverages, and he imbibed it at every opportunity. I led my flight out onto the airfield, stopping only to say goodbye to Angelica.

I took her in my arms and kissed her.

"Come back safe," she whispered.

"I will."

"I love you."

"I love you too."

She blew me a kiss as I turned away and headed for my kite.

"Why does it have to be blasted East Anglia all the time?" Jonty complained as I caught up with him.

"Don't you like it?" I asked.

"Good God, no. It's a dreadfully dull sort of place and completely flat," he replied in disgust.

Jonty had developed a distaste for provincial living, although he put up with it. He came from aristocratic stock and had led the high life before the war by all accounts.

"Stop moaning. Orders are orders," Willie told him.

"I wasn't precisely moaning."

"Well, it sounded like moaning…"

Anticipating yet another argument between Willie and Jonty, I left them to it and headed swiftly for my Spitfire. I climbed up onto the wing of my kite and was then helped into the cockpit by Leading Aircraftman Dominic Redwood.

"It's all right and tight for you, sir — she's been well maintained and is ready for action," he told me.

"Thanks, Techie," I said.

"Sorry that you lost your old plane," he said, helping me to strap in.

"You win some, you lose some," I replied philosophically.

"Hopefully you'll win some today then, sir."

"I hope so too."

Redwood jumped down from the wing and I fired up the Spitfire. The Merlin engine roared to life, joining the noise of the other five Spitfires in the patrol. It was a beautiful sound.

We taxied to the end of the runway and took off. Once we were airborne, the others settled into formation.

I set a course for Clacton and kept my eyes on the horizon. We scanned the sky constantly for bandits, which made it difficult to fully appreciate the clear blue, cloudless day. It was quite a warm spring day, too, though we didn't feel it up in the clouds.

Clacton passed beneath us, and I turned northwards, intending to fly up the coast as far as Cromer and head for home. It was an all too familiar run — Jonty was correct on that score. We had patrolled it many times in pursuit of the Ace Raider. However, single-plane incursions had dropped off. Instead, Jerry seemed to want to send over several to make a nuisance of themselves.

As we passed over Aldeburgh and headed for Lowestoft, there wasn't another aircraft in sight.

"I don't think we'll be seeing Jerry today, Skipper," said Jonty after a while.

"Here we go again. Must you do that?" Willie protested at once.

"Do what?"

"Jinx it by saying we won't see any Germans," said Willie. "Every time you do, some bloody Jerries appear out of nowhere."

"I say, steady on —" Jonty began, but his objections were cut short.

"Bandits at three o'clock, coming in fast," said Dylan, who was pretty sharp-eyed when it came to spotting enemy planes.

"See, I told you!" said Willie in disgust.

"Never mind all that," I said. "Break, break, engage."

We peeled off to meet the incoming Wulfs — six enemy planes, closing in rapidly. The Germans seemed to have come for a fight, as they made a beeline towards us.

As usual, I picked a mark and tried to manoeuvre so I could get behind him; however, the German was doing the same thing. It was a matter of who would be quicker.

Gunfire broke out between the other planes as I headed straight for him, and he for me. Who would break off first?

As it happened, neither of us did. As we got within touching distance, I passed right under him and pulled a tight turn. I looked back and saw he was doing the same. We tried again in a ridiculously foolish action, heading for each other, almost as if we were playing a game of chicken.

I had had enough and let rip a salvo which he evaded easily, but it put him off his stroke. He turned his kite away, and I managed to get behind him after all.

He quickly went into a steep dive. I followed, then he made a steep climb. I stuck on his tail and fired a couple more times, missing on both occasions.

"Yes!" I heard Dylan say triumphantly. "I've got him!"

That was one down. Five to go. Meanwhile, the Wulf I was pursuing was weaving this way and that, trying to shake me off.

"Come on, damn you," I muttered, hoping he would make a mistake.

He suddenly flew skywards at a tremendous rate. I didn't follow but turned away, knowing he was trying to loop over and catch me. I wasn't playing that game.

As I came out of the turn, the Jerry was nowhere to be seen. The others in the flight were seeing off the remaining Wulfs. Beneath us lay the smoking remains of the one shot down by Dylan.

The rest of my patrol flew towards me, ready to form up. Suddenly, Olek shouted, "Scottish, watch out!"

I looked up to see the Wulf I'd been chasing bearing down on me in a steep dive. He'd come out of nowhere. I banked on instinct as he opened fire. The bullets missed my plane by inches. However, Jonty was on the ball.

Tracers streamed out from his guns, hitting the German amidships. The Wulf exploded into a fireball.

"Ha! That'll teach you, you rotten Hun," exclaimed Jonty jubilantly.

"Thanks, Jonty," I said, rather relieved at his speedy reflexes.

Was I getting slow, I wondered? I watched what was left of the stricken plane smash into the ground.

"Form up," I said to the others. "Let's go home."

I put the doubts out of my mind. Two near misses in as many days were bound to rattle me. It was simply bad luck.

I set a course for Banley, and Jonty burst into song.

"Oh, I went out to Clacton Town for some Germans to find me. The Jerries came, we shot them down and left them all behind me…"

"Must you do that?" said Willie, who invariably complained about Jonty's singing.

Jonty was undeterred and continued with his ballad. "The Jerry thought he'd got a plan to dive onto our Skipper. But I was ready for his tricks and hit him with a ripper…"

"Please, Scottish, for the love of God, can't you order him to stop?" Willie pleaded.

I sometimes did intervene, but on this occasion, I declined.

"I think he's deserved it, Kiwi, don't you?"

"That's a matter of opinion!"

Jonty wasn't fazed and was well into his fourth verse. Willie subsided as we made our way back to Banley.

As luck would have it, we passed over several fields of livestock from local farms near Banley. It was then that Jonty, buoyed up by his recent success, decided to kick up a lark.

"Jonty," I said as he dropped out of formation, "what are you doing?"

"Just having some fun, Skipper," he informed me as he headed for the nearest field full of cows.

"Oh God," said Willie. "Here we go…"

"Jonty, I don't think you should —" I began, but it was no use. Jonty in full flow was impossible to curb.

"It's all right, Skipper, you'll see," he said gaily.

He opened up his throttle and roared over the field as low as he could go. The cows scattered in every direction as he passed over them at full pelt. My heart sank as I noticed the farmer in his tractor shaking his fist.

"Oh, Heavens," said Arjun. "Now we're in trouble."

"We?" said Willie hotly. "No, not us! Just Jonty!"

"Jonty," I said firmly, regaining control of the situation, "I order you to return to formation at once!"

"Wilco, Skipper," he said airily, settling back into position as if nothing untoward had occurred. "I say, that was a jolly good laugh. Did you see the way they all scattered?"

"I don't think the farmer was impressed," put in Jean.

"Really? Oh blast!" said Jonty.

"We'll discuss this when we land," I told him.

Jonty subsided, although it was impossible to keep him down for long. He was completely irrepressible. My first thought, however, was that if this latest prank came to Bentley's ears, there would be hell to pay. I wasn't optimistic about him not finding out, either.

We landed in short order. I taxied to my standing, killed the engine and jumped down from my kite.

Angelica pelted over to meet me and hurled herself into my arms.

"Oof!" I said. I had never quite got used to her boisterous greetings.

"I'm glad you're safe," she said. "I was worried when you encountered those Wulfs."

"I'm fine, thanks to Jonty," I said. "Talking of which, I need to have a word with him."

"Oh dear. What's he done now?"

"Only gone and buzzed a herd of cows," I told her as I started after Jonty and Willie, who were heading back to the hut. Angelica slipped her hand into mine.

"Oh, Jonty, what a silly boy," she said, in the manner of a mother talking about her favourite child.

"Jonty!" I called after him. "Hang on."

"Skipper?" he said, turning to me with an innocent expression.

"Jonty," I said, "whatever possessed you to do something so bloody stupid?"

He shrugged. "I don't know, Skipper. It just seemed like a good idea at the time."

"Well, for God's sake, curb your blasted antics. All we need is for Bentley to find out..." I trailed off since I had spied the CO striding towards us, along with Audrey.

"Oh well," said Jonty, "he wasn't there, and what he doesn't know won't hurt him."

"I wouldn't be so sure," I replied as I clocked Bentley's demeanour, which looked decidedly choleric.

When he arrived, he stopped and took out his pipe. "Ah," he said in a deceptively mild tone, "Butterworth."

"Sir," said Jonty, snapping a salute. We all followed suit.

Jonty watched him empty, scrape and fill the pipe with some trepidation.

"I just had a lengthy telephone call from a Farmer Brown," said Bentley, lighting the pipe and taking a few puffs.

"Really, sir?" said Jonty.

"Do you know why he called me, Butterworth?" Bentley asked, continuing to give the appearance of unruffled calm.

I was not taken in by this because I could see a twitch developing below his right eye, a sure sign of impending wrath.

"I'm not sure I do, sir. I'm not familiar with the individual in question," said Jonty.

Bentley ignored this, although I noticed the twitch below his eye becoming more pronounced.

"He called me on account of his favourite cow, Daisy. I wonder if you're acquainted with *her*?" said Bentley.

"Well, sir, I'm not really familiar with any farm animals, if I'm honest."

I glanced at Willie, whose face held an expression of justified foreboding. Jonty was treading on thin ice, and any moment now the ice was going to crack.

"Hmm. I see. And do you know *why* he wanted to speak to me about his cow?"

Bentley's tone was ramping up several notches. I knew it would not be long before he cut loose.

"No, sir. I —" Jonty began

"No, sir? No, sir!" thundered Bentley suddenly, brandishing his pipe in an accusatory fashion in Jonty's startled face. "Well, you *should* be bloody well familiar with his cows, since you practically had tea with them earlier. I'll tell you why Farmer Brown called me, Butterworth. He called me because his favourite bloody cow, Daisy, had a cardiac arrest in the field when you elected to spook his prized dairy herd with your blasted Spitfire."

"Oh… I… How did he know it was me?" said Jonty with something akin to foolhardy valour.

I could see Willie imperceptibly shaking his head at this.

"Because the insignia of the squadron is painted on the side of your damn plane, you idiot. The insignia that *you* designed!" roared Bentley. "There's not another pilot in this squadron who would do something so damnably foolish."

"I —" began Jonty.

"Do not," said Bentley through gritted teeth, "attempt to deny it."

The CO was fairly bristling now and puffing on his pipe at an alarming rate. I wondered if he was going to emulate the ill-fated cow and have a heart attack himself.

"Sir, perhaps what I did was rather unwise," said Jonty lamely.

"Unwise? Un-bloody-wise? I'd say it was the hare-brained act of an imbecile," said Bentley, not mincing his words.

"Yes, sir," said Jonty, since there was nothing else he could say in the face of such a scathing assessment.

Bentley took a few more puffs of his pipe. This had a calming effect, and I was relieved to see his eye had stopped twitching.

"What possessed you?" asked Bentley.

"I don't know, sir. It just came to me…" Jonty trailed off.

"Well, we'd all be a damn sight better off if you ceased to act on every daft notion that comes to you, don't you think?"

"Yes, sir," said Jonty.

"Your pranks are idiotic enough at the best of times, but this particular farrago will cost the RAF money, since Farmer Brown has demanded compensation. I will have to pay up, as the last thing I need is the top brass coming down here demanding to know why my pilots are engaging in the most addled tomfoolery this side of London. Perhaps in future you could refrain from scaring animals with your plane, Butterworth?"

"Yes, sir, it won't happen again," Jonty averred.

Willie rolled his eyes at this.

"Harrumph," grunted Bentley. "I've heard it all before. If it does happen again, then it will be coming out of your pay packet. Understood?"

"Yes, sir."

"Dismissed," said Bentley wearily.

Jonty saluted and left with Willie in unseemly haste.

Bentley sighed and turned his attention to me. "Is there nothing you can do to stop that fellow and his blasted pranks, Angus?" he asked.

"Believe me, sir, I've tried and I will speak to him again," I said without much conviction.

"The times I've thought of kicking the bounder out of the squadron, but where else could he go?" said Bentley. "He'd end up right back here again anyway. So, we're stuck with him."

"Yes, sir."

"Anyway," said Bentley, "some good will come out of it. Since we're paying for it, I've ordered that farmer to deliver the cow to the mess. That way, we'll all benefit from some roast beef and so on."

"An excellent idea, sir," I said.

"Yes, but I don't want Butterworth thinking he can improve the mess supplies with his foolish antics," said Bentley.

"Indeed not."

"Very well … carry on, and well done on shooting down a couple of Jerries," he said.

"Thank you, sir. It was Butterworth and Davies who shot them down," I told him.

"I suppose that partially redeems Butterworth, but not entirely … not by a long chalk!" he said.

Without further ado, Bentley strode away with Audrey by his side.

Angelica burst into laughter as soon as Bentley was out of earshot.

"Really, darling," I said, "it's not funny."

"Oh, but it is," she said. "Jonty's face!"

Her laughter was infectious, and soon I was laughing too.

CHAPTER TWO

Jonty's misdemeanour was soon forgotten; in the past, he'd pulled some even sillier pranks than that.

As a bonus, there was beef on the menu in various guises at the mess for several days. Jonty remarked upon it one lunchtime when we were enjoying some rather delicious beef stew, mashed potatoes and vegetables.

"I say," said Jonty, "this is rather splendid. All this beef all of a sudden — I wonder where they got it from."

Willie stared at him. "Really?" he said. "You've no idea?"

"Well, it's not like beef is going begging around here."

Angelica shook her head and laughed. "Oh, Jonty, you're quite impossible, you silly boy," she said.

"Try and have a think, Jonty, as to where they might have come by a cow recently," I said.

Jonty looked perplexed for a moment, and then the penny dropped. "You don't mean … oh! Oh, I say," he said.

"Don't you go getting any ideas!" I told him.

"Absolutely not, Skipper. I will never buzz a herd of cows again," he said.

"Or sheep," said Willie. "Or pigs … goats … chickens…"

Angelica burst out laughing, and we all followed suit.

"Dear Jonty," she said at length. "Where would we be without you?"

"We wouldn't be getting roasted by Bentley for a start," said Willie.

Jonty looked inclined to take him up on this but was forestalled by Audrey, who came up to our table.

"Sir," she said to me, "there are two gentlemen…"

"The Marx Brothers!" said Angelica at once.

"Yes," said Audrey, smiling.

"Back again, like the bad pennies they are," Angelica continued.

The Marx Brothers were two spies from Military Intelligence. I had dubbed them 'Harpo' and 'Chico' on account of not knowing their real names. As far as I knew, they were not aware of this. The two agents were not favourites of mine or Angelica's, since their arrival usually meant there was a difficult, if not impossible, mission in the offing. Bentley went practically apoplectic at the mention of them. Suffice it to say he had cause on account of their dissembling behaviour. With the Marx Brothers, nothing was ever as it seemed.

"I'll just finish my lunch and we'll be along," I said, unwilling to forgo the rest of my stew.

"Yes, of course," said Audrey, and she perched on a chair at our table. "Is that the cow which…"

"Yes, it is," said Willie, waving his fork to cut her off.

We all started laughing again. Then, when I had finished my lunch, Angelica and I accompanied Audrey to the main building and the familiar room in which I'd met the Marx Brothers several times before. It had also served as our HQ during recent secret missions.

The two agents were sitting at ease, smoking cigarettes. Both wore dark suits and white shirts, though one had a blue tie, the other red. Their fawn trench coats were draped over the backs of their chairs, and their hats rested on the table. I didn't smoke and nor did Angelica, but we had become inured to the tobacco cloud that accompanied them everywhere they went.

"Ah, Flight Lieutenant and Section Officer Mackennelly, long time no see," said Harpo. Neither of them got up, but that was their way. I was used it by now.

"Pull up a chair," said Chico, motioning for us to sit.

I did so and waited while they smoked in silence. Angelica, however, didn't possess my tolerance as far as the Marx Brothers were concerned.

"What is it this time?" she demanded, fixing them with a baleful stare.

"Oh dear," said Harpo.

"She's not very pleased to see us," said Chico.

They frequently operated as a double act, so we were quite used to this behaviour.

"And as to long time no see," Angelica continued, "it's not very long at all, by my recollection."

"Is it not?" said Chico laconically.

"Time passes so quickly in this war," added Harpo.

I could see that Angelica was quickly losing her cool. One reason for her annoyance with regards to the spies was that they invariably placed the squadron in all kinds of danger. She felt them to be quite reckless, as she had informed me on more than one occasion.

"I assume you're here for a particular reason," I said in slightly less belligerent tones than my wife.

"You assume correctly," said Harpo.

"He's got it," said Chico with a smile.

"Which is?" I said, hoping that we'd finally get an answer.

Harpo took a pull on his cigarette and let the smoke curl skywards before answering. "Offensive," he said.

"I beg your pardon?"

"We want your flight to go on the offensive... Well, it's not just us, naturally. This is all coming from the top."

"Could you possibly elaborate on that?" I asked, slightly perplexed.

"Indeed, we can. You'll be carrying out sorties over Northern France and possibly Belgium and Holland too. Bentley will be calling a briefing. He'll explain it all there."

"In which case —" said Angelica, firing up.

"You're wondering why we wanted to see you," said Harpo, interjecting.

"Yes," Angelica replied through gritted teeth.

"Since we were here for the briefing, we wanted to give you advance warning," said Chico.

"Advance warning of what?"

"Of the fact that we've also got something else lined up for the Mavericks."

This was getting us nowhere. "Would you care to share?" I asked him.

"I'm afraid that as much as we'd like to, we can't at this point," said Harpo. "But it's going to be a lot of fun."

Angelica rolled her eyes.

"'Fun' isn't exactly the word that springs to mind with any of our previous missions," I retorted sarcastically.

The two agents were unperturbed and continued to smoke their cigarettes in the most insouciant fashion.

"Take it from us, we think you and your chaps are going to like it," said Harpo.

"That remains to be seen," I told him.

"He's such a sceptic," Chico said to his colleague.

"Indeed," Harpo agreed.

I could see that Angelica was becoming immensely irritated and decided the best course of action was to beat a hasty retreat.

"If there's nothing else?" I asked them.

The two of them shook their heads in unison.

"No. See you at the briefing," said Harpo affably.

"Right."

"Toodle pip," he continued.

"Chin-chin," said Chico.

I nodded and hustled Angelica out of the room before she could say something untoward. The two spies remained seated, smoking their cigarettes as if they didn't have a care in the world.

"I swear that one day I'll —" said Angelica hotly once we were outside the main building.

"You'll what?" I interrupted, catching her in my arms.

"I'll do those two a mischief! They make me so cross sometimes," she continued.

"Will this help?" I asked her, planting a kiss on her lips.

"It certainly goes some way towards it," she said when we pulled apart again. "But I think you'll have to try it again to make sure."

I laughed, and then a discreet cough interrupted us. It was Audrey.

"There's a briefing, sir, in the hangar in about twenty minutes," she said.

I wasn't surprised to hear this after our meeting with the Marx Brothers.

"Thank you, Audrey," I said.

We made our way to the hangar while Audrey returned to the main building. We arrived to find all the pilots and ground crew assembled from both M Flight and the main squadron, led by Flight Lieutenant Judd.

"What-ho, Skipper," said Jonty as soon as he saw us. "Any idea what's afoot?"

"To be honest, no," I told him.

He looked disappointed but persevered. "Didn't you go to see those two spy Johnnies?" he asked.

"Yes, we did," Angelica cut in, saving me the trouble of explaining it further. "Much use that was. They didn't tell us anything."

"Oh blast," said Jonty.

"You'll find out soon enough," Willie told him. "Here comes Bentley."

Sure enough, Bentley strode into the hangar, along with Audrey and the Marx Brothers. "At ease," he said, taking to the podium placed there for his use.

He immediately took out his pipe and began the familiar routine. We all waited patiently, including the Marx Brothers, who smoked their cigarettes and looked around nonchalantly.

Bentley finished filling his pipe and lit it. Only once he was puffing away on it satisfactorily did he elect to speak.

"I've called you all here to inform you that we've been given some new operational orders," he said. "Fighter Command wants us to take the fight to the enemy, in order to cause whatever disruption we can to their forces in France and the Low Countries. As such, you will seek out and attack what we might term 'targets of opportunity'."

He paused to allow this to sink in. Jonty put up his hand.

Bentley fixed him with a jaundiced eye. "Yes, Butterworth?"

"If I might ask, sir, what do you mean by targets of opportunity?" said Jonty.

Bentley's eye developed an immediate twitch. He puffed furiously on his pipe, which seemed to calm his temper.

"I was about to explain," he said acidly. "However, since you ask, Butterworth, it means that you can attack what you damn well please."

He paused to let this sink in before adding, "I should have thought that some of you would relish the idea of roaming unfettered across the enemy landscape doing exactly what you want."

He looked directly at Jonty as he said this, who suddenly seemed to find that his collar was too tight.

"However, for clarification, what we mean are *military targets* or those targets which might be of use to the military. That includes trains, enemy encampments, installations, convoys of troops and so on."

The CO paused again, and his gaze fell once more upon Jonty.

"What it doesn't mean, just for the record, is attacking farmers, their livestock, the general populace or anything else you might think would be fun to shoot at just to kick up a lark. Do I make myself clear, Butterworth?" he barked in his best parade-ground voice.

"Yes, sir, perfectly, sir," said Jonty, snapping to attention.

"And that goes for the rest of you," Bentley continued, pointing the stem of his pipe at the assembled party. He paused to take a puff before continuing, "I will ask our colleagues here from MI6 to explain a little further."

Harpo and Chico, who had been listening to this with interest, simultaneously discarded their cigarettes and stepped forward.

"As I'm sure you probably know, the German Sixth Army surrendered to the Russians at Stalingrad in February," Harpo began. "According to intelligence reports, this is a bitter blow to the German High Command, particularly Hitler himself."

I glanced at Angelica. We had heard the news of the defeat with no small spark of joy and a burgeoning hope.

"As a result, it seems a good idea to capitalise on this defeat by harrying Jerry a little more on the home front, as it were," said Chico. "Hence the idea of flying across the Channel, picking a target, and causing as much mayhem as you can."

I had some questions about the manner in which this was to be carried out, but the Marx Brothers were ahead of me.

"We know you've previously flown Rhubarbs and Rodeos," said Harpo.

The Rhubarb was a two-plane mission, the Rodeo a fighter sweep, both designed to lure out the Luftwaffe. Neither of these was popular with the pilots. I'd been shot down on a Rhubarb.

"We're not suggesting either of those," said Chico. "We're also not suggesting you try to tempt out the Luftwaffe — quite the contrary. You need to go in, hit a target and get out, preferably without engaging the Luftwaffe at all."

This did somewhat clear things up, but they hadn't finished.

"We will leave operational issues to you. Squadron Leader Bentley and the flight leaders will decide on the number of planes and the plan of attack for each sortie. We will endeavour to supply intelligence on likely targets, then you take your pick," said Harpo.

"It goes without saying that you need to keep all that on the Q.T.," added Chico. "The codename for this series of missions will be Operation Wagtail."

I couldn't quite fathom the reason for that name, but we'd certainly had some worse ones. Operation Fish Bait was a notable codename to which Bentley had taken great exception.

Bentley glanced at them when they didn't say anything further. He decided they must have finished and took over the briefing again.

"Are there any questions?" he asked, looking directly at Jonty.

There was silence. Jonty was unlikely to try his luck a second time.

"Very well," Bentley said. "Flight leaders, come and see me once you've had a chance to think about how you want to approach Operation Wagtail. Dismissed."

He left the podium in short order along with Audrey and the Marx Brothers.

"Well," said Angelica once they had gone, "looks like you've got some planning to do."

"Yes," I agreed, not relishing the thought.

"I'll help you," she added with a smile, tucking her hand into mine.

She was always a great help and confidante. I smiled back at her.

"I say, Skipper, that's a bit of a good show, don't you think?" said Jonty, coming up to us. "Pick our targets, go in, shoot 'em up and get out. What's not to like about that?"

"Yes, Jonty, but just keep in mind what Bentley said. No potshots at cows," I told him.

"Skipper," he replied, trying unsuccessfully to look wounded by my remark, "all that is behind me. From now on, I'll be a model pilot."

Willie, who had joined us, snorted in derision. "That'll be the day!"

"I will, you'll see," Jonty averred.

"Just do your job and we'll all be happy," I told him, cutting off the burgeoning argument.

"When are we going on the first sortie?" asked Jonty, changing the subject.

"Give the man a chance," said Willie. "He's only just heard about it."

"Soon enough," I told Jonty, shooting Willie a grateful glance.

"Why don't we go and have some tea in the mess, darling?" Angelica asked me helpfully.

"Yes, good idea," I said.

We quickly excused ourselves before Jonty could quiz me further. There was a lot to think about now that we'd been given our orders.

We arrived in the mess to find Olga having tea with Maria. Olga waved at us, and so we made our way to their table and took a seat.

Olga and Maria could have been sisters since they were similar in looks, both with blonde hair and blue eyes. Olga was Polish and Maria German, but since she was Jewish, Maria had been seen as an enemy of the Nazi state. In return for her life, she had been forced to act in propaganda films for Goebbels, something she wasn't proud of. The two of them had formed a firm friendship since arriving at Banley.

"Hello," said Maria, smiling.

"Let me order you some tea and cake," said Olga. "We were just about to get a fresh pot."

"Ooh, lovely," said Angelica.

I didn't demur, and in short order the four of us were chatting quite amiably when Olga, who had been talking about the latest news from Eastern Europe, suddenly stopped and stared over at a table in the corner.

I followed her gaze. A sergeant was sitting on his own, smoking a cigarette and nursing a mug of tea. He was rather burly, with black hair and a full moustache.

"Who's that?" she said quietly.

I shrugged. "I have no idea," I replied. "Why?"

"I haven't seen him before," she said.

Maria looked around briefly to take in the stranger, and so did Angelica. I saw nothing particularly remarkable about him. There were plenty of personnel on the base whom I didn't know.

However, Olga's duty was to mind her charge. She took a great deal of interest in everyone. Since we'd already had one assassin on base, she was forever on the alert.

The man quickly became aware that he had become the object of attention, and instead of ignoring us, he got up and walked over to our table.

He saluted as he came up to us, and I returned the salute.

"Can I help you, Sergeant?" I asked.

"Sir, I couldn't help noticing you all here might be eyeing me a bit askance," he said.

"I wouldn't say *that*," I said smoothly. "We were a little curious, as we'd not seen you around before."

I noticed that Olga was watching him intently.

"Sergeant Nicholas Willis, at your service," he said.

"You're new here?"

He laughed. "You've got me bang to rights there. Just passing through, sir, that's all. Thought I'd take a cup of tea at your rather nice mess."

I glanced at Olga. Her expression became even more guarded. Angelica, however, simply looked amused.

"Passing through?"

"I work for supplies and logistics. I'm one of these people you never see, making sure things get delivered to airbases when they are needed."

"Oh right…" I trailed off. It seemed quite reasonable on the face of it.

"We've a supply office over in the Nissen huts at the edge of the field. You've probably not spent any time there, being a pilot an' all," he added by way of explanation.

"I must admit to not having had cause to do so," I replied.

It was a while since I'd been anywhere near them, and that was only when chasing a suspected spy.

He hesitated for a moment. "Well, you'll likely be seeing more of me in the future," he said. "Here and there around the base, making sure everything is all right and tight."

"Yes, I see. Well, welcome to Banley," I said with a smile.

"Sir." Willis nodded, saluted again and returned to his table.

I picked up my cup of tea and took a sip.

"I don't like him," said Olga darkly.

"Oh? Why not?" asked Angelica.

"Just something about him — I don't know. You develop a sense for these things in my line of work," Olga told her.

That was probably true. It was her job to be suspicious of everyone. The Marx Brothers had told me that spies were the people you'd least suspect. They'd certainly been right. But was Sergeant Willis a spy or even a threat to Maria? He didn't seem particularly suspicious to me.

I glanced over at where Willis had been sitting, but he was no longer there. I thought no more about it because I had more pressing matters to attend to, like attacking unspecified targets in France and Holland. It was all very well for Bentley to tell us to just go and find targets, but I wanted to be a little more specific than that if I could.

It meant we would need a little more intelligence about the enemy's movements. A thought struck me. Maria had been extremely helpful to us with the capture of the Ace Raider. She had a degree from a German university, where she'd also studied aeronautics and navigation. With her expertise, we had put together precise navigation and timings that had enabled us to trap the errant pilot once and for all.

"Do you think you might assist us in a little project?" I asked her.

"I'd love to," said Maria, brightening up. "It's frightfully dull just sitting around all day, and I've read so many books…" Her face took on a slightly stricken expression, and she put out her hand to Olga. "I don't mean…"

"It's fine," said Olga. "I know what you're saying. It would be good to have something meaningful to do."

"If we can obtain some intelligence and photographs of Northern France, perhaps you can help identify some prospective targets for us?" I continued.

"What a splendid idea," said Angelica, catching on. "I can get the intelligence."

She had a high security clearance, and so this would be no trouble.

I went on to explain a little more about Operation Wagtail to them both. They seemed more than keen to participate. After tea, Angelica and I returned to the hut.

"That was rather opportune," she said as we walked.

"Yes, it was. Serendipity, perhaps?" I replied.

"Rather like when you met me," she said with a glint in her eye.

"Oh, but that was more than serendipity," I said with a laugh. "That was good fortune."

She stopped and wound her arms around my neck. "That's the right answer," she said, before indulging in a playful kiss.

CHAPTER THREE

Until Bentley gave us orders to the contrary, we still had patrols to fly. I rounded up my usual crew, and we were soon airborne.

"East Anglia again, is it?" asked Jonty as we made our way towards Cromer.

"Yes, I'm afraid it is," I told him.

"Don't jinx it either," Willie added.

"I'll be as silent as the grave," Jonty vowed, to my amusement.

It wasn't long before we passed over Cromer. I turned us south, following the coastline down to Winterton, Great Yarmouth and Lowestoft. The skies were fairly clear, and so far we had seen nothing of Jerry. I wasn't particularly unhappy about that; after all, not every sortie had to result in a skirmish or a dogfight.

As we headed towards Felixstowe, Dylan sent up a cry.

"Bandits on our thee o'clock... No, wait ... not bandits... What on earth are those?"

I looked over to see a full squadron of what appeared to be fighters with American markings. They weren't a type I'd seen before either; they were rather squat and thickset aircraft with two wings poking out of the side. They looked rather ungainly.

"Who on earth are they?" said Jonty. "Where have they come from?"

I turned towards the flight of planes to get a better look. As we got nearer, we could see one or two of the pilots waving.

"They seem friendly enough," remarked Arjun.

I waved back and decided to break contact; after all, it wasn't any of our business if Americans were flying their own sorties. They were obviously not on our frequency, as they didn't attempt radio contact.

We left them behind us. I didn't think anything more of it. By this time, we were over Felixstowe and I decided to call it a day.

I was just about to say so when our luck ran out.

"Bandits, real ones this time, on our nine o'clock!" shouted Willie.

I sighed inwardly. Sure enough, several Focke-Wulfs were approaching us at speed.

"Break, break, engage," I said, dropping out of formation.

The others followed suit, and we flew towards the Germans on the attack. As usual, I singled one out and made a beeline for it. In moments, the air was filled with gunfire.

The Wulf I was heading for took a sharp turn, and I went after him. He was an agile pilot, weaving this way and that as I tried to keep him in my sights. I fired once, twice, but missed.

"That blighter's pinged me," said Jonty over the radio.

I glanced over to see if he was all right. He was engaged in looping his plane over, followed by another Jerry.

In fact, from what I could see, the Germans seemed to be mainly the ones in hot pursuit. I turned my attention back to my quarry. He was leading me a merry dance. The radio was filled with chatter.

"Get off my tail," said Jean, who was being chased.

Then came the words nobody leading a patrol would want to hear.

"I'm hit," said Olek. "I'm going to bail."

I saw a Spitfire diving to earth with smoke pouring out of it. The Wulf in front of me was still evading my guns, and I was running low on ammo. I conserved my bursts until I felt sure I might hit him. My attention was claimed by another problem.

"Watch out behind you, Skipper," said Jonty.

In my mirror, I saw that there was a Jerry coming after me. I cursed inwardly, caught in the middle of two enemy planes. Then, the radio crackled to life.

"I'm hit! He's hit me!" said Dylan.

"Bail, bail!" cried Jean.

My heart sank. I flicked my Spitfire away as the Wulf behind me fired. The Wulf I was chasing turned towards me. It was now two against one.

I opened up the throttle, aware of briefly seeing two parachutes drifting to earth. Dylan and Olek had made it out of their planes. That was good news, at least. The bad news was that we were two planes down, with only four of us left.

I started to weave left and right, aware that with two planes after me, the odds of evading them both had considerably reduced. I made sure I was over land just in case I was hit. The idea of bailing yet again didn't fill me with joy.

However, just then, to my surprise, one of the Wulfs behind me erupted into a fireball. Then the second followed suit.

I turned sharply to see the American squadron joining our fight with all guns blazing. Another Wulf was hit, while a fourth had smoke pouring from the engine. Outnumbered, the Germans abruptly broke contact and headed out over the Channel.

"Tally-ho! That was a lucky strike," said Jonty. "The Yanks came just in time."

Down below us, I could see two figures waving. Olek and Dylan had made it safely to earth. The Americans pursued the Germans briefly and then headed back towards us.

"Let's go home," I said, and the four remaining planes formed up.

The American squadron formed up around us and flew alongside. I looked over at the leading plane. The pilot looked somewhat familiar.

"Oh, the Yankees saved our bacon, the Yankee doodle dandy planes, they came flying out of the sky, giving the Jerries a punch in the eye, oh…" sang Jonty to the familiar tune of 'Yankee Doodle Dandy'.

There was a groan from Willie, but he didn't demur. After all, it was true. The Americans had been in the right place at the right time — though by chance or providence, I wasn't sure.

Banley came into view. I got clearance from the control tower before bringing those of us left in the patrol in to land. As we began our approach, the Americans dipped their wings and continued onwards to the base next door. The penny dropped. I thought I had recognised the pilot.

It had to be Captain Sandford Booker from the American bomber base. We had flown escort missions with them, and they had helped us out on several occasions. However, by my recollection, they flew Spitfires, so this was something new.

We landed and taxied to our standings, and I jumped down from the wing. Angelica was waiting as usual, and as soon as she saw me she ran to me, hurling herself into my arms. I braced myself for the impact.

"Oof!" I said, embracing her.

"You're safe," she said. "Thank God for that."

"Thank God for the Americans," I told her. "They appeared in the nick of time."

"Olek and Dylan?" she asked anxiously.

"They got down safely as far as I could see."

Further conversation was cut short by the appearance of Bentley. I saluted while he took his pipe from his pocket and lit it. After puffing away for a moment, he said, "I gather that you've had quite a rum do."

"You could say that, sir, yes," I replied.

"And those two who bailed?" he asked in quieter tones.

"I was just telling my wife, sir, they're safe and will no doubt make their way back here in due course."

"Hmm." He ruminated for a moment. "Two more bloody planes gone for a burton."

I didn't answer. Bentley was quite possessive about his aircraft, although he knew it couldn't be helped.

"I heard that you were saved, as it were, by the cavalry," he continued.

"The Americans, yes, sir," I replied.

"Just as well."

While he puffed on his pipe, I elected to change the subject.

"They seem to have new planes, sir — I've never seen that kind before," I said.

"New planes, eh?" he replied. I noted a calculating expression appearing on his face.

"I'll go over and see Captain Booker to thank him, shall I?" I ventured.

"Yes," he replied quickly. "Yes, indeed, and ask him if any of his Spitfires are going spare. That's the ticket."

I smiled inwardly. Bentley was nothing if not resourceful when it came to getting equipment for the Mavericks.

"I will, sir," I replied.

"Jolly good. Carry on, then. Glad you made it back in one piece," he said, saluting and turning on his heel. He left briskly with Audrey at his side.

"I say, Skipper," said Jonty, appearing at my elbow along with the others in the patrol, "what did old Bilious Bentley want this time?"

"I don't think he'd appreciate you calling him old, Jonty, or bilious," said Angelica with a laugh.

"I suppose not, but he does have a dreadfully bad temper," said Jonty, with some justification.

"Only because you keep pulling stupid stunts," put in Willie.

"There is that..." Jonty trailed off.

"Bentley was concerned for our downed pilots, Jonty," I told him.

"Oh yes, well, that was jolly bad luck," said Jonty, as if this came as a surprise. He knew as well as any of us how much Bentley cared about the people under his command.

"Even worse luck if they'd been killed," I added, reminding him of the realities of war.

Jonty didn't reply but looked decidedly down in the mouth. I knew that wouldn't last long.

"Come on, you reprobate, let's have some tea," said Willie, putting an arm around his friend's shoulder. The two of them walked to the hut along with Arjun and Jean, chatting amiably.

"Let's go and find Fred," I said to Angelica, using the general nickname for Sergeant Gordon.

Gordon wasn't hard to locate. He was at ease in his jeep, smoking a cigarette and reading a book. I wasn't fooled by this nonchalance. He seemed to get an incredible amount done during the day.

"Hello, sir," he said. "Need a ride?"

"Yes please, Fred. Take us over to the American base, if you would."

"With pleasure," he replied.

We jumped in beside him. Gordon let out the clutch, and we were off.

"Any particular reason for your visit, sir?" he asked me as we bowled along.

"I want to find out about these new planes they've got," I told him.

"Ah, yes. I'd heard something of the sort," he remarked.

This didn't surprise me. Gordon was a fount of knowledge when it came to the goings-on at the base. A thought struck me.

"Have you heard of the new sergeant that's appeared on our base recently?" I asked him.

"Sergeant Nicholas Willis," added Angelica.

"I'd heard about him, yes, but I haven't met him directly, sir. Isn't he from logistics?"

"So he says," I replied.

"Was there something you wanted me to find out?" he enquired tentatively.

"Olga doesn't like him," said Angelica.

He looked a little surprised by this. "Oh? Did she say why?"

"No," I said. "But I suppose being a spy, she has a nose for these things."

"In that case, I'll enquire further and report back," he said.

If anyone could find out about the newcomer, it would be Gordon.

The journey to the American airbase had not taken long, and we passed the sentries at the gate without any trouble. Gordon, in particular, was a familiar figure to them. We drove over to the main building, which contained the offices of various ranked personnel, including Captain Booker. Angelica and I then left Gordon in the jeep and headed to Sandford's office.

He was sitting at his desk when we entered and jumped to his feet at once, his face wreathed in smiles. He and I were of equivalent ranks, though the United States Army Air Force still held onto the army ranking system, hence his being a captain.

"Angus *and* Angelica," he said, sounding pleased. "Good to see you both."

"Good to see you too," said Angelica.

He came around and shook our hands warmly, then bade us take a seat. We sat down around a small coffee table while he called out to his corporal to bring us refreshments. These would invariably consist of Coca-Cola, along with glasses filled with ice.

"What brings you here?" he said.

"We're here to thank you, for one thing," I began. "I take it that was your squadron helping us out earlier?"

"Glad to be of service," he said with a smile. "We've got these brand-new planes, and we haven't figured out how to change the radio frequency yet, so I couldn't contact you, I'm afraid."

"That's all right," I said. "I'm just grateful you were there. We were taking quite a beating at the time."

Beside me, Angelica's mouth turned down a little at the corners. She didn't like to hear that I had been in a sticky situation. She liked to feel that I was somehow invincible. It helped her deal with the worry, she told me.

"Of course," I added quickly, "we could probably have shaken them off, but it was getting difficult."

I shot Angelica a reassuring smile and was rewarded with a smile in return.

"McClusky saw you were in trouble," said Sandford. "We were about to head back to base when he said, 'Hey, boss, the

Mavericks are getting shot up — shouldn't we go over there and show these Jerries some muscle?'"

Angelica and I laughed at this perfect imitation of Second Lieutenant Joe McClusky, one of Sandford's more outspoken pilots.

"So, we did," Sandford added.

"I'm glad you did," I told him.

The corporal brought the drinks, which were as I predicted. Angelica poured her Coke into the ice-filled glass and took a sip with some relish.

"You've got new planes?" I said, after sipping my own drink.

"Yep," said Sandford. "P-47 Thunderbolts. We're one of the first squadrons to get them. The big cheeses want us to try them out."

He and Bentley had a similar irreverence for the higher-ups.

"What's the verdict on them so far?" I asked him.

"Well, apart from the fact that — as McClusky put it — 'they're the ugliest damn planes this side of the United States', they're not too bad. Top speed similar to a Spitfire Mark IX. Pretty similar in terms of flight ceiling and armaments. They can take drop tanks and be used as fighter bombers." He paused and took a sip of his own drink. "And they handle pretty well in combat, as we've now found out," he added.

"Noted," I replied with a smile, and he laughed.

"I'll take you out to see one, if you like, when you've finished your drinks."

"Sure, I'd like that. It would be interesting to see one close up."

I glanced at Angelica. I still had to ask Bentley's question, and now seemed as good a time as any. "What are you going to do with the Spitfires?" I said as casually as I could.

Sandford eyed me shrewdly. "Did Bentley send you here to ask that?" he said.

We all burst out laughing. He knew our CO almost as well as we did.

"I cannot tell a lie," I said, putting my hands up in mock surrender.

"To be truthful, we hadn't thought about it," he continued. "We might keep some as spare planes, but as for the rest, I could make enquiries. After all, they'll just be sitting there otherwise. Might as well give them back as keep them in the hangar, gathering dust." He sighed, sounding a little regretful. "I'll miss those things, to be honest. I'd kind of got used to flying a Spitfire…" He trailed off thoughtfully.

I didn't know how I'd feel if we were asked to fly a different plane. I'd got so used to the Spitfire and how it handled, it now seemed like second nature. It would be hard to give it up. Fortunately, being in the Mavericks, we'd probably be at the back of the queue for any new innovations. Unless, of course, we were earmarked to fly a particular mission.

We finished our drinks and headed over to the main hangar to look at the new planes.

I had to admit that McClusky's description had some merit; they weren't the most attractive design. They were teardrop-shaped and quite stout in appearance, with a big snub nose and short, stubby wings. Quite a contrast to the sleek Spitfire.

"If it handles well and shoots down the enemy, then that's all that matters," said Sandford as we walked back to the jeep where Gordon was waiting.

"You're right," I agreed.

"We will figure out the radio," he said. "So next time we'll be able to talk to you in the air."

"Sure, that would help," I replied.

We were shaking hands when another thought occurred to him.

"I'll get McClusky to fly one over to your base, if you like. Then your boys can take a proper look at it."

I was about to demur since I had a feeling that it wouldn't stop at simply looking at it, particularly where Jonty was concerned. The thought of explaining to Bentley how one of the new American planes had been damaged wasn't something I relished. As expert a pilot as Jonty was, he seemed to attract calamities wherever he went. However, Angelica forestalled me with great enthusiasm for the idea.

"That would be marvellous," she said, cutting in. "I'm sure they would love it."

Thus, as the Americans put it, she sealed the deal.

"Great," said Sandford. "In that case, I'll arrange it and let you know."

"Yes, excellent," I replied, shaking his hand with a feeling of foreboding.

The following day, Dylan and Olek were restored to the Mavericks, none the worse for their experience. The two of them arrived in a farmer's truck, having been offered a lift.

By sheer coincidence, it turned out to be Jarrod Carpenter who brought them back.

"You chaps are making a habit of landing in my fields," he said, laughing.

"I can assure you it wasn't on purpose," Dylan told him.

I asked Jarrod if he'd stay for a cup of tea, but he declined, saying he had to get back to his farm.

"Molly looked after us well," said Olek. "Thank you."

"She was glad of the company," said Jarrod.

He shook our hands in turn and got back into his truck.

"Well, that was a stroke of luck," said Dylan as we watched him leave.

"It certainly was," I agreed.

Later on, Sandford was as good as his word, and the promised visit by McClusky took place.

All of M Flight were in our hut when we heard the whine of a plane engine. I looked up; the noise was different.

"Is that who I think it is?" asked Angelica, who often spent time with me in the hut when she didn't have other duties.

"It certainly might be," I said.

We piled outside and watched as a P-47 circled the airfield and then landed.

"I say," said Jonty. "That's one of those new American planes, isn't it?"

"Yes, Sandford said he'd send one over for you lot to have a look at," I told him.

"Well, what are we waiting for?" said Jonty, hurrying over to where the Thunderbolt had come to a halt.

A familiar figure jumped down from the wing of the aircraft and was soon enveloped in a crowd of pilots. The rest of the crew from Judd's squadron joined the fray.

"Shall we go over?" Angelica asked me, sounding amused.

"I think we can leave them to it," I said. "We've seen the plane already."

We went back inside for some tea. One by one, the others joined us. I listened to the chatter.

"What an ugly plane," said Dylan.

"I wouldn't like to fly it," put in Arjun. "It's lacking in sleekness, not like the Spitfire."

"Ah, give me a Spitfire any day, not these American planes," said Tomas. He walked over to me with a cup of tea in hand.

"Scottish, come on, what do you think of this new plane, eh?" he asked.

I paused to listen to the sound of the P-47 taking off before answering him. However, I didn't get to tell him what I thought of it because at that moment McClusky entered the hut.

"Chief, good to see you!" he said, coming over and vigorously shaking my hand.

I stared at him, a little stupefied, since we could all hear the sound of his Thunderbolt circling the airfield.

"Good to see you too, McClusky," I said. "But if you're here, then who's that flying your plane?"

He looked a little sheepish. "Ah, well, Chief, you know, Jonty seemed so keen on the new jalopy that I thought…"

"You'd let him fly it," I finished for him.

He shrugged. "Something like that. You know how Jonty can be, and he promised me a ballad."

I knew perfectly well how Jonty could be, and although I knew that McClusky was very fond of Jonty's ballads, I didn't have time to reflect on it just then.

"Right, well, perhaps it wasn't that wise a course of action," I told him, hurrying out of the door.

"Sorry, Chief, if I'd known you wouldn't like it…" McClusky called after me.

Willie was standing on the edge of the field, watching the Thunderbolt circle around.

"I told him, Scottish, I told him not to do it," he said as I came up beside him, along with Angelica and the rest of M Flight, who had come to watch the spectacle of Jonty trying out the plane.

"Is there going to be trouble, Chief?" McClusky asked me as he appeared at my elbow.

"As long as Bentley doesn't find out, I suppose we might be okay…" I began, but trailed off as I spotted the familiar figures of Bentley and Audrey striding towards us.

"Senior officer present," said Willie as we all snapped to attention.

"At ease," said Bentley, in a fairly genial mood. "I heard one of those new planes was paying us a visit, so I came to see for myself," he said. He lit his pipe and watched as the Thunderbolt pulled a daisy cutter down the airfield, went up high and looped the loop.

"Hmm, that's quite a bit of manoeuvrability," he remarked, not having noticed McClusky.

The American began to edge surreptitiously away, but Bentley caught the movement.

"Aren't you the pilot of that plane?" he asked, pointing the stem of his pipe at McClusky.

McClusky saluted. "Yes, sir, that's me. I brought it over to show the men, sir," he said.

"If you're on the ground," said Bentley, "then who the bloody hell is flying it?"

He scanned the faces of the assembled crew of M Flight, who were somewhat reluctant to let on.

"Angus?" he said, when an answer was not forthcoming.

I was about to inform him of the circumstances when he stopped me.

"Wait," he said. "Don't tell me, I know exactly who it is. It's Butterworth, isn't it?"

"Yes, sir," I replied.

"Sir, it's my fault, I —" McClusky began.

"No, don't explain," said Bentley, developing an immediate twitch below his right eye. "I'll say no more, as long as he brings it back in one piece with not so much as a scratch on it."

"Yes, sir," I said, hoping this would be the case.

"Or I'll have his guts for garters," said Bentley, upon which, to my relief, he strode away abruptly.

"Oh dear," said Angelica.

"I knew it," said Willie with a sigh. "I knew this would happen."

"I'm sorry, Chief," said McClusky mournfully. "I didn't mean to get you into trouble."

"Don't worry about it," I said. "If Jonty wanted to fly that plane, he'd have found a way to do so, and none of us could have prevented it."

So saying, we watched as the Thunderbolt circled around the field once more, then come down for a near perfect landing. It taxied over to where we were standing. The engine died abruptly, and shortly afterwards Jonty climbed out of the cockpit. He jumped down and made his way over to us.

"I say, that was a jolly wizard flight," he declared enthusiastically. "It was bloody marvellous. That plane flies better than it looks."

I let Jonty chatter on for a few minutes, talking to the others until they eventually dispersed back to the hut.

He noticed me at length. "What-ho, Skipper," he said. "I hope you don't mind me taking McClusky's plane out for a spin."

McClusky eyed me warily, wondering what I would say.

"Could I have stopped you from doing it if I had?" I asked Jonty.

"Well, now that's a question I've often been unable to answer. Old Bagshot, my housemaster, used to say much the same thing —"

"Jonty," I said, cutting him off, "Bentley was here, and he knows you took that plane up."

"What? Oh blast!" he said. "And what did he say?"

"He said you'd best bring it back in one piece," I told him.

He brightened up on hearing this. "Well, Skipper, as you can see, it's all right and tight," said Jonty.

McClusky, perhaps thinking that discretion was the better part of valour, decided it was time he departed. "I'd better be going," he said to us.

"Thanks again, old sport," said Jonty, shaking his hand warmly.

"Yeah, okay, but don't forget my ballad," said McClusky.

"I won't," said Jonty. "And I'll make it a good one."

With that, McClusky climbed into his aircraft and left in short order.

As I re-entered the hut with Angelica, Tomas came up to us.

"Scottish," he said, "when do you think we are going to start flying these new missions?"

It was probably a question on all the minds of M Flight. Judd's squadron had also been given the same task. Yet, to all intents and purposes, we operated independently. Judd would make his own plans. I had to make mine. We would liaise to ensure our plans did not clash, but other than that, we did things our own way. So far, that had worked very well.

"Soon," I told him.

"Okay, but how is it going to go?" he asked. "How many planes, for example?"

Tomas could be quite persistent when he wanted. The other pilots in the hut had also stopped to listen. I needed to say something, although I hadn't completely made up my mind.

"I imagine that it will either be the full squadron or at least six planes," I said. "Half of the number will attack targets. The other half will ride shotgun in case we are attacked."

My biggest concern was Luftwaffe retaliation. In order to avoid it, we'd have to fly in low and fast, probably at first light. We would carry out our attack and then leave as quickly as we came. We did not have air superiority over enemy territory and would have to fly the missions by stealth.

"That's a good plan, Scottish," said Tomas, clapping me on the back.

"I will be briefing everyone before the first mission," I said. "Before that, I want to identify potential targets, which is what we're currently engaged upon."

I was about to say more about it when Audrey appeared in the hut.

"Bentley wants to see Pilot Officer Butterworth," she said.

"Oh dear," said Angelica.

I sighed. This was exactly what I had hoped would not happen.

"Jonty," I called. "A word."

I went outside with Angelica and Audrey so as not to be overheard by the others. We were soon joined by Jonty and Willie.

"Jonty," I said, "why would Bentley want to see you?"

"Really, Skipper? I can't imagine," said Jonty, trying to look innocent.

"Can't you?" I said in a voice laced with sarcasm. "Well then, I suppose we'd best go and find out."

The four of us accompanied Audrey. Angelica, because she was just as curious as I was about what Jonty had done this time; Willie, because for all his complaints, he would stand by Jonty through thick and thin.

We entered Bentley's office and stood to attention in front of his desk.

As soon as he saw us, he started on his pipe routine. Empty, scrape, tamp and fill. Once it was lit and he had taken a few puffs, he surveyed us with interest.

"Come mob-handed, I see, Butterworth," he said with deceptive mildness.

"Sir, they just tagged along..." Jonty trailed off on seeing Bentley's less than friendly expression.

"Did they? Well, if you want an audience, then you shall have one, I suppose."

Jonty sensibly remained silent. Bentley puffed a little harder on his pipe before speaking again.

"I just had an interesting phone call, Butterworth," he said, "from the commanding officer of the American base next door."

"Did you, sir?" said Jonty.

"Yes, I did," said Bentley. "And do you know why he phoned me?"

Jonty elected to continue to feign innocence, although I was sure he knew perfectly well what Bentley was alluding to. "I can't imagine, sir."

Bentley's right eye began to twitch alarmingly, a sure sign that he would shortly erupt with fury. "Can't you?" he said in a voice of icy calm. "Well, then let me tell you why, in that case. He phoned me because some damned fool in an American fighter plane had flown a low-level pass over General Grimthorne's house just this afternoon. General Grimthorne naturally wasn't happy about it..."

General Grimthorne was retired from the army and had a sizeable property close to our airfield. At one time most of the Maverick pilots had amused themselves by buzzing over his house, but Bentley had put a stop to this pastime after the venerable old general had made one too many phone calls to complain about it.

"Well, sir, I may have gone over the general's house a bit too low when I borrowed that plane," said Jonty.

Bentley catapulted out of his seat and began to pace the room. "May have?" he roared. "The way he tells it, you practically took his chimneys off and brought them home with you!"

"Well, I hardly think —" Jonty began, but Bentley was in full flow.

"I gave explicit instructions that pilots were to cease and desist from buzzing Grimthorne's house. God knows I've had my fill of his complaints. What addle-brained notion appeared in that head of yours, Butterworth, to make you think it was a good idea to disobey my orders?"

"Sir, I don't know," said Jonty.

Predictably, this answer did not sit well with Bentley.

"Yes, that's the problem, Butterworth, you don't know. Yet you continue to engage in antics unbecoming of an officer of the RAF. Don't you think I'm somewhat tired of you acting the giddy goat on every hare-brained scheme you come up with?"

"I apologise wholeheartedly, sir," said Jonty, looking abashed.

"Yes, you bloody well should!" Bentley shouted. "I'm trying to foster good relations with our friends next door, not make them think we're a pack of incompetent idiots. Do I make myself clear?"

"Yes, sir, perfectly," said Jonty.

Having sufficiently vented his spleen, Bentley puffed on his pipe for a few moments, which seemed to calm his ire.

"You will write a heartfelt letter of apology to the commanding officer of the American base," he said to Jonty. "And you will never do anything so stupid again. Do I make myself clear?"

"Yes, sir," said Jonty.

"Dismissed," said Bentley with a sigh.

We left in short order while Bentley returned to his desk and began to sift through his papers.

"Phew," said Jonty, once we were outside the main building. "That wasn't too bad."

"Jonty," I said with a wry smile, "you're like a cat with nine lives, but I don't know how many you've got left as far as Bentley is concerned."

"Scottish is right," said Willie. "You're an idiot and that dressing-down was well deserved. Come on, let's get some tea in the mess."

Angelica and I watched them go.

"Poor Jonty," she said. "He never learns."

"No, unfortunately, he doesn't," I agreed, knowing full well that this would probably not be the last time Jonty was on the carpet.

CHAPTER FOUR

Over the following week, Angelica obtained a large stack of intelligence photographs and gave them to Maria to look over. It was time to make some decisions. To that end, we were seated in Maria's living room.

As always, Olga served us tea with fruit cake, which she was rather good at making. Her culinary skills were excellent; originally she had been working undercover as a chef in the mess.

"Have you found anything helpful?" I asked Maria as I stirred my tea.

"It's difficult," she said. "The types of targets you want are not abundant."

"Many of Hitler's forces are on the Western Front," said Angelica. "Their presence in Europe is reduced, by all accounts."

"It's enough to keep the population under control," said Maria bitterly. "I am glad he's losing in Russia!"

She was very aware of Hitler's policies against the Jews and other minorities, and was still distressed about the part she had been forced to play in the propaganda films which perpetuated the lie that the Aryan race was superior to all others.

"Just summarise, perhaps, what you think we should do," I said, gently moving the conversation back to the topic in hand.

"I would suggest," she said, "that you stick to the coastal towns — at least to start with — like Calais, Dunkirk, Boulogne. The obvious targets would be railway terminuses, barracks and so forth. Many of the German installations are in bunkers, which would not suit your purpose."

She was right; we couldn't attack bunkers. Our mode of operation would be to get in, strafe the target, and get out. We wouldn't even be dropping bombs like the Germans had during the 'tip and run' raids, which had been undertaken by lone Focke-Wulfs.

I sipped my tea and sighed. "It's one thing for the Marx Brothers to tell us to go and find targets to attack," I said. "It's quite another to find them."

"I'm sorry, it's not so easy," said Maria. "The Germans will be moving troops around. You can't always tell where they'll be."

"That's why they're called targets of opportunity, I imagine," said Olga wryly.

"You know an awful lot about the military," I said to Maria in surprise.

"Yes," she replied. "I was around military people during the time I made those films…" She hesitated. "They talked, you know. I listened. Stupid women aren't always quite so stupid."

"Is that how they saw you?" I asked her. "As stupid?"

"Naïve, perhaps, but unworthy of much attention other than being a useful adjunct to their system of oppression. Women are for breeding the new Aryan race for the future Thousand Year Reich, didn't you know?" She fairly spat the words in disgust.

"*Lebensborn*," said Angelica. "The Nazi breeding program."

"Good God," I said.

"Women must produce children," said Maria. "But only as long as they are 'racially pure'."

This was far beyond anything I had imagined. It was easy to become focused simply on one's own role in the war and forget the bigger picture. I realised I was less informed than I thought and resolved to quiz on this Angelica further.

"Anyway," said Maria, "that's my advice. I've marked up some of these photographs with potential targets."

She handed me a sheaf of photos with red writing and arrows on them. There was another pile, which were evidently the ones she had discarded.

"Thanks for doing this," I said. "It's saved us a lot of trouble."

"You are welcome," said Maria. "I'm always happy to help with anything that can bring about a Nazi defeat."

"I don't exactly think it will do that," I said.

"It's probably along the lines of harassment," said Olga. "Hitting them while they are down."

"Did the Marx Brothers tell you that?" I asked her.

Naturally, spies would talk to other spies. Olga just smiled. I took it as affirmation.

"Do you know how long you will remain with us?" Angelica asked Maria, changing the subject.

Maria shrugged. It was obviously a sore point. She hadn't seen or heard from her husband since he'd gone to the United States. I wondered why there had not been moves to take her there too. Perhaps her collaboration with the Nazis, though forced, stood against her after all.

"I'm sorry," I said.

"Don't be," Maria said. "The war is … the war."

In that statement, she encapsulated how we all felt about it. There was nothing we could do except keep fighting.

Angelica and I took our leave shortly afterwards and walked together towards the main building.

"What now?" Angelica asked me.

"I suppose we'd better get on with it," I said. "But first, I need to run the plans past Bentley."

There was no time like the present, so we went to Bentley's office. Audrey let us in then resumed her seat at a desk near Bentley's. She carried on typing, but I knew she was taking everything in.

Bentley looked up from his papers and motioned for us to sit. Then he commenced his pipe ritual. We knew better than to say anything until he was smoking it contentedly.

"Angus," he said, leaning back in his chair, "what brings you here?"

"I wanted to outline our plan of campaign for Operation Wagtail, sir," I said.

"Go on."

I told him my thoughts and showed him the photographs which Maria had marked up. He leafed through them with interest and handed them back.

"So," he said at length, "those bloody spies want us to go and distract the Jerries, is that it?" He had picked up on this immediately. I might have guessed he would.

"I gathered as much," I replied.

"Some blasted jumped-up Johnny windbag upstairs comes up with a brilliant plan. Then who do they get to carry it out? The Mavericks, of course. Not one of their prize bloody squadrons, no. The Mavericks, because after all we don't matter quite so much..."

"We've carried out some very successful missions, sir," I reminded him. I didn't want us to be seen as the spare parts of the RAF.

"Yes, yes, I know all that," he said dismissively. "But it doesn't change the attitude of the top brass towards us one iota."

I elected to remain silent. Bentley knew more than I did about the machinations of the Air Force.

"So, Maria assisted you, did she?" he said with interest.

"Yes, sir. She's proven to be very useful."

"I wonder how long she's staying," he mused and then answered his own question. "For the rest of the war, probably…"

I could only agree with him on that point.

"Oh well," he continued. "It's our job to make sure she's comfortable while she's here and keep her safe."

"Yes," I said. "Indeed."

"All right, Angus. Run your first mission when you're ready," said Bentley.

"Yes, sir, I will hold a briefing with M Flight."

"Let me know when that is," he said.

"What about Judd, sir?" I asked tentatively.

"What about him?"

"I assume he's running missions, too? I planned to liaise with him to make sure we didn't clash."

Bentley said nothing for a moment and then, "I've stood him down from Wagtail, temporarily, until you've proven the idea."

"I see," I said, not sure whether to be pleased about this news.

"Put your hackles down, Angus," he said perceptively. "Your squadron is the more experienced one for the job — that's all there is to it."

He turned his attention back to his papers. It was an indication that we should leave, and we did so.

Angelica and I went to our bench at the edge of the airfield and sat for a few moments. Out over the fields beyond the perimeter fence, a gentle breeze was blowing through the long grass. I could hear the lowing of cattle. It was a perfect spring day. Angelica leaned into me as I put my arm around her shoulder.

"Do you think there will be another attempt on Maria's life?" she asked after a few moments.

"I don't know," I said. "The assassin is dead, but we've no idea if her location has been given to the Nazi regime."

Angelica looked pensive, so I tried to reassure her.

"There have been no attacks on our base since," I replied. "After all, what purpose would it serve to kill Maria now, other than revenge? Her husband won't stop working with the Americans, regardless."

"Olga will keep her safe," said Angelica.

"Yes," I agreed. Olga was probably Maria's best bet. I put it from my mind. There were other more pressing matters to consider, like our first opportunistic raid.

The following day I gathered M Flight together for a briefing in our mission room. Redwood and his technicians were present, while Angelica sat in the front row along with Bentley and Audrey.

"I've assembled you all here to discuss Operation Wagtail," I said. "I've come up with a plan of action, at least for the first mission."

"Does that mean it could change, Skipper?" asked Jonty.

"It does," I replied. "We've not done anything like this before, and as such, we don't know how it's going to go."

Angelica smiled at me reassuringly, and Bentley nodded in approval.

"Reconnaissance photographs haven't told us as much as I'd hoped," I continued. "So, for the first mission, I've decided we will attack an obvious target, the main railway terminus at Calais."

There was a large map on the wall behind me, showing the port of Calais.

"We will leave at dawn," I said, indicating the route, "and fly at low level all the way to the Channel and across it, to remain under the radar."

I saw Jonty perk up at this. He liked nothing better than risky flying.

"We will cross the French coastline between Calais and Grand-Fort-Philippe, to avoid detection if possible. Then we'll take a straight route to the railway line at Les Attaques, which is, coincidentally, an appropriate name."

There was some laughter at this.

"We will then fly up the railway line towards the Calais terminus and open fire on any military trains we see. If there are no such trains on the line, we will strafe military positions and railway ordnance at the main terminus and then get out of there *tout de suite*."

"Scottish," said Arjun, "how will we know if they are military trains?"

"It's likely they'll be well defended," I told him.

Bentley spoke up at this point. "I'm sure you're all well aware that the current bombing campaign is not entirely focused on military targets. A mission like this has the potential for casualties. Unfortunately, it's a risk we have to take, no matter how careful we are."

It was a sobering thought. Bentley was simply reminding us that niceties didn't necessarily apply in wartime.

"We will fly two six-plane formations, with two sections in each," I continued. "The first formation will be the attack flight, and the second will ride shotgun. Calais is surrounded by airfields. We should expect a swift response.

"Our job is to get in and get out. It's not our job to engage the Luftwaffe, unless it becomes necessary to do so. In which case, the shotgun flight will fight a rearguard action as we retreat back to Blighty. Any questions?"

"Who is in which flight?" asked Dylan.

He would naturally want to be in the attack formation. I had made my decision on that score.

"Attack flight will be me, Kiwi, Jonty, Arjun, Jean and Dylan," I said. "Shotgun flight will be led by Tomas, and those I have not mentioned will be flying with him."

I saw Dylan smile at this. He liked to be in the thick of it.

"You can count on me, Scottish," said Tomas at once.

"Thank you," I said. "Anything else?"

"When are we going?" asked Jean.

"Tomorrow morning," I said. "At first light. Make sure you get a good night's sleep. We won't be flying any patrols today."

I didn't want to risk losing any men, plus it gave the ground crew more time to prepare.

Bentley, who had been engaged in emptying and filling his pipe, now brandished the stem in the direction of the assembled crew. "Needless to say, I wish you all good luck," he said. "I know you'll do your best — and bring those bloody planes back in one piece, or I'll have your guts for garters."

There was general laughter, since he was smiling as he said it.

"Remember, this is all hush-hush," I told them. "So keep it to yourselves."

Since there was nothing else to discuss, I called an end to the proceedings.

"Well done, Angus," said Bentley before he left. "And good luck. I'm counting on you."

"Yes, sir."

Angelica and I watched him go, as members of the flight approached.

"I say, Skipper, this sounds like a jolly damn good wheeze," said Jonty.

"You just like shooting things up," said Willie, who had accompanied him.

"I don't like that we might kill innocent people by accident," said Arjun, joining the group.

"Innocent people die all the time," Tomas put in. "That's how it goes in war."

"We do what we have to do, Arjun," I told him. "A French Resistance fighter once told me they'd rather die by British hands if it meant that Nazis died too."

It was a telling remark from a conversation I'd had when I had been forced to land my plane in France.

"You think too much, my friend," said Tomas, clapping Arjun gently on the shoulder. "For me, if the Air Force tells me to jump, I ask, 'How high?'"

We all laughed. It broke the tension. In the end, I knew we'd all carry out our mission regardless.

"Come on," said Tomas. "I'm going for tea. What is it you British say? Tea cures everything."

There were murmurs of agreement at this. He headed for the hut with the rest of the flight. Angelica wound her arms around my neck.

"I love you," she said softly.

"I love you too," I replied.

"Don't get killed on this mission," she whispered.

When we reached the hut, there was an argument in progress between Willie and Jonty. This was hardly unusual, but it seemed rather heated.

"Well, someone must have taken it…" Jonty was saying.

"Don't be daft. It's just been misplaced," said Willie.

"It's gone, I tell you!" Jonty protested.

Angelica and I made our way over to the squabbling pair.

"What's gone, Jonty?" I asked him.

"The king is missing from the chess set. It was there the last time we played, but now it's gone," he said.

He seemed genuinely distressed, which ruled out this being one of his pranks.

"When did you last play, Jonty?" asked Angelica reasonably.

"We played yesterday and I won," said Jonty at once.

"You didn't win — you cheated," countered Willie.

I sighed as they started up again.

"All right," I said, intervening. "So, it was there, but it's not there now?"

"Yes, Skipper. Someone has taken it!" said Jonty.

"Has anyone seen the king from the chess set?" I asked the rest of the hut.

The others shook their heads.

"Have you searched the hut?" Angelica asked Jonty.

"Of course I have," said Jonty, aggrieved.

"He did," said Willie, then he asked, "How do we know it wasn't your parrot?"

"Percy?" exclaimed Jonty, looking shocked. "He hasn't even been out of his cage! Besides, he would never do such a thing."

I regarded him sceptically while Willie went over to check Percy's cage. He shook his head. The parrot, to be fair, hadn't exhibited any signs of kleptomania so far.

"Who on earth would want to take a chess piece?" I said.

Jonty suddenly looked as if he'd had a brainwave. "I bet it's over at the other hut," he exclaimed. "Those bounders!"

Before I could protest, he was out the door.

"I'll go after him," said Willie. "Try and stop him getting into trouble."

"All of this for a chess piece," said Tomas, shaking his head.

"Oh Lord," said Angelica. "I hope he doesn't annoy Judd."

The chances of Jonty not annoying Judd were slim. I was contemplating following Jonty to the other dispersal hut when, thankfully, he reappeared. He looked crestfallen.

"They haven't got it," he said.

"Yes, and you nearly made an idiot of yourself," Willie added. "Judd wasn't happy."

I sighed, fully expecting that at some point I would hear about it from Bentley.

"What on earth are we going to use now?" said Jonty. "We don't have another king."

I cast around for some object that we might use, but Tomas saved the day.

"Here," he said, taking an empty cartridge case from his pocket. "You can use this." Tomas placed the case upright where the king belonged in the manner of a conjurer. "Here you go. Now play."

I didn't like to ask why he was carrying an empty cartridge case in his pocket. However, Tomas supplied the answer.

"It's for luck, Scottish," he said. "Now perhaps it will bring luck to Jonty."

A talisman — that explained it. Most of us carried one. Mine was a letter from Angelica, which she had written to me long ago.

Jonty and Willie settled down to play chess together quite happily. Now that order was restored, I went outside to get some fresh air along with Angelica.

"What did you make of that?" she said.

"What should I make of it?"

"It seems odd, doesn't it?" she continued. "The piece going missing like that?"

"It does, but I can't think who would have taken it, or why," I told her.

It was a mystery. I had no time to think about unsolvable mysteries, so I put it aside. I had a mission to finalise.

"Let's go and see Techie," I said. "We'll make sure the planes are all right and tight for tomorrow."

Once we'd done that and everything seemed settled with M Flight, I elected to return to Amberly with Angelica. Gordon was in the jeep as usual, reading a book and lighting a cigarette.

"Ready to go, sir?" he asked, taking a drag from his smoke.

"Yes please, Fred, take us home," I replied, helping Angelica into the jeep and climbing in beside her.

Gordon slipped the jeep into gear, and we headed down the road back to Amberly Manor.

"I made some enquiries, sir," said Gordon as he drove. "Into Sergeant Willis."

Angelica perked up on hearing this.

"And?" I asked him.

"He seems genuine enough, from what I can gather," Gordon replied. "Keeps himself to himself. He's definitely from logistics."

"Oh," I said.

"Would you like me to dig a little deeper, sir?" he asked.

"No, thank you, Fred. Probably no need."

It didn't sound as if Willis was a spy, at least. The Marx Brothers had said that the spy was usually the one you least suspected. Other than being a strange face, Willis wasn't particularly suspicious, although there was the fact that Olga had taken him in dislike.

Later that night Angelica lay in my arms, both of us happy. The war seemed far away, in another place.

"Why on earth would someone take a chess piece?" she exclaimed suddenly.

"Really? That's what you've been thinking about?" I said with a low laugh.

"Not really, no," she said. "But it's very odd."

"Yes, it is," I agreed.

"I have been thinking about *other* things," she continued softly.

"Have you?" I asked.

"Yes," she said, her lips now almost touching mine.

"Show me," I whispered.

The sky was clear the following morning, which augured well for a low-level flight into enemy territory. Despite it being very early, we had breakfast at the manor, which had been arranged by Gordon.

"Going into battle on an empty stomach isn't advisable, sir," he informed me.

I was extremely grateful to the staff for serving us.

"Thank you, Ellie. This is an ungodly hour for you," I said to one of the maids as I tucked into my eggs on toast with beans.

"That's all right, sir," she replied with a smile. "You're doing your duty, so we're doing ours. Besides, it's not so early for us. We're always up before the crack of dawn."

I had not registered how hard the staff worked or the hours they kept. I had been brought up in circumstances where they were simply there.

"You're doing a wonderful job," I said.

"Thank you, sir."

She curtsied and smiled. There was no time to ponder the accidents of birth, however. We had a mission to fly.

"Looks like it will be a nice day for it, sir," said Gordon as he drove us to Banley.

There was a chill in the air, but that would soon go as the sun came up. Mist was rising off the fields as we bowled along the silent, empty lanes.

"Let's hope so, Fred," I told him.

I began to feel the familiar tension that always came before a mission. I glanced at Angelica. I could tell she was feeling it too. I took her hand in mine. She squeezed it tight as if she never wanted to let go.

"Good luck, sir," Gordon said as we jumped down from the jeep at the airfield. He lit up a cigarette and waved, watching us leave.

At the hut, I was surprised to discover that Bentley was waiting, along with Audrey. He was smoking his pipe as usual.

"Came to see you off, Angus," he said without preamble. "It's a while since you've flown a mission into enemy territory. So take care of these reprobates, will you?"

He gestured with the stem of his pipe towards the others, who were standing in a group waiting for the off.

"Yes, sir, I will," I said.

"Good luck to you all," said Bentley with a smile. I knew that he cared very much for the men under his command.

I checked my watch. The grey light of dawn would be emerging very shortly.

"All right, chaps," I said. "We know what we have to do, so let's go and do it."

I turned to Angelica as the others started to make their way to the planes. She put her arms around my neck and pulled me close.

"Come back safe, darling," she whispered.

"I will, I promise. I love you," I replied.

"I love you too."

On those final words, I turned, slowly letting go of her fingers and walking to my Spitfire. I climbed up onto the wing and Redwood helped to strap me in.

"All the planes are in tiptop condition, sir," he said. "I've made sure of it myself."

"Thanks, Techie," I replied with a smile.

"Fly safe. Give the Jerries hell."

"We'll do our best."

Then it was time to go. I fired up the Merlin and listened to the purr of the engine. Eleven other planes added to the stirring sound.

"Control, Panther Leader requesting clearance," I said. We had chosen the codename for the mission. We were the hunters, so it seemed fitting.

"Panther Leader, you're clear to go," said the control tower.

"Panthers, let's get airborne," I said, taxiing my kite down to the end of the runway. I waved at Angelica, who was watching us, along with Bentley and Audrey. She waved back.

I opened up the throttle, and in moments I was airborne. The rest of the flight joined me, and we formed up in two groups of six, just as we'd planned.

"Here we go," I said, dropping the kite to treetop height and throttling up.

The ground flashed by beneath us at a tremendous rate. This type of flying required focus and precision. You couldn't take your eyes off the terrain for a moment.

"What fun this is, Skipper," said Jonty after a few moments.

"You need your head examined," retorted Willie, "if you think this is fun."

I smiled at the banter. It broke the tension just a little. It was quite a short run, which took us down past Chelmsford, then across the Thames at Tilbury. Down below us were a host of naval ships in the river. We dipped our wings. I could see some sailors waving.

"Glad I'm not in the Navy," said Jonty.

"Why's that?" asked Dylan.

"Too much water, for one thing…" Jonty replied.

There was a crack of laughter from several of the others. I understood what he meant. Flying had always been my dream.

We took a straight line past Chatham, Rainham, Sittingbourne, Faversham, Canterbury and then on to Dover. Dover Castle loomed up in the distance, but we passed by.

"All right, Panthers," I said as we crossed over the blue water of the Channel. "This is it, radio silence."

I dropped down as low as I dared, not quite to wave-top height but close enough. Hopefully, Jerry wouldn't see us coming, at least by radar. I knew they had lookouts at various points along the coast, so we might still be spotted. Hopefully, we'd be in and out before Jerry could react.

Hitler was having a vast array of defensive bunkers built along the Atlantic coastline, known as the 'Atlantic Wall'. It was supposedly to prevent an Allied invasion. I had a hunch that, in the end, this would not work.

The journey over the choppy waters of the Channel took no time at all. I headed for the beach between Calais and Grand-Fort-Philippe. The white sand flew past beneath us, and then we were once more over fields. Now we had to stay on the alert for Luftwaffe patrols, in case we'd been seen by the Atlantic Wall lookouts. So far, there had been no incoming fire, so perhaps we would be lucky.

I took a heading that would place us in the general vicinity of Les Attaques, but in reality, we had to simply fly east until we hit the railway line. The route I had chosen was, thankfully, empty but for fields and the occasional farmhouse.

"Panthers, keep an eye out for the track," I said.

We didn't use a codeword for the target, since 'track' could mean anything to the Jerries.

"There it is," said Arjun moments later. "Dead ahead."

Sure enough, the railway line stretched out some way in front of us, going north and south.

"And there's a big choo-choo, right on cue," said Dylan.

As we approached, the smoke from a steam engine was visible in the distance. The train would directly cross our path. Could this be some kind of serendipity? I felt the adrenaline kick in, and my pulse started racing.

"Panthers stand by," I said, slipping the safety off the guns.

This was hopefully a prime target. As we closed in on it, a long train came into view. It consisted of truck after truck of closed wagons with slatted sides.

"Shall we take it, Skipper?" asked Jonty eagerly.

"Wait," said Jean. "There are people in that train."

I saw hands and arms frantically waving through gaps in the wooden slats. What were they doing in there? I had no time to think about it. These were obviously not troops. I made a snap decision.

"Stand down," I ordered. "We'll fly up the tracks as planned."

We passed over the train and I banked around, preparing to follow the tracks of the railway up to the Calais terminal. The train disappeared into the distance. I positioned our formation directly over the line. This made it a lot easier to follow.

"There's another one," said Willie suddenly.

Sure enough, the smoke from a second engine was visible in the distance, coming towards us.

"Is it military?" asked Arjun.

Before I could answer him, tracers streamed out from the approaching train.

"Panthers Alpha group, attack," I said without hesitation, breaking left and circling around to hit the train from the side.

"Beta group, break right," said Tomas, taking his part of the flight into a holding pattern.

The train was coming down the line at some speed. As we turned towards it, the bullets really started flying. I hoped that none of us would get hit. It was, however, an opportunity I couldn't pass up.

We fanned out in a line; there was no time to lose. The train was now well within range, so I gave the order.

"Fire!"

The ammunition from six planes kicked up the dirt as the guns found their mark. The train was a heavily armed troop train; nevertheless, we got a lucky strike on the engine. The train ground to a halt with steam escaping, enveloping the rest of the railcars and reducing visibility for the defenders. German soldiers spilt out of the carriages as we passed overhead.

"We'll give it one more go," I said, turning for another sweep.

Tomas's group were circling out of range, waiting to escort us home. We closed with the train once more, firing several bursts, cutting through the scattering troops. There was an explosion as a fuel tanker blew up, followed by several more. The back of the train was loaded with Panzers, obviously going somewhere. The fuel was for them. Now they would be at a standstill for a while — we'd got a lucky strike.

We passed over the train and beyond it. There was some more firing from the Germans on the ground. Fortunately, they all missed.

"Shall we go again, Skipper?" asked Jonty.

"No, we've done enough. Panthers, let's get the hell out of here," I said, turning away from the flaming wreckage. I didn't .want to push our luck.

"Panthers Beta group, on station," said Tomas, settling in behind us.

It was now a question of escaping before the Luftwaffe could respond. I throttled up, keeping low and heading west of Calais. We reached the Channel a few minutes later.

We were halfway over the water when Olek said, "Bandits on our six o'clock."

I checked my mirror and saw several Focke-Wulfs in the distance behind us.

"Keep going," I said. "If they get too close, Panther Betas will engage."

We seemed to be outrunning them when, thankfully, the cliffs of Dover came into view. Then we were once more over British soil, and the Wulfs turned away, back to France. I breathed a sigh of relief.

"I say," said Jonty as we headed for Banley. "That was bloody marvellous."

Before Willie could object, Jonty burst into song.

"Oh, we went on a jolly jaunt to France, to run some Jerries down. Their train went by in the blink of an eye and…"

"No!" groaned Willie as Jonty started his second verse.

I let it go. We all had our own way of letting off steam, and this was Jonty's. I took the squadron back to normal height now that the mission was over. It had been a success. My thoughts returned to the train we had let go by. Who was in it? Where were they being taken? I didn't know the answers.

By the time we landed, Jonty had lapsed into silence. As I taxied my plane to the standing, I could see Angelica pelting over the field to meet me.

"Oof!" I said as she landed on my chest.

"You're safe," she said. "Thank God you're safe."

I enveloped her in an embrace, lost to the world for a moment. A cough caused us to draw apart. It was Bentley, accompanied by Audrey. He was engaged in lighting his pipe.

"Back in one piece, I see," he said, puffing away and smiling.

"Yes, sir, though we did have some return fire from the troop train we shot at."

"Yes, I can see the holes all over Butterworth's plane," he said, pointing them out with the stem of his pipe.

I followed his gaze and sure enough, Jonty's fuselage did have several bullet holes in it. Jonty hadn't mentioned this, which was typical of him.

"I'll make sure it all gets patched up," I told Bentley.

"See that you do," he replied a little acerbically. "The raid was a success, by all accounts. Well done."

"Thank you, sir, and yes, it was," I replied.

"Jolly good. Onto the next one then." He turned on his heel and left in the abrupt manner he often did.

"I suppose there'll be a next one," said Angelica quietly.

I pulled her in closer. "Yes, I suppose there will."

CHAPTER FIVE

There was a commotion in the mess. I'd gone there for lunch following the mission with Angelica, Willie, Olga and Maria. Raised voices emanated from the kitchen.

We had been sitting enjoying a portion of beef pie, mashed potatoes and vegetables.

"That sounds like the chef, Charlie," said Olga, who knew most of the crew in the mess. "I'll go and find out what's wrong."

"I'll come with you," said Willie, getting up from his seat.

Olga and Willie left us and made their way to the kitchen. The shouting stopped soon afterwards.

"I wonder what could be wrong?" said Maria.

"We'll know soon enough," I replied, turning my attention back to my pie.

"That cow Jonty killed has lasted a long time," remarked Angelica, changing the subject.

"Jonty killed a cow?" Maria asked, intrigued.

I had just finished explaining the circumstances, much to her amusement, when Olga and Willie returned and resumed their seats.

"What was all that about?" I asked Olga.

"Charlie's pocket watch," she replied. "It was an heirloom from his grandfather. I remember him showing it to us. It's gone missing."

Angelica and I looked at each other. After more than one instance of spying on the base, we'd learned to pay attention to small details. Not that this seemed like a case of spying, but I was curious. I finished my food and resolved to discover a little more about the circumstances.

"Do you think Charlie will mind if I have a word?" I asked Olga.

"No, I'm sure not. He seemed pretty upset."

Angelica and I entered the kitchen. It was spacious, with long worktops and large pots bubbling on the stove. Over in one area, a couple of staff were busy washing up. Sitting on a chair, looking rather mournful, was a man I took to be Charlie. He was wearing a white smock and apron, with a white chef's hat on his head. He was a little rotund in stature and had a shock of black hair peeping out from under his cap.

"Charlie?" I said tentatively, going up to him.

He sprang to attention at once and saluted. "Corporal Charlie Wescott, sir — how can I help? Is it the food? Not to your liking?" he asked anxiously.

"Not at all," I said, reassuring him. "The food is delicious."

"We came to ask you about your pocket watch," said Angelica.

His face fell at once. "Oh."

"We heard it was stolen."

He gestured helplessly towards a row of hooks where the staff obviously hung their various garments. "Yes, it's gone. I always hang it up there when I'm cooking, to keep it safe. It was there this morning, and then I just noticed it was missing."

He sighed lugubriously, as if the weight of the world had descended upon his shoulders.

"Are you sure you brought it in today?" asked Angelica gently.

"It never leaves my side," he replied. "Except, of course, when it's hanging up there and when I'm in bed…"

"Do you have any idea who might have taken it?" I asked him.

"No. I've questioned everyone here; they swear they never touched it," he replied.

I guessed that the raised voices we had heard had been Charlie's way of questioning the staff.

"Do you believe them?" said Angelica.

"Yes, I've no reason not to. I've been working with these people for months. They wouldn't…" He trailed off.

"Have you noticed any strangers hanging around, anything like that?"

"No, nobody comes back here really."

"Who *does* come back here?" I asked him.

He thought for a while. "Well, there's the staff, of course. Olga … she's a great chef. The odd person here and there on business. You know, bringing in supplies, that sort of thing."

Angelica and I exchanged a glance.

"Sergeant Willis?" I said casually.

His face brightened up at the mention of Willis's name. "Oh yes, he's in here a lot, making sure we've got everything we need. He's a good sort." He paused for a moment and looked at me. "It wouldn't be him, if that's what you're thinking. Salt of the earth."

"Of course," I said. "I wasn't implying anything, just checking who had been back here."

"Has to be some sneak thief," said Charlie. "If I catch them, well, they'd just better watch out, that's all."

His eyes fell on some large knives lying on one of the worktops, and I caught his drift without him elaborating on his intentions.

"Right," I said. "Well, thanks for your time."

"Do you think you might be able to investigate it?" he said hopefully.

"I'll see what I can do," I replied.

"Thank you, sir, I appreciate it. I appreciate you coming and asking me too," he said.

We rejoined the others.

"We've ordered apple crumble for dessert," said Willie.

"You're a lifesaver, Kiwi," Angelica told him.

"Well?" said Olga, who was more interested in our conversation with Charlie.

I told her what Charlie had said. Olga said she had elicited much the same information. We talked about the odd occurrence of the missing chess piece.

"I don't see there's much we can do," I said at length.

"You could talk to Bentley," suggested Angelica.

"I could," I replied without much enthusiasm.

"He ought to be made aware, at least," she added with a smile.

She was right, though I anticipated that any hint of an investigation would be met with a frosty reception.

"All right," I agreed. "I'll have a word with him about it, but I don't hold out much hope that anything will come of it."

Having enjoyed the rather delicious apple crumble, I made my way to Bentley's office. Audrey opened the door and ushered me in, then returned to her desk. I stood in front of Bentley's desk and waited. He was busy reading a memo. As soon as he saw me, he picked up his pipe and began to scrape out the bowl.

"Ah, Angus," he said. "Take a seat."

I waited patiently while he tamped in a fresh batch of tobacco and lit it. I wondered what would happen if he and his pipe were ever separated. I suspected there would be hell to pay. It didn't bear thinking about.

"What brings you here?" he said, puffing out clouds of acrid smoke.

"Sir, there may be a problem on the base."

He didn't bat an eyelid but carried on smoking his pipe and regarding me with interest. "What kind of a problem?" he said.

"Well, things are going missing…"

There was a slight twitch below his right eye on hearing this. "What things?" he asked, leaning back in his seat.

I relayed the circumstances of the missing chess piece and Charlie's missing pocket watch while he listened patiently.

"So, a chess piece and a watch. Is that right?" he said when I'd finished.

"Yes, sir."

"Hardly a crime spree, is it?" he said acerbically.

"Well, no, but —"

"The chess piece was probably mislaid by that blasted reprobate Butterworth, for a start," he continued.

"That's possible, sir, but we did search high and low for it," I persisted, feeling I was fighting a losing battle.

"*Did* you?" he said in a tone laced with sarcasm.

"Yes, sir."

"Even if you are right, what do you suppose I should do about it?" he said.

This was the nub of it, and to be fair, I hadn't thought it through, expecting to be rebuffed.

"I don't know, sir, conduct a search perhaps?" I said, clutching at the first thought that came into my head.

"I can't just go searching the place for a pocket watch and a chess piece," he said. "And I can't authorise a search without any sort of evidence."

I had to acknowledge his point was completely reasonable.

"No, sir," I said.

"Right, well, is there someone you suspect?" he said.

I hesitated about mentioning the new sergeant, but in the end, valour won over discretion. "Well, there's a new man around the place," I said.

For the first time Bentley showed some signs of irritation, something I had been hoping to avoid. He began to puff on his pipe a little faster, which was a sure sign of his rising temper. "What new man?" he asked.

There was nothing for it but to come out with it. "Sergeant Nicholas Willis," I said.

At the mention of his name, Bentley leapt from his seat and began to pace the room. "Sergeant Willis?" he roared. "Oh, yes, I know all about *him*. I received orders recently notifying me that he will be looking after logistics. Do you know how many times that man has been in my office, insisting I go over the inventory with him? Well, *do* you?"

"No, sir," I replied, rather taken aback by his reaction.

"Too many bloody times, that's how many!" he barked, brandishing the stem of his pipe in my direction. "As if I've not enough to do running blasted missions. But no, they have to send some bloody toffee-nosed bureaucrat to dot all the I's and cross the T's. Well, I've had my fill of blasted Sergeant Willis and no mistake!"

He returned to his seat and sat down heavily. He discovered with some annoyance that his tobacco was spent. I waited for him to refill his pipe. Fortunately, this action seemed to calm him down somewhat.

"What are you insinuating, Angus?" he asked in milder tones. "That Willis might be the thief? Taking watches and chess pieces? A little far-fetched, don't you think?"

I sighed. "I don't know, sir. It's just that this wasn't happening before he arrived," I said.

"Nevertheless, there's no evidence to go on. We can't just go making assumptions. You, of all people, should know that."

"Yes, sir," I said. He was right, of course.

"Look," he said, "I appreciate you bringing this to my attention, but unless there are further thefts of a similar nature, it's not something I want you to spend your time on. File a report and be done with it."

"Yes, sir," I replied.

"You've got missions to run, so concentrate on that," he said in kindlier tones.

"Yes, sir."

"If anything else does happen, though, let me know," he said.

This was something of an olive branch. At the end of the day, his frustrations with Willis weren't of my making.

Bentley turned his attention back to the memo on his desk, a sign that our discussion was over. As soon as I closed the office door behind me, Angelica accosted me in her usual style.

"Well?" she said eagerly. "What did he say?"

"Let's go to our bench," I suggested. "And I'll tell you."

"From your tone, it doesn't sound promising," she said, smiling.

"You don't know the half of it," I replied.

She tucked her arm into mine, and we made our way to our favourite spot. When we were sitting looking out onto the fields, watching the wild spring flowers wave in the breeze, I told her what had transpired.

"So, Willis isn't Bentley's favourite person," she said when I had finished.

"It appears not," I said. "Though he's far from being pegged as our thief."

"Then we will just have to wait and see. If the thief strikes again, then we can go back to the CO."

"Even so, he's reluctant to act without evidence," I told her.

"Then we'll have to try and get it," she said.

"If you say so."

"I do say so. Now, kiss me…"

I was more than happy to oblige her in that and steer the conversation away from trying to catch petty thieves. But I knew that once Angelica had taken a notion into her head, she wouldn't let it go.

In the meantime, I had another mission to organise in Northern France. We couldn't hit Calais again so soon, so I decided to look at Dunkirk or Boulogne. I knew we had got lucky with the train — that had certainly been a 'target of opportunity'. I wasn't convinced we'd be as fortunate a second time.

Meanwhile, we still had patrols to run, since keeping the skies free of bandits was one of our ongoing duties. If we ceased to patrol the skies, then Jerry might get the wrong idea.

A couple of days later, I prepared to take six planes out along the coast of East Anglia once more. I had the usual crew with me, except Jean, who had reported for duty that morning with an obvious fever. I ordered him to see the medical officer and substituted Pilot Officer Clive Roberts.

"You're not fit to fly," I told Jean. "Go and get yourself seen to."

"Scottish, come on," he said. "It's just a patrol."

"I need you to be fit; you're one of my best pilots. Now go!"

I watched him make his way towards the medical unit and hoped that the rest of the crew didn't come down with the same thing. Most of the time we were lucky; the squadron wasn't particularly plagued by ill health.

Angelica came to see me off. "Fly safe," she said, planting a kiss on my lips.

"I will. I love you."

"I love you too," she murmured.

She was smiling as I made my way to my Spitfire with the others. I climbed onto the wing and into the cockpit. Redwood strapped me in.

"Good luck, sir," he said.

"Thanks, Techie."

I spun up the prop and taxied out to the end of the runway, along with the rest of the patrol. We were soon airborne. I set a course for Felixstowe.

"East Anglia again!" said Jonty predictably as we headed for the east coast.

"Yes," said Willie. "So you might as well stop complaining."

"We've got a job to do," I told Jonty, forestalling any argument. "And that's to keep the Luftwaffe out of our skies."

"Wilco, Skipper," Jonty replied.

He subsided reluctantly. The town of Felixstowe soon came into sight, sitting as it did across the harbour from Harwich. It was another port for the Navy and, as such, a prime target for the Germans.

"Well…" began Jonty.

"Don't say it," said Willie, forestalling Jonty's prediction about not seeing any Germans.

"Don't say what?" Jonty replied.

"You know what," said Willie. "I don't want you jinxing it."

"No need for that," said Clive, interrupting them. "Bandits coming in fast on our three o'clock."

I flicked a glance over to my right and sure enough, there were half a dozen Focke-Wulfs streaking in at low altitude towards Felixstowe. I had no doubt this was a sneak attack to bomb and strafe the port.

"Break, break, engage," I said, dropping out of formation.

"Tally-ho!" said Jonty joyfully.

We were bearing down on the Wulfs as they made the harbour entrance. For some reason, we hadn't been spotted. Ack-ack and machine-gun fire opened up from the coastal defences, but the German planes were low and coming in fast. They weren't an easy target for the gunners.

I picked my mark and opened fire. The tracers streamed out towards the leading Wulf, striking his wing. Now our presence was revealed, he executed a tight turn, which proved to be his undoing.

Ack-ack fire hit him amidships, and his plane exploded. The other planes continued on towards their intended goal, undeterred.

Jonty and the rest of the patrol had managed to get behind them. Bullets spewed out from their Spitfires, striking two more Wulfs. The engine of one began to smoke, but these pilots were determined and they simply carried on.

Seconds later, they released their payload, scoring hits on the port and one of the ships. Smoke billowed up into the air. Their mission complete, the Jerries turned away for home.

"Don't let them escape," said Dylan, whose blood was up. "Let's get after them."

Arjun flew in from the side, fired, and shattered the canopy of the Jerry plane, which had slowed due to a hit on its engine. It skewed right and dived into the water, impacting with a tremendous splash. The four remaining Wulfs continued on. They were pulling away at a rapid rate.

I was about to tell the others to break off as the Germans streaked out across the Channel, heading for Holland, when Clive managed to get close enough to take another shot. I held off giving the order.

It was a decision I was to regret.

Without warning, one of the Wulfs suddenly executed a tight turn, and in seconds, Clive was in his sights. The German was obviously a skilled and experienced pilot. I should have reckoned on that.

"Watch out!" yelled Willie, but it was too late.

The German opened fire, ripping into Clive's fuselage. Moments later his plane caught fire and dived into the sea. Clive wouldn't have known anything about it.

Meanwhile, the German, sure of his kill, resumed his escape.

"Damn you, you rotter!" shouted Jonty in a voice filled with fury. "I'll get you for that!"

He gunned his Spitfire forward, but the Germans now had quite a head start. I took control of the situation.

"Leave it, Jonty, stand down," I said, not wanting to lose another pilot.

"But Skipper —" Jonty protested.

I wasn't having it. The further out over the Channel the Germans got, the more likely they were to call up reinforcements. Jonty would simply be putting himself in danger for nothing.

"Disengage — that's an order!" I told him. "That goes for the rest of you. Form up and let's go home."

"Wilco, Skipper," said Jonty, reluctantly turning away from the fleeing German planes.

I set a heading for Banley while the others joined me in formation. Nobody spoke. It was the first casualty we'd had for a while. Perhaps for that reason, it hit hard.

We landed in a sombre mood. As usual, Angelica was waiting when I climbed down from my plane. Instead of running at full pelt, she walked up to me slowly. I waited for her arrival, and she gently wrapped her arms around my neck.

"I'm sorry," she whispered, pulling me in for a kiss.

"It's my fault," I told her when our lips parted.

"No, it's not," she said fiercely. "You did your job."

There was a discreet cough beside us. We pulled apart to see Bentley and Audrey standing next to us. Bentley pulled out his pipe and lit it.

"A rum do, Angus," he said quietly.

"Yes, sir. Roberts —"

"I know," he replied shortly. He took a few puffs on his pipe before pointing the stem at me. "And don't go thinking you're responsible."

The CO was his usual perceptive self, but I did still feel it was my mistake.

"I could have told him to disengage, sir. I thought he would get the Jerry … so I didn't … and instead Jerry got him," I said, getting it off my chest.

Bentley wasn't about to let me wallow. "Listen to me," he said. "I've told you before, you can't go taking every death on your watch personally, otherwise you'll never fly again. I can't have that. You're too valuable to this squadron. Roberts took his chance, as we all do. It so happens that Lady Luck wasn't smiling this time. That's all there is to it."

"Yes, sir," I said.

"He's right, you know," Angelica said quietly.

"Of course I'm right," said Bentley, catching what she'd said. "Listen to your wife; she's got some common sense."

"I always do," I said with a wry smile.

"As it should be," said Bentley with a nod. "Now, put all this behind you. We'll have to get you another pilot and a plane, but never mind. War is war."

On that note, he departed, along with Audrey.

"I told you," said Angelica. "You take too much upon yourself."

For once, Bentley hadn't complained about the loss of a plane. He would feel the loss of one of our pilots as keenly as I did.

It being close to the end of the day, Angelica and I went to find Gordon and return to Amberly Manor.

He was sitting in his jeep as usual, reading a book. Gordon had an uncanny knack for being in the right place at exactly the right time. I didn't know how he did it.

"Ready for home?" he asked, putting his book down.

"Absolutely, Fred," I replied.

We climbed into the jeep, and I sat beside Angelica. Gordon pulled a cigarette out, struck a match and lit it. He took a few puffs with some satisfaction.

"You don't usually use matches, Fred," said Angelica.

"No," said Gordon. "Thing is, I seem to have mislaid my lighter."

Angelica and I exchanged a glance.

"Really? Since when?" she continued.

"Yesterday or the day before. Couldn't find it anywhere. Must have put it down, but now it's gone. Shame, really — it was a nice silver Zippo lighter. Got it from one of the chaps at the American base."

"I remember it," said Angelica. "Very stylish."

Gordon shrugged as if it were of no consequence. "These things happen."

His approach to life was rather philosophical. However, I wasn't about to let it go so easily. It was too much of a coincidence for my liking.

"You know, it's not the first item to have gone missing recently," I said. "There's the chess piece and Chef Wescott's pocket watch. Don't you think it's odd?"

"Yes, I suppose so, but if these items were stolen, where would you even start?"

He turned the engine over, and it sprang into life. He slipped the jeep into gear, and we set off.

"I spoke to Bentley about it," I said as we headed back to Amberly Manor. "He told me to let it go. Said it wasn't exactly a crime spree."

Gordon laughed. "He's right about that." He took a pull on his cigarette. "I take it you're not minded to let it go, sir?"

"I was," I replied. "But not now that your lighter has gone missing."

"What do you propose we do?" Angelica asked, naturally including herself in the investigation. I had a ready answer to this.

"I suggest we pay Sergeant Willis a little visit," I replied.

"On what basis?" she asked.

"I'll think of something," I replied.

"If it is him, sir, he'll have covered his tracks well," said Gordon.

"Well, it won't hurt to look around his place, will it?" I said, although a small voice in the back of my head told me that Willis probably wouldn't regard us prying into his business with any equanimity.

CHAPTER SIX

The following morning I paid a visit to the medical officer, Dr Vivek Ramachandran. I wanted to find out for myself if Jean had been to see him and what the verdict was. Jean hadn't been in evidence since before the sortie, so I assumed he'd taken to his bed. In addition, I needed to make sure it wasn't something the rest of the squadron needed to worry about.

Dr Ramachandran was sitting at his desk when I entered his office. He was a mild-mannered, distinguished-looking man of some fifty years with grey hair and a beard. He looked at me over the top of his gold-rimmed spectacles.

"I've come to ask about Pilot Officer Tarbon," I said. "I sent him to see you yesterday."

"Ah, yes, Jean," he replied. "An interesting case."

His turn of phrase made me concerned at once.

"Interesting case? What does he have, Doctor?" I asked him.

"He has malaria," came the calm reply.

"Malaria!" I exclaimed. "How on earth did he get malaria?"

The doctor sat back in his chair and replied in the patient manner he had. "He already had it. It's a recurrence of the disease, which can happen and frequently does."

"How did he get it in the first place?"

"Apparently when he visited the tropics before the war. He recovered but, unfortunately, it stays in your system. I've seen it before in India." He smiled at me reassuringly, as if it wasn't as serious as it sounded. "Do sit down, Flight Lieutenant."

"What? Oh … yes." I took a seat in front of his desk and then asked the obvious question. "Will he recover?

The doctor nodded sagely. "Yes, with the right medication, which I have had sent from the local hospital. But I'm keeping him here until he is well. It's not infectious, if that's what you're wondering."

The thought had crossed my mind. However, I still had some questions. "How long will it take for him to get well?" I asked.

Dr Ramachandran shrugged. "I can't say for sure. A few days, a couple of weeks perhaps."

"And assuming he does recover, can he fly again?"

The doctor nodded. "He can fly once he's fit, though I can't say he won't get another bout of it."

"That's something, anyway," I replied with relief. "I know very well he would hate it if he weren't allowed to serve anymore."

"It'll take a little more than that to keep him from the front line," said the doctor. "Now, if you want to see him, he's in room number two."

"Thank you, Doctor," I said. I paused because there had been something else on my mind.

"Is there anything else I can help you with, Flight Lieutenant?" the doctor asked.

"Well, Doctor, I've been a little concerned about my reactions in combat recently. I've had a couple of near misses lately and wondered if I was getting slow," I told him.

Dr Ramachandran regarded me keenly. "Fatigue, tiredness, and all sorts of other things can affect our reaction time," he said.

"But are there some tests you could do, Doctor?" I persisted. "To set my mind at ease?"

"Tests?" he said with a smile. "You want a test?"

"Well, yes…"

Without warning, his right hand came up and he flung a tennis ball straight at my face. Without thinking, I put my own hand up in defence and caught it.

The doctor laughed. "There's nothing wrong with your reactions, Flight Lieutenant. Now go on, get out of here."

Somewhat abashed by his unorthodox methods, I took my leave and made my way to room number two. Jean was lying in a single hospital bed, looking a little pale. Beside him on a small table was an empty bowl, which I presumed had contained his breakfast.

"Hello, old chap," I said.

He smiled up at me weakly. "Sorry, Scottish, that you're seeing me like this."

"It can't be helped," I said, taking a seat beside his bed.

"Damned mosquitos, they did for me. I thought I'd got over it last time…" He trailed off.

"It doesn't matter," I told him. "What matters is that you get well."

He struggled up onto one elbow and looked at me anxiously. "Please let me fly when I'm better, Scottish. I don't want to be grounded," he said.

"Well, you're grounded until you recover," I told him. "When the doctor says you can fly, then you'll be allowed to fly."

Jean looked relieved and lay back on his pillows.

"Can I get you anything?" I asked him.

"A book to read, perhaps," he replied.

"I'll get the chaps to come and visit, bring you some reading matter."

"How did the patrol go?" he asked suddenly. He obviously had not heard.

"Clive bought it," I said. "Shot down by a Focke-Wulf near Felixstowe. We caught the Jerries attacking the port. We shot down two of theirs — some consolation, I suppose."

"Damn," he said. "I liked Clive. He was a good sort."

"Concentrate on getting well," I told him. "I'll come and see you again soon."

"Thanks, Scottish," said Jean, closing his eyes.

I left him, as I could see he was tired. Hopefully, his condition would improve with treatment. Since Doctor Ramachandran didn't seem particularly ruffled, I decided not to worry.

As I left the medical unit, Angelica sidled up to me. She slipped her arm into mine.

"How's Jean?" she asked.

"He's has malaria," I told her.

"Malaria?" Her eyes widened.

I explained what the doctor had told me and that I had seen Jean myself.

"Oh dear," she said. "I hope he gets better."

"So do I, because we're two pilots down now."

Bentley wouldn't be pleased to hear the news, although he'd be sympathetic about Jean's condition.

"Where are we going?" Angelica asked me, since I wasn't leading her towards the hut.

"We're going to find Gordon, and then we're going to pay Sergeant Willis a visit," I said.

"Oh … oh, yes!"

Her face brightened at this news. Angelica rather enjoyed a spot of intrigue. We found Gordon in the mess, chatting with one of the WAAFs attached to the mess crew. Angelica shot me a knowing look. We both knew Gordon was something of a ladies' man.

He spotted us approaching and said goodbye to the WAAF before joining us.

"Were you looking for me, sir?" he asked me.

"Yes, Fred, we were thinking of going to see Sergeant Willis."

"One of your lady friends, Fred?" Angelica asked in a teasing tone, nodding towards the WAAF.

"Oh, you know…" he said, shrugging off the question.

"We *do* know, Fred," said Angelica, undeterred.

"Shall we go?" I said, intervening.

"I'll lead the way," said Gordon, looking relieved to have been rescued from any more awkward questions.

Sergeant Willis evidently spent much of his time in the supply huts. These were a series of Nissen huts on the perimeter of the base. Gordon, who obviously knew his way around, took us to one of them.

We entered by the main door into a surprisingly spacious interior. Windows set into the prefabricated sides let in the daylight. The hut was full of shelving containing all kinds of items which were needed for a functioning airbase. At one end of the hut was a desk, behind which stood a number of filing cabinets. The desk was covered with stacks of files and paper. Sitting at the desk, illuminated by a desk lamp, was Sergeant Willis.

As soon as he saw us enter, he stood up and came forward to greet us. We exchanged salutes.

"Can I help you, sir?" he asked politely.

I had to admit that I had not thought the plan through beyond turning up at his supply hut, and so for a moment I was a little lost for words. Fortunately, Gordon stepped smoothly into the breach.

"Inspection," he said. "We're here for an inspection."

"Inspection?" said Willis. "I wasn't told about this."

I looked at Gordon. He smiled encouragingly, so I took up the refrain.

"Yes," I said. "The CO likes to be sure everything is right and tight, so he asked us to take a look around."

"He wants you to take a look around?" said Willis in disbelieving tones. "A pilot…"

"Flight Lieutenant Mackennelly is often asked to carry out other duties by Squadron Leader Bentley," said Angelica.

"Is he?" said Willis.

"Yes," replied Angelica simply.

Realising that he couldn't cross the line into insubordination, Willis softened his attitude a little. It was clear, however, that our presence in his domain was unwelcome.

"Well, if Squadron Leader Bentley has ordered it, then naturally, feel free to take a look around. You'll find it's all in order," he said.

"Thank you," I replied.

Now that we'd cast ourselves in the mould of inspecting the premises, we had to do exactly that.

The three of us wandered around the Nissen hut, conducting a cursory examination of the various items on the shelves and asking spurious questions. Willis answered them with as much equanimity as he could muster.

"Yes, that's spare cutlery for the mess… No, the various tins are in the hut next door if you'd like to take a look… The uniforms are in hut three…"

We eventually arrived at Willis's desk. I looked down at the tidy piles of papers and the exceptionally neat handwriting in the pages of a ledger which lay open on the desktop.

"You keep it all very organised," I said.

"I like to think so, sir," responded Willis.

"Squadron Leader Bentley will be most impressed," said Angelica, furnishing him with one of her sweetest smiles.

It was then that I spotted a door in the wall just behind the desk.

"What's that?" I asked Willis.

He bristled a little at the question. "That's my sleeping quarters when I stay over. Naturally you're welcome to inspect that too, if you *must*."

I glanced at Angelica and Gordon. Although I dearly wanted to take a look inside, I felt that it would be a bridge too far, under the circumstances.

"No, I don't think that will be necessary, Sergeant," I said.

"As you wish, sir," Willis replied, looking suspiciously relieved. "Would you like to see anything else, inspect the other huts?"

I decided that we'd seen enough, and if he was the thief, we were not going to catch him out so easily.

"No," I told him. "That will be all. We've seen enough to know that you've got everything in perfect order."

As we left the hut, he watched us from the window, perhaps wanting to be sure that we actually left.

"He was acting very suspiciously," I said once we were out of earshot.

"Or he could just be a tad possessive over what he considers to be his area of responsibility," Gordon replied, playing devil's advocate.

"I agree with Angus," said Angelica. "I think he's hiding something."

"Female intuition?" I asked her with a smile.

"Angelica's intuition," she countered.

"Well, in that case…" said Gordon, and we all laughed.

However, I couldn't really see a way forward. "Even if we do suspect him," I said, "we can't really do much unless we've got some evidence to go on."

"If I might venture an opinion," said Gordon. "A criminal is bound to slip up at some point. They get cocky or careless, and that's when your evidence will appear."

I smiled at this. Gordon was wise as usual. It seemed prudent to wait rather than to act precipitously.

"You're right," I replied. "We'll just have to be patient."

Angelica and I parted company with Gordon and went to the hut to inform the others about Jean's illness. They were all extremely solicitous and promised to pay him a visit.

"Grapes, Skipper, that's what he needs," said Jonty, who seemed to regard the fruit as some kind of panacea for all ills. "I shall go and acquire some forthwith."

"I'm coming with you," said Willie.

I watched the two of them head off to where Jonty parked his Morgan three-wheeler. I didn't like to ask where he imagined he would find grapes at this time of year. Far be it from me to cast a damper on his enthusiasm.

It wasn't much later when Audrey appeared. Angelica and I were sitting outside the hut, drinking tea.

"Bentley wants to see you, sir," she said without preamble. "And Angelica."

"Why me?" Angelica asked her.

"He's had a visit from Sergeant Willis," said Audrey, as if that explained everything. Which, of course, in this case it did.

Obviously, the good sergeant had taken it upon himself to see Bentley directly after our visit, no doubt to frame some kind of complaint.

"How is Bentley's temper?" I asked Audrey as I set down my mug and stood up.

"It hasn't been improved by Willis," she said frankly.

"Right, well, I suppose we'd better go and face the music."

We accompanied Audrey back to the CO's office and stood to attention in front of his desk. Bentley seemed in no hurry to acknowledge our presence, but I knew this was just his way.

"Ah, Flying Officer Mackennelly and Section Officer Mackennelly," he said at length, almost as if he had not kept us standing there for several moments. "Do take a seat, why don't you?"

We complied and sat patiently while the pipe of doom was replenished. It was the precursor to a Bentley lecture. Angelica stole a glance at me, and I tried to smile back reassuringly.

Bentley finally lit his pipe and leaned back in his chair. "I saw Sergeant Willis not long ago," he said casually.

"Really, sir?" I replied. "Was he here for a particular reason?" I was reluctant to own up to anything without knowing the tack Bentley was going to take.

"He came specifically to ask me why I had ordered an inspection of his premises without giving him any notice. I wonder if you know anything about it?" he continued, coming to the point.

"Well, sir, I —"

Bentley cut me short. "I thought I asked you to leave this whole thievery business alone, Angus?"

"Well, yes —" I began.

"Yet here you are conducting some blasted clandestine investigation disguised as an inspection which I am supposed to have ordered."

"Sir, it's on account of Sergeant Gordon's lighter," said Angelica, entering the fray.

"His lighter?" said Bentley, sounding nonplussed. "What the devil has Sergeant Gordon's lighter got to do with it?"

"His lighter went missing, sir. He couldn't find it anywhere. It was one of those clever Zippo ones," Angelica explained.

"A Zippo lighter, eh?" said Bentley, who held a certain reverence for any artefact associated with smoking. "I can understand how that might be missed... But even so, why on earth did you hotfoot it over to see Willis?"

"It was my idea, sir," I said. "It just seemed opportune."

A note of scepticism crept into Bentley's tone. "Opportune to do what? Did you imagine that, even if he had taken it, he'd have all his stolen goods on display?"

"Well, no," I admitted. "I just thought, perhaps, there might be a clue..." I trailed off somewhat lamely since, in hindsight, it didn't seem the best plan after all.

"I take it you didn't find any evidence," he said in a slightly less acerbic tone.

"No, sir, he keeps the place rather tidy," I admitted.

"Hmm, well, that's as may be," said Bentley. "But the net result of your, shall we say, ill-judged actions is that I had to endure yet another session with Willis bending my ear for far longer than I was able to tolerate with any equanimity!"

"I apologise for that, sir," I said.

"Yes, well, I told him that I'd order inspections whenever I damn well wanted, that this is my airbase and I'm in charge of what goes on here. Sent him away with a flea in his ear, by Jove," he continued with some satisfaction. "However, in future, if you're going to put my name to some hare-brained scheme, then at least have the decency to ask me first."

"Yes, sir, I will, sir," I replied, rather glad that Bentley had kept his temper for a change.

"I understand these things are important to you," he said, "but there is also a war on. Don't forget that."

"No, sir, I won't, sir," I said. Then I remembered Jean. "There is another matter, sir…"

"Well?" he said, eyeing me a little askance.

"Sir, Pilot Officer Tarbon has malaria."

There was silence while Bentley received this intelligence. He took several puffs on his pipe before speaking. "How the deuce did he get malaria, for God's sake? Have we experienced a sudden plague of mosquitoes in this country?"

"No, sir, he already had it and recovered. This is a recurrence," I explained.

"Right, I see. Well, what's the prognosis?"

"He'll be fit to fly again once he recovers. The doctor is treating him with appropriate medication."

"So now I'm two bloody pilots down," said Bentley. "I never should have let them transfer Pilot Officers Franklin and Smyth to other squadrons."

Bentley was right. We had been given extra pilots while running a pair of twenty-four-hour standby planes to protect Maria from the assassin. However, once that threat had been eliminated, the standby operation was stood down. We thus had two spare pilots, which were soon taken off us by Fighter Command, much to Bentley's annoyance.

"No, sir," I replied, knowing he'd had no real say in it.

"Well, it can't be helped," said Bentley. "I'll get you some replacements as soon as possible. In the meantime, you need to continue to fly patrols and carry out your next mission … with or without the extra pilots."

"Sir," I replied, without much enthusiasm at the thought of flying a mission with ten planes instead of twelve. Then I had a thought. "Perhaps I could ask Captain Sandford…"

He pounced on this at once. "Yes! Then perhaps you could ask him when he's going to deliver the Spitfires he promised us?"

He and Sandford had evidently discussed handing over the spare planes.

"Yes, sir, I will. If that's all, sir?" I said, hoping to make a quick exit.

"Yes, go over there *tout de suite* and find out where my planes are, that's the ticket," said Bentley, who now had the bit between his teeth. "And don't spare the horses."

Angelica and I took our leave as rapidly as we could.

"That was a lucky escape," she said, once we were outside the main building.

"Yes," I agreed. "Fortunately, we got away with the Willis business."

"Do you still suspect him? Because I certainly do," she said.

"I don't know. There's something about him, just like Olga said."

"Well, if he is a thief, then it's only a matter of time before he slips up, just as Fred implied."

"No doubt," I agreed. "Let's go and find Fred in any case. We'd better get over to the American base and ask them to expedite the transfer of those planes."

It turned out that Sandford was more than happy to lend a hand. In fact, he offered his whole squadron if we thought it would help. I was happy to accept. Angelica and I sat in his office discussing the possibilities, and all seemed to be going well. However, when I finally asked about the redundant Spitfires, he went a little quiet.

"There are complications," he said, sipping his Coca-Cola.

"Complications?" I said, frowning.

He sighed. "Well, the powers that be at the USAAF don't want to give them back."

I glanced at Angelica. She looked equally flabbergasted.

"What? Why ever not?"

"Well, you know, it's that old thing about finders keepers…" He trailed off, since he knew that was not a reasonable explanation.

"This isn't exactly finders keepers, though, is it?" I protested hotly. "The RAF gave you the Spitfires in the first place, so technically we could say that they were on loan."

"I know all of that," said Sandford, looking shamefaced. I felt sorry for his embarrassment, since it was not of his doing.

"Bentley isn't going to be pleased," I said.

"He's going to be livid," put in Angelica.

Sandford grimaced at the thought. "I know, and I promised him. Now I can't keep my promise. I'm sorry."

"So these bloody planes are just going to gather dust in your hangar because someone on your side doesn't want to give them up?" I said, pardonably annoyed.

"I wouldn't quite put it like that," said Sandford.

"Then how would you put it?"

Sandford thought for a moment and then shook his head. "Okay, I *would* put it like that. You're absolutely right. Unfortunately, the base commander doesn't want them gone."

"Is he keeping them as souvenirs or something?" I demanded.

Sandford shrugged as if it were out of his hands. I also couldn't understand why his commanding officer would suddenly make such an arbitrary decision. Until now, the two bases had got along very well.

"You know that Bentley won't leave it there," I said. "There'll be something of a stink."

"I know, but the new guy does everything by the rules, so…" He shrugged again.

"New guy? What happened to the old guy?"

"He's still here, technically the CO, but now there's a base commander above him. A damn shame — he was easy to work with as COs go."

"Does this spell an end to cooperation?" I wondered out loud.

Sandford was quick to reassure me on that point. "Oh no. We'll be supporting you on your missions, no questions asked. Those are in standing orders all the way to the top."

"And you can't think of any way around this issue of the Spitfires at the moment?" I asked him. "Just when we need them, too."

"I can't. I've tried, the CO has tried, but according to the new head honcho, there's nothing in the Army manual to support your request, and if it's not in the Army manual or standing orders, then…"

I finished my drink and stood up. "Well, I suppose there's no more to be said," I said. Suddenly, the American base didn't seem quite as welcoming as it had previously.

"I really am sorry," he told me, looking contrite.

"It can't be helped," I replied. "I'll be in touch about the mission soon."

We took our leave and returned to the jeep, where Gordon was waiting.

"Hello," he said, taking in my expression. "Did things not go well, sir?"

"I'll say they didn't go well, Fred," I replied, still irritated by the entire proceedings.

"They won't give our Spitfires back," said Angelica, as we climbed into the jeep.

"What? Captain Sandford?" said Gordon with surprise.

"No, his new base commander," I told him. "Stickler for the rules, apparently, and there's nothing in the rules to say they have to return them."

"Hmm, that doesn't sound good," said Gordon, starting up the jeep and slipping it into gear.

"Not good? It's catastrophic," I replied as we made our way past the sentries and then onto the road leading to Banley. "Bentley is going to hit the roof."

"Perhaps we don't have to tell him today," suggested Angelica.

"That sounds like an excellent idea," I said. "We'll wait until tomorrow."

Given that we'd already had one uncomfortable session with Bentley, I didn't relish another quite so soon. To which end we made ourselves scarce and returned to Amberly Manor. We were always contactable by telephone, should there be something requiring urgent attention. The problem of the new base commander's intransigence seemed insurmountable. I didn't relish the inevitable interview with Bentley on the morrow.

Naturally, when we arrived at Banley the next morning, Audrey was on the lookout for us. She came up to the jeep at once.

"Don't tell me," I said. "Bentley wants to see me."

"He was looking for you yesterday too," she told me, which didn't augur well.

I sighed. Bentley's blood was definitely up over the Spitfires.

"Lead on," I replied, jumping down from the jeep, followed by Angelica.

"Good luck, sir," Gordon called after us.

"I think we're going to need it," I said to Audrey.

In no time at all, we were sitting in Bentley's office while he conducted a prolonged ritual with his pipe.

"Ah, Angus," he said once he was puffing away, releasing clouds of smoke into the room. "No doubt you're eager to report on your mission to the American base."

Since he forbore to ask where I had been the previous afternoon, I accepted the tinge of sarcasm in his tone.

"Yes, sir," I said, a little reluctant to come to the point.

"And how was your mission?" he asked.

"Well, Captain Booker is happy to participate in our next raid, sir. He'll even bring his full squadron," I said, trying to defer the moment of truth.

Angelica glanced at me, as if to say, *just get on with it.*

"Yes, yes," Bentley replied testily. "No doubt he is, but what about the Spitfires? When can we get them?"

"Well, sir, it's like this…" I began.

Perceiving that my response was not going to be as he'd hoped, Bentley pointed the stem of his pipe at me like a dagger. "Go on, spit it out. What did Captain Booker say?"

I metaphorically girded my loins. "He said, sir, that we can't have them," I told him.

"What?" said Bentley. "What did you say?"

"Sir, he said that the base commander refuses to return them to the RAF."

The twitch below Bentley's eye became very pronounced at that moment. He started to puff clouds of smoke at an alarming rate. Moments later, he catapulted out of his chair with a roar.

"He won't return them? Is that what you said? He won't give the RAF back our bloody planes?"

"Yes, sir, that's about the gist of it," I replied.

"I'll give him the bloody gist! On what blasted authority does he think he has the right to keep our aircraft? I've never heard such poppycock in all my life. What sort of clown show are they running over there? Won't give back our planes? It's absolutely outrageous!"

"Apparently, sir, the CO was all for giving them back, but they've got a new base commander and he's a stickler for Army protocol," I explained.

"Protocol? I'll give him some blasted protocol!" he roared. "Who the hell does he think he is? We're running a war here, not counting bloody rivets. Who is this base commander?"

"I'm afraid I don't know, sir," I said.

"Audrey, find out who the American Base Commander is on the double," ordered Bentley. "I'll have his guts for garters."

"Yes, sir," said Audrey, springing into action and picking up the telephone. She was no doubt inured to Bentley's starts.

In the meantime, Bentley resumed his seat and proceeded to refill his pipe while muttering darkly about 'jumped-up American scoundrels who think they own the place.'

We listened to Audrey's side of the conversation as she obtained the required information. She wrote it on a piece of paper and put down the phone.

"Well?" said Bentley, lighting his pipe. After a few puffs, he thankfully seemed much calmer.

"It's Colonel Dougan Todd," said Audrey, reading from her paper.

"Is it?" said Bentley acidly.

"Yes, sir."

"Well, I suppose we're going to have to pay Colonel Todd a visit," he said. "Take the bull by the horns, as it were."

I didn't like the way he said 'we', since meeting the base commander of the US Airbase was the last thing I wanted to do.

"Will that be all, sir?" I asked him tentatively.

"No, Angus, that will not be all. When I said 'we', that includes you and Section Officer Mackennelly. *We* will be going over there to find out what he's playing at!"

"It's just that I've got a patrol to run, sir, and a mission to plan," I protested.

"Yes, and you're two planes short, in case you hadn't noticed. So, you need those Spitfires, don't you?"

"Could I at least run the patrol first?" I asked him hopefully.

He made a noise of exasperation. However, duty was duty — even Bentley knew that.

"Fine, but don't go disappearing afterwards," he said. "And don't go getting yourself shot down or killed either; you're coming with me, and that's the end of it!"

Knowing that this was simply his extreme agitation over what he perceived to be a wrong being done to our squadron, I took this in good part.

"Yes, sir," I said. Angelica and I stood up and saluted.

"Very well, dismissed, but get back here as soon as you can," he said. "I'll be waiting."

We left in short order. Clearly, we were not going to escape Bentley's expedition. One which I already felt was going to be fruitless.

M Flight was now down to ten active members with Jean in the infirmary and Clive having been killed. At the hut, I caught up with Tomas.

"How was your patrol yesterday?" I asked him.

"We saw some Jerries in the distance, but they did not come close. I think maybe they were put off their attack by our patrol," he said.

"Makes sense," I said. "Where was this?"

"Just north of Lowestoft," he replied. "Anyway, will we be getting some new pilots and planes?"

"In due course," I replied. "We're trying to get the Americans to give the Spitfires back."

"Ah, the Americans…" He trailed off, but the look he gave me spoke volumes. I wondered if news had travelled or if there was some other reason for his cryptic remark.

"I say, Skipper," said Jonty, joining the conversation. "Have you heard that we're not allowed in the American mess anymore?"

"What?"

"Yes, some new chap in charge says we can only go there on official business," Jonty continued.

"You see," said Tomas. "People are your friends until one day … they are not…"

I looked at Angelica and she pursed her lips. This wasn't good news. Cooperation was the key to any good relationship. It seemed that Colonel Todd was putting paid to that at a rapid rate.

"That's as may be," I said, "but the Americans are welcome on this base any time they want."

It didn't do to stoop to the same level, and I hoped Bentley would feel the same. I picked out Willie, Jonty, Dylan, Arjun and Pilot Officer Stanley Turner to join the patrol, and I put the issue with the American base firmly from my mind for the moment.

Outside the hut, Angelica and I said goodbye, although I never liked to think of it as something quite so final.

"Come back safe," she said, embracing me.

"I will."

"I love you."

"I love you too."

We parted and I made my way to my kite. Redwood strapped me in. I fired up the engine as soon as he was clear. The Merlin sprang to life, and I taxied down to the end of the runway. A minute or so later, I was airborne, along with the others.

I set a course for Lowestoft on a hunch that if the Jerries had been deterred the previous day, they'd be highly likely to try again.

"I say, Skipper —" Jonty began.

"Don't complain or jinx it," said Willie at once.

"For your information, I was going to say what a jolly nice day it is for a run out to East Anglia," Jonty retorted.

"Pull the other one," said Willie.

"Let's keep our eyes peeled," I said, intervening. "Those bandits from yesterday might well come back."

The flight to Lowestoft was uneventful. The seaside town lay spread out below us. It sported a harbour. There were several naval bases there by all accounts, which included the Royal Naval Patrol Service. I could see boats and small ships below as we passed over them. I decided to linger around the area for a little longer before going north.

"We'll take a circle out into the Channel," I said, turning my kite.

We traversed in a loop which ran parallel to the shore, but some way out over the blue water. There was no sign of the enemy. I was about to give up and head back to shore when the radio crackled to life.

"Bandits," said Stanley. "Three o'clock low."

I looked down and saw three Focke-Wulfs streaking in at low level, presumably to attack the port. It was another sneak attack, or perhaps a 'tip and run' raid.

"Break, break, engage," I said, dropping out of formation and heading towards the Wulfs.

They had slipped underneath us and were now not far from the port. I was determined not to let them get there. The six of us opened fire at the same time from behind the Germans, who had not seen us.

We scored a hit on one, and the other two broke off their attack. They headed straight up in the air, turning away from their intended target. The Wulf which had been hit landed in the water with a splash.

I left him to it as we went in pursuit of the other two planes. A boat would no doubt pick him up if he managed to get out of his plane.

In the meantime, we gave chase to the remaining Wulfs, who were trying to make a getaway.

"Tally-ho!" said Jonty, gunning his Spitfire forward.

He and Willie got on the tail of one of them. The German weaved and turned, avoiding shot after shot. The third Wulf was clean away and off into the distance.

I noticed we were getting further into the Channel when I spotted some distant specks on the horizon. More enemy planes. If we kept going, we'd engage a whole fresh set of bandits. That would be foolhardy.

"Disengage, break it off," I said.

"I've almost got him, Skipper. Just one more minute," said Jonty.

"Leave it. That's an order," I told him. "Let's head back."

I turned away, keeping a weather eye on my mirror. We might be low on ammo, and the new Jerries would likely outnumber us.

"Those Jerries are getting closer," said Dylan, who'd been watching them too.

"Keep going," I said, heading back to the port. If the Germans carried on, they'd be in range of the ack-ack, so I doubted they would follow us all the way in.

Below us, a Naval Patrol Service boat was picking up the downed pilot. His plane was slowly disappearing below the waves.

As we crossed back over British soil, the planes behind us were once more receding. They'd thought better of engaging us over the port, something for which I was thankful. We had prevented a raid, that was the important thing. There had been a few more incursions than normal recently. Shortly, we were to embark on one of our own.

We arrived back at Banley without further incident. Jonty didn't sing either, for a change, which probably made Willie happy.

After we landed, Angelica pelted over to see me. I took the usual impact as she flung herself into my arms.

"I suppose you'll never tire of that," I said, laughing.

"Would you want me to?" she said, her eyes dancing.

"I suppose not. I'm glad you're pleased to see me."

We embraced and kissed, then we made our way to the hut. I divested myself of my life jacket, and then it was time to bite the bullet.

CHAPTER SEVEN

"Are we off to see Bentley?" asked Angelica as we walked towards the main building.

"I wouldn't dare not go," I said. She laughed.

Audrey was standing at the entrance to the building and said, "I've ordered a staff car. You can follow in the jeep."

"All right," I replied.

We went to find Gordon, who was fortuitously waiting in the jeep, smoking a cigarette.

"We're off to the American base with Bentley," I told him.

"Righty-ho, sir," he said. "Hop in."

We followed Bentley's staff car to the American base, where it was stopped by the sentries. I could hear Bentley getting annoyed at being questioned as to why he was visiting.

"I'm here to see Colonel Todd," we heard him say. "Yes, it is official business… What the bloody hell do you think I'm here for, a social call?" His voice began to get louder. "No, I do not have an appointment, and I don't need one. I'm the commanding officer of Banley Airfield — now let me through!"

The sentry who was asking the questions hesitated for a moment and then waved him through. We followed behind.

"Have the sentries become more difficult, Fred?" I asked Gordon.

"Let's just say they are scrutinising identification more closely," said Gordon. "I must admit I won't be frequenting the base as often as I did."

This spoke volumes. The edicts of Colonel Todd were having an impact. We drove on to the main office building, where we pulled up next to Bentley.

"What a bloody farrago that was," the CO raged as he got out of the staff car. Then he looked around. "I wonder where this blasted colonel's office is."

We need not have worried. A corporal appeared almost at once from the building entrance and saluted.

"You're here to see Colonel Todd, sir?" he asked Bentley.

Obviously, the sentries had forewarned the base commander's office.

"Yes," said Bentley. "Kindly take us to him."

"All of you?" said the corporal, looking at the rest of us.

"Yes, all of us," said Bentley, who was already in a tetchy frame of mind. "Shall we go?"

"This way, sir," said the corporal, leading us into the office building. Gordon stayed with the jeep, along with the WAAF driving the staff car. I could hear them striking up a conversation, and her laughter faded away as we entered the building.

We were ushered into a large office, the door of which proclaimed it to be that of 'Colonel Todd, USAAF Base Commander' in gold letters. Inside, it was spacious, with an American flag on a pole behind an oversized desk. On the wall hung a painting which appeared to depict Colonel Todd wearing his best military uniform and striking a pose not unlike that of Napoleon. Everything in the office seemed to have been placed there for his exaltation.

Colonel Todd was a florid-looking man. He had a comb-over of blond hair to cover his receding hairline. He looked a little portly as he stood up, his uniform replete with various decorations and medals.

Bentley snapped a smart salute, and we followed suit. Todd flicked a lazy salute in return and eyed us with interest.

"Colonel Todd, Base Commander, at your service," he said.

We remained standing since he had not asked us to sit, while he resumed his seat behind his desk. There were, in fact, a couple of sofas in the room which could have accommodated us all, so I assumed this was deliberate.

"Squadron Leader Bentley, Commanding Officer of the Mavericks squadron next door," said Bentley.

I noticed that he did not get out his pipe, perhaps in observance of some kind of protocol.

"Ah yes, the British next door," said Todd in a dismissive tone.

"We have a long-standing arrangement of cooperation with your airbase," said Bentley. "We've supported many of your bomber missions, trained your fighter pilots, and in general assisted wherever we can."

The CO's tone was deceptively polite. The colonel was two ranks above him and, as such, a senior officer. However, this point seemed to galvanise the colonel into action.

"Where are my manners?" he said. "Please, take a seat, all of you. I'll order up some coffee."

He motioned to the sofas while picking up the phone and giving his adjutant instructions for refreshments. Then he came around from his desk and sat down in a large easy chair.

"Yes," he continued. "So nice to be here in Britain. I remember when I was here the last time…"

He proceeded to regale us with a litany of his achievements during the Great War.

I was rather relieved when the coffee arrived complete with sugared doughnuts to interrupt his monologue. Audrey and Angelica served the coffee and resumed their seats.

"I love these doughnuts," said Todd. "I had the chef make them specially. I'm a great chef myself, as it happens. Doughnuts … I can make those easy. There's not a lot I don't know about cooking…"

Apparently, he knew a lot about everything. We sipped our coffee politely and continued, perforce, to listen. Talking was something the colonel was very good at.

A quick glance at Angelica told me that she was enjoying her doughnut immensely. The refreshments were the only consolation in the dismal meeting so far.

Bentley, who had been showing definite signs of suppressed agitation, put his empty coffee cup down on the table.

"Ahem," he said. "I wonder if we might discuss the small matter of returning our planes."

"Your planes?" Todd looked at him blankly.

Bentley controlled his temper with an effort. Todd must have known perfectly well what he was talking about.

"Your unit was loaned some Spitfires by the RAF for your fighter pilots to use. Now that you've got the new planes, I'm sure you have no further use for them. So, we would like them back, because *we* certainly have need of them."

Todd stood up and went over to his desk, where he picked up a memo. "Well, you know, I'd like to help you, I really would. Of course, we like to help our allies. But the planes, according to this document, were given to us until we no longer need them and then to dispose of as we see fit."

"What?" said Bentley, sounding nonplussed.

"It's all here. See for yourself," said Todd, handing the memo over to Bentley.

Bentley took it and scanned through. I could tell that he was extremely annoyed.

"Yes, I see what it says, but we need those Spitfires for operational missions," he said.

"Sure, but what if *we* need them?" said Todd. "Then we won't have them, don't you see?"

"But you don't need them, sir," Bentley protested. "You have got a whole squadron of new planes. We have just lost two Spitfires."

"The thing is, though, we might need them, and then we won't have them, because you will. Do you see?" said the colonel. I wondered if he was being deliberately obtuse. "You know I can't just go giving away US Army property…"

Bentley flushed scarlet and spoke through gritted teeth. "Those spitfires were not US Army property in the first place," he said. "When your fighter crew landed, they had no planes, so we lent them planes because there's a war on, and that's what you do. Now we need planes, and we're asking you to return the favour."

"You know, I wish I could help," said Todd. "But my hands are tied."

The colonel wasn't going to cooperate, that much was clear.

"We are fighting a war, sir," Bentley repeated, trying to remind him of his duty. "In wartime, extraordinary things are expected of people. There is a common enemy here, and it's the Germans!"

"You're right, of course, but unless I have orders to the contrary, the planes are going to stay here."

The colonel was not going to be moved. Bentley knew when he was defeated, at least for the moment.

"That's your final answer, is it?" he asked in clipped tones.

"Yes, I'm afraid it is, bud," said Todd, sounding very offhand once more.

"In that case, I thank you for your hospitality, and we will take our leave," said Bentley.

"Anytime," said Todd. "The door is always open."

I refrained from pointing out that, due to his orders, this was no longer the case. Instead, we all snapped a crisp salute and left his office. Todd watched us go with the demeanour of a man who wasn't particularly bothered either way.

As we left the building, I saw Sandford standing in the doorway of his office. His expression was apologetic. Meanwhile, I was sure that Bentley was on the verge of having an apoplectic fit.

"Let us return to the base," he said, getting into the staff car, "where we will meet to discuss this further."

"How did it go, sir?" Gordon asked as Angelica and I climbed into the jeep.

"Badly, Fred, very badly indeed," I replied.

When we arrived at Banley, Bentley got out of the staff car, smoking his pipe. His agitation had not lessened, and I could tell from Audrey's expression that he had already articulated some of his ire.

He spotted us jumping down from the jeep and marched straight over to us. "What did you make of that, Angus?" he demanded.

"Sir, I felt that the colonel was being somewhat obtuse," I replied diplomatically.

"Obtuse? I'll say he was bloody well obtuse. This is supposed to be an alliance of cooperation against a common enemy! Instead, we've got some bloody starched shirt holding onto *our* planes just because he feels like it!"

"It's an awkward situation, sir, I agree," I said.

This only served to fan the flames.

"I'll say it's awkward. Very awkward that I'm two Spitfires down and no more spares, when there are planes sitting not more than a bloody mile away doing *nothing*! Blasted jumped-up bureaucratic nonsense. There's a blasted war on, and what's he doing? Serving us coffee and doughnuts!"

Apparently, this gesture was perceived by Bentley as some kind of insult. I remained silent while he puffed on his pipe at an alarming rate, sending clouds of smoke billowing into the breeze.

"This is not the end of it, Angus," he said, waving his pipe around as if it were a weapon. "Not by a long bloody chalk."

"Should we still involve the Americans in our mission?" I asked tentatively.

"Damn right you will. I will have my pound of flesh one way or another in the meantime," he said. "Anyway, I'm off to make some calls. We'll see if we can't bring that blighter back into line."

He turned on his heel, and I watched him stride away with Audrey by his side.

"Do you think Bentley can get the higher-ups to order Todd to return the Spitfires?" asked Angelica when he had gone.

" Let's hope so," I replied, without much optimism.

The workings of Fighter Command and the War Office were something of a mystery to me. Bentley could simply order more Spitfires from the factory as he normally did. As an operational unit, we would get the supplies we needed.

However, he had now taken Todd's intransigence as a personal affront. I was sure he wouldn't give up until all avenues were exhausted.

"I've met the colonel's sort before," said Gordon, who had listened patiently during the trip back to Banley while I regaled him with the details. "There are ways of dealing with people like him."

This caught my interest. "There are?"

"Care for a cup of tea, sir?" he said.

I took his meaning at once; a visit to Annie's Kitchen was in order. Annie's was a cosy tearoom close to Banley, which had become something of a favourite of ours.

"A splendid idea, Fred," said Angelica, catching on. She was particularly fond of the venue after I had introduced her to it.

Not long afterwards, the three of us were seated around our usual table at Annie's splendid establishment. On the table sat a steaming pot of tea, hot crumpets, butter and homemade jam. Angelica reached for a crumpet and spread it with butter and jam. Gordon and I followed suit.

There was a moment of silent reverence as we each savoured the delicious combination.

"These truly are magical," said Angelica, swallowing the first mouthful.

"As I always say —" Gordon began.

"The best crumpets this side of London," said Angelica, finishing for him.

We poured the tea and waited expectantly for Gordon to give us the benefit of his excellent advice.

"The thing with these kinds of men," he said at length, setting down his cup, "is that you won't get anywhere using threats. We had one such officer in the Great War. Never listened to a word of advice … always had to do things his way … got several men killed with his intransigence…"

"And what happened to him?" I asked.

"He was shot by a sniper after we'd advised him to keep his head down," said Gordon.

We laughed, but I wasn't really catching his drift.

"I don't quite see…"

"Ah, well, the point is, sir," said Gordon, taking another sip of his tea, "that whatever you advise them to do, they'll do the exact opposite. In that case, it worked in our favour."

"Okay…" I picked up my own cup and took a sip. Annie's tea always seemed to taste better than any other.

"So, I fear that bringing pressure to bear on the colonel from on high is likely to make him even more intransigent," he said.

"Well, how do we persuade him then?" Angelica asked, reaching for another crumpet.

"You have to appeal to his vanity," Gordon told her. "You have to make whatever you want him to do seem like his idea. But more than that, you've got to make it so that he appears to be the hero. If there's some personal glory in it, then he'll do whatever you want."

"Good God," I said, much struck by this logic.

"You're a genius, Fred," said Angelica.

We consumed our second round of crumpets thoughtfully.

"That's all very well, but how do you propose we do that?" I asked.

"Well, there's the nub," said Gordon. "You have to work out a way to do it."

"And?" I said expectantly.

"And I've no idea," he said, smiling.

I sighed. "Perhaps I can pick Captain Booker's brains. He might have some inside knowledge. In the meantime, we've got the mission to Boulogne to plan. The Americans will help us on that raid — I can ask him then."

"Good idea, sir," said Gordon. "In the meantime, Bentley might prevail."

I suspected we all knew that Bentley's efforts would come to nothing. I ordered up a fresh pot of tea and crumpets as consolation.

I had given the raid on Boulogne a lot of thought. The most logical idea was to strafe the port area to at least disrupt it. We'd fly in soon after dawn at low level, attack what we could and get out. Since I was down to ten active pilots and planes, I had asked Sandford to support us. It was dangerous, and the port was heavily defended. There was a strong possibility we might lose someone in the process. However, I hoped that the element of surprise would be on our side.

To that end, I invited Sandford and his crew over to attend a briefing, along with M Flight. Bentley was also in attendance. When everyone was assembled in the mission room, I got up to speak.

"Our next mission as part of Operation Wagtail," I said, "will be carrying out a surprise attack on the port of Boulogne. Due to the size of the port, the raid will be supported by our American colleagues, led by Captain Booker."

There were murmurs of approval on hearing this. Sandford turned around to acknowledge them. I noticed that Bentley's expression remained rather stony while he puffed on his pipe. His efforts with the higher-ups had, unfortunately, not prospered. I had gone over the mission plan with him beforehand, and he had agreed to it without comment.

"We will leave at dawn in two days' time," I said. "We'll fly at low level and come at the port from the north side. M Flight will take the lead, augmented by two planes from Captain Booker's squadron. His planes will fly behind us and ride shotgun. We will strafe everything we can and get out in one pass."

I paused and glanced at Angelica, who smiled at me encouragingly.

"The port is heavily defended, as is Boulogne itself. I can't stress to you enough the importance of sticking to the game plan. We want everyone to come back in one piece," I told them. "There are photographs to study so you can get an idea of the lay of the land. Any questions?"

"Our planes are fighter bombers," said Sandford. "We could drop some ordnance behind you."

"Why not? That sounds like a good idea," I said. "But conserve your ammo. You might need it to fight a rearguard action against the Jerries if they send out air cover."

"You got it," said Sandford.

I waited to see if anyone else had any questions.

"Can I ask when we'll be getting some replacement Spitfires and pilots?" asked Dylan.

"No, you cannot, Pilot Officer Davies," said Bentley in quelling tones, pointing his pipe at Dylan.

It was an awkward moment. Dylan subsided at once. The issue of the Spitfires obviously still rankled. I caught a glimpse of the chagrined expression on Sandford's face. The entire episode had cast a damper on Anglo-American relations, at least in our neck of the woods.

"Any questions related to the mission?" I said pointedly.

There were a couple about logistics and so forth, but generally it was pretty straightforward. Overall, I didn't know how much damage we could really do to the port, but we had to try. We might get lucky and hit some fuel dumps. At the very least, our attack would be disruptive.

I glanced at Bentley in case he wanted to speak. He stood up and puffed on his pipe for a moment or two.

"You might be thinking to yourself, what's the wisdom in this mission?" he said. "What damage can we really do to a port? Well, if you're thinking that, then it's the wrong attitude. When we are asked to do a job, we do it. We step up and make the best of it. When we're asked to cooperate with the Allied forces, that is exactly what we do!"

He paused, looking directly at Sandford, who coloured up slightly.

"This war will be won because of squadrons like the Mavericks, who carry out their designated missions regardless of the risks. Don't think that your dedication and bravery are unappreciated. That is far from the case. I appreciate it, for a start, and I expect every man to make it back to Blighty in one piece!"

Bentley's blood was obviously up, and much of what he said was for the Americans' benefit as much as anything. It was also noticeable that he had excluded them from his appreciation, signifying his discontent with their base commander.

"Good luck and Godspeed, as they say." With that, Bentley sat down and resumed puffing on his pipe.

"All right," I said. "If there's nothing else, let's get to it. We've patrols to fly. Familiarise yourselves with the reconnaissance photographs, and we'll convene again before sunrise in two days."

M Flight and their American counterparts departed the mission room along with Bentley and Audrey, leaving me alone with Angelica and Sandford.

"That was something of a fiery speech," said Sandford, coming up to me with a smile.

"Yes, I'm afraid Bentley is not at all happy with the current state of affairs regarding our two bases," I said.

"I'm sorry again," said Sandford. "I've tried and my CO has tried, but there's no shifting the colonel on the issue of the Spitfires. Apart from which, he's not making too many friends at the base. People are getting tired of his petty orders. Plus, he's holding briefings every day to tell us how great he is…"

"I gather he has something of an inflated sense of his own importance," I observed.

"That's one way of putting it," said Sandford with a wry smile.

"We need to get him in a more receptive frame of mind," said Angelica.

"And how do you propose to do that?" Sandford asked her.

"I'm still thinking about it," said Angelica.

"Good luck with it then."

Sandford smiled. He was out of ideas. He didn't really believe we could change anything regarding his base commander, but then he wasn't aware of quite how resourceful Angelica was. Although we had not discussed it since our conversation with Gordon, she had obviously been searching for a way to win the colonel over.

"Why don't you come over to our mess and have something to eat?" I suggested to Sandford. It was my way of burying the hatchet and showing that on the British side of the fence, we could still be hospitable.

"Sure," he said. "I'd like that very much."

The morning of the Boulogne mission, we took an early breakfast once again, arranged by Gordon. The atmosphere was quite cheery, with Willie, Jonty and Dylan joining us in the dining room.

"Hope it's a nice day for the bunfight, Skipper," said Jonty, tucking into eggs, spam and beans on toast.

I accepted my plate and started to eat.

"I hope so too," I replied, happy that at least it wasn't raining.

"Let's show those Jerries what we're made of," said Dylan, who, like Jonty, was always up for the fray.

In spite of their seeming insouciance, they were both excellent pilots, dedicated to their task.

After breakfast, we made our way to Banley. It was still dark, and the country lanes were silent as we bowled along. The air was quite balmy, and the stars were still shining, although the sky was beginning to lighten. I sat in the jeep with my arm around Angelica. We didn't say much, enjoying the silence and being together.

"Good luck, sir," said Gordon upon arrival at the airfield.

Once at the hut, M Flight assembled around me for a final briefing. I kept it short. Everyone would have gone over the photographs and timetable more than once.

"All right," I said. "You know the drill. Let's make this one count."

I turned into Angelica's embrace as the other pilots headed for their planes.

"Come back safe," she said with a kiss.

"I love you," I replied.

"I love you too."

Our fingers slowly parted, then the goodbye ritual was complete — my good luck charm. I walked to my Spitfire as the sky began to turn grey, climbed in and let Redwood strap me in.

"Have a good one, sir," he said.

"We'll do our best, Techie."

I spun up the prop, and the engine roared to life. It was time to go.

"Badger Leader requesting clearance," I said to control tower, using the codename we'd picked for the mission.

"You're clear. Good luck," came the response.

"Badgers, let's go," I said.

Then we were off. I waved to Angelica, who blew me a kiss, then taxied down to the end of the runway. Moments later, we were airborne. I circled around, waiting for the Americans. They arrived in short order.

" Badger Leader, this is Coyote Leader," said Sandford. "Coming on station."

"Roger, Coyote Leader," I said. "Nice to see you."

"Coyote Two joining the main pack," said McClusky as his plane joined our formation.

"Coyote Three joining the pack, too," said First Lieutenant Eugene Rockwell, also making up part of our flight.

"We're right behind you, Badger Leader," said Sandford.

I glanced around and checked the formation in my mirror; I could see Sandford's squadron.

"Roger," I replied. "Let's go." I dropped the Spitfire down to hedge height and opening up the throttle.

We flew fast and low, M Flight leading with the Americans behind us. Trees, hedges and telegraph lines all zipped past, taking up most of my attention.

"Hey, this is fun," said McClusky.

"Yeah, well, don't get too carried away. Keep your eyes on the ground in front of you," Sandford told him.

"Roger," said McClusky.

I smiled. McClusky and Jonty were of a similar disposition — happy-go-lucky, ready for a fight.

We took a direct route down past Basildon, crossing the Thames at Tilbury. The endless procession of naval ships up and down the river played out below us. Sailors waved as we roared overhead.

Then it was on to Maidstone and Ashford, aiming for Dungeness. I kept us over flat fields as much as I could, which made the low flying far easier. The sky began to lighten even more, with sunrise set to break soon enough.

Dungeness loomed up ahead, stretches of sand going out to the point. The white sand slid by beneath us, and then we were over the Channel.

"Keep them peeled," I said.

Despite flying under the radar, we needed to keep a weather eye out for Jerries. The lookouts might spot us, but as we'd be going straight into the attack — spending very little time over enemy territory — it would hopefully all be over before they could react.

We were skimming the waves, keeping as low as I dared. Ships were the other problem, but fortunately, we saw none. I had told Angelica I wasn't worried, but now my pulse began to quicken.

We were on a course directly for Boulogne. We'd approach from the side, then turn in to the attack down the wide port entrance. As we ate up the miles, the coastline of France came into view, getting closer by the second. I went over the plan of attack in my mind, visualising what we had to do. Moments later, it became all too real.

The port wall loomed up in front of us. I slipped off the safety on the guns.

"Badgers, Coyotes, on me, attack formation," I said, turning left and then heading straight for the open harbour. There were docked ships and boats, men running for cover as we approached.

I took us up a little higher in order to strafe the decks of the ships. The Americans would follow us in and drop their payload behind us. It was potluck what we hit, but hopefully we'd cause some damage.

"Incoming," said Dylan as streams of tracers erupted from the ships and the port defences.

"Stay on target," I said.

We were closing in fast. Once we were level with the port entrance, I gave the order.

"Fire!"

Twelve planes opened up on the port, with tracers now flying both ways. Bullets ripped across ship decks and the port wall. We passed over the port with speed and fired another salvo into the buildings on the other side.

Sandford's flight followed us in. I heard him say, "Bombs away."

Seconds later, there was a series of explosions as the ordnance went off. The air was full of smoke. We'd managed to cause some mayhem at least. It was time to leave.

"Let's get the hell out of here," I said, turning for home.

We'd been lucky so far. But then our luck ran out.

"I'm hit, I'm hit! Going down…" It was Eugene. I glanced to my left and saw his plane dropping into the Channel, the engine on fire. We were too low to bail. His plane hit the water with a tremendous splash. There was no time to linger; I hoped he would make it out alive.

I throttled up and continued on a heading for the English coast, still keeping low. We would soon be out of range of the guns on the shore.

Suddenly there was another explosion beside me. Shards of metal came flying past my canopy. Another of our planes had been hit.

"We've lost Badger Five," said Dylan.

It was Pilot Officer Berek Drabek's Spitfire, gone for a burton.

"Keep going," I said. There was nothing else we could do.

Halfway across the Channel, I heard a cry from First Lieutenant Jack Carter in the American flight behind us.

"Bandits, on our five o'clock," he said.

"Leave them to us, Badger Leader," said Sandford. "This is our job now. Break, Coyotes, break. Let's take them."

In my rear-view mirror, I saw his squadron peel off and turn towards the incoming Germans. Sandford was right — that was what he was there for, to have our backs.

"Keep going, Badgers," I said, maintaining a dogged course for Blighty.

"Can't we just —" began Jonty.

"No," I said sharply. "Remain in formation — that's an order."

I could hear the chatter on the radio as Sandford's crew engaged with the German fighters.

"I've got him."

"He's on my tail."

"Watch out!"

"Now I've got you!"

I noticed that McClusky had left us to join his squadron and engage in the fight. I hoped he had enough ammo left. It wasn't for me to stop him. The P-47s carried more rounds than our Spitfires; they could probably last twice as long before running out.

The dogfight receded behind us, and the radio chatter grew less. Dungeness came into view once more. Then we were over the sand and back over the fields. I took us up to a more reasonable height now that we'd made friendly skies.

"Disengage," I heard Sandford say. "Let's go home, boys."

It sounded as if they'd fared okay. I hoped they hadn't lost any more pilots. Losing Eugene would be a bitter blow. He'd been there from the start.

Bentley would not be happy to hear that Berek had died. We'd be another pilot and Spitfire down. I didn't see how we could run any more of these missions without more pilots and more planes. The issue of the disputed Spitfires was becoming more pressing.

We landed at Banley Airfield shortly afterwards, and then the remaining Americans roared over us. They had not been far behind.

Angelica was waiting as usual. She came running over to me with a smile on her face.

"You're safe," she said. "Thank God for that." She wound her arms around my neck and kissed me. "I'm sorry about Berek," she added softly.

"I am too," I replied.

We disengaged as I noticed Bentley and Audrey striding towards us. He stopped in front of us, took out his pipe and went through his ritual of emptying and filling it. He lit it and took a few puffs.

"Lost another pilot," he said shortly. "A rum do."

"Yes, sir. The Americans lost a pilot too," I said.

"Yes," he replied in a tone which indicated that as much as he sympathised, he wasn't in a forgiving mood.

"And now we've lost another plane," he observed.

"Yes, sir."

Bentley took a few more puffs before continuing. "I've requested some replacements from Fighter Command," he said at length.

It was an indication that he'd given up on the colonel. This annoyed me, not because of Bentley, but because it seemed so unfair. There had to be a way to get the planes back.

"Anyway, carry on, Angus," said Bentley. "You can stand down from further missions for the time being until we are back up to strength. Can't expect the Americans to bail us out all the time, hmm? That point is abundantly clear."

"Sir," I said, saluting.

Angelica and I watched him leave, Audrey at his side.

"My goodness," she said, "he's a little down in the mouth."

"Yes, I think the colonel's attitude has affected him more than I thought," I replied.

"Then we're going to have to change that," said Angelica, raising her chin in a determined fashion.

The problem was that I couldn't for the life of me think of how we could.

CHAPTER EIGHT

After commiserating with the rest of the flight, Angelica and I went to find Gordon. I stood M Flight down for the day and elected to return to Amberly.

Gordon was parked in his usual spot, leaning against his jeep, enjoying a smoke. "How was the mission, sir?" he asked.

"It went well, I think, except that we lost another pilot, Berek," I told him.

"I'm sorry to hear that," he said. "Are you for home?"

"Yes," I replied. "We've been stood down from further missions until the pilot and plane shortage has been resolved."

"No luck with the colonel then, sir?"

"No, unfortunately not."

"Jump in then, sir, ma'am," he said.

We climbed into the back of the jeep, and Gordon started it up. In no time we were making our way down the country lanes to the manor house.

When we arrived, we walked in through the main entrance and up the staircase only to run into Lady Barbara Amberly. We had not seen Barbara for months. She still looked a picture, I had to admit, with auburn hair, a flawless complexion and green eyes. Beside me, I felt Angelica bristle, as well she might. She took my hand possessively.

"Oh, Angus," said Barbara. "And Angelica, too, how lovely to see you."

"Barbara," I replied with a nod.

She inclined her head and then looked at Angelica and smiled. "Darling, no need to look at me like *that*. I know we were rivals once, but that's all in the past," she said. "Can't we just be friends?"

They hadn't parted on the best of terms. However, Barbara seemed to want to bury the hatchet.

"Hello, Barbara," said Angelica. I glanced at her, and it seemed her hackles had receded just a little.

"How are you settling in?" Barbara asked us. "Is the suite all to your liking?"

"It's very comfortable, thank you," said Angelica.

"Well, if there's anything else you need, just ask," Barbara replied. She hesitated and then asked, "Have you both eaten?"

"Well, no," I admitted.

I felt Angelica squeeze my hand, indicating she wanted me to demur.

"Then you must come and have lunch with me — fill me in on all the gossip," Barbara said lightly.

"Well, we don't want to put you to any trouble," Angelica told her, not wanting to refuse outright, though I could tell she was reluctant to agree to the idea.

Barbara had other plans. "Oh, no, I insist. Come and join me up in my private dining room. I'll get the staff to organise some extra settings."

There was really nothing else to do but comply. Barbara in full flow wasn't a woman who was easy to refuse, as I knew to my cost.

Angelica kept hold of my hand as we followed Barbara to her private dining room. The small salon brought back memories I would rather have forgotten.

"Have a seat, do," said Barbara as she went to call the maid.

Angelica and I sat down beside each other. Barbara positioned herself opposite us.

"So?" she said as the maids arrived to set our places and bring in the main course. "How have you both been?"

Angelica informed her that we couldn't be happier and that we'd settled very well into marital bliss. Barbara didn't bat an eyelid and said she was very pleased. I knew this conversation was simply Angelica stamping her supremacy as my wife upon my former mistress.

After this, Angelica looked a great deal more comfortable and was happy to partake of a decent portion of roast chicken with all the trimmings.

"You know, I'm part of SOE now," said Barbara. "That's why I've not been around so much, but it means you can tell me anything regarding the exploits of the Mavericks and it goes no further."

The Special Operations Executive was a highly secret organisation set up by Churchill to engage in espionage and other missions behind enemy lines. I knew Barbara had been recruited by MI6, but I had not known in what capacity.

"Well, as far as the Mavericks go," I said at her prompting, "we've engaged in a number of missions since you've been gone…"

I went on to give her a potted history of events while we finished off the main course, with Angelica interjecting a few titbits every so often.

"Goodness, that does sound rather exciting," said Barbara.

The maids cleared away the main course and brought in the dessert, which consisted of rhubarb crumble and custard.

"What about you?" Angelica asked her, tucking into the rather delicious crumble. "What have you been doing?"

"Oh, well, I can't really give too many details," said Barbara. "But I've learned more than a dozen different ways to kill a man, and to use all kinds of spying equipment, radios and so forth. I'm fluent in French and German, with some Flemish too…"

"Impressive," I said. "I take it that you've been in Nazi Germany?"

"Yes," she said. "Yes, I have. I've met a few… people, you know…"

I didn't really know, but I assumed she meant high-ranking Nazis. If anyone could pull it off, she could.

"So, what are you doing back here?" Angelica asked Barbara as she pushed away her empty plate.

Seeing that we were finished, Barbara rang for tea.

"After my last mission, I needed to make myself scarce for a while — let's just put it like that. After that, who knows? Probably not Germany for a while anyway."

She smiled, but I could sense that she'd done things and seen things that the old Barbara could never have imagined. What had she done in Germany that meant she could not go back? I dreaded to think.

A thought struck me. "You might know this," I said to her. "We recently undertook a raid on the railway leading into Calais. One of the trains — I let it go — but it consisted of what looked like cattle cars … except that there were people inside. We saw arms waving from between the slats…"

Barbara went quiet. The maids cleared the dessert and placed a pot of tea, milk and sugar on the table along with cups. There was a little plate of petit fours — little truffles and small sweets.

Angelica reached out, took one and popped it into her mouth, being partial to chocolate. Barbara lit up a cigarette, and I served the tea.

She took a few puffs on her smoke while we sipped our tea.

"There are things," she said, "things we know in Intelligence, not for public consumption. Things that I've seen and heard while sleeping with the enemy … as it were."

She smiled. I knew that the metaphorical phrase would be more than just that in her case.

"We're not exactly the public," I told her.

"I can't tell you much," she replied, "except this. I'm sure you're aware of Hitler's antipathy towards the Jews."

"Yes."

"Well, they are being rounded up, shipped by train to places … camps…" She trailed off.

"And then?" said Angelica.

"They don't come back," said Barbara, unwilling to put a name to what we all knew she meant.

"Where are they taken?" I asked her.

"To places in Germany, Poland … that's all I can tell you."

"Good God," I said, shocked.

"When we win the war," Barbara continued, "certain things will be revealed that are beyond anyone's imagining."

These disclosures rather killed the conversation. I drank my tea, and Angelica reached over for another of the petit fours.

"Anyway," said Barbara brightly, "it's been lovely to catch up like this. No point in dwelling on what we can't do anything about, at least not right now. It sounds like the Mavericks are doing a splendid job."

"We would do an even better one if the Americans would give our Spitfires back," I said, recalling our present conundrum.

"They're not giving them back?" said Barbara, intrigued. "Do tell."

Angelica and I furnished her with an account of the present circumstances and Colonel Todd's intransigence.

"Oh dear," she said when we'd finished. "He sounds like a terribly pompous old bore."

"He is," I averred. "We have an idea of how we could get him to change his mind, but we can't really see the means to do so."

"And what is that?" she asked, lighting up another cigarette.

Angelica poured another round of tea, and since nobody was touching the petit fours, she eased the plate over to her place in order to reach them more easily. I smiled at her affectionately.

"Actually, it was Fred's idea…"

I explained how Todd might be persuaded to part with the Spitfires if it placed him in some kind of favourable light.

When she heard this, Barbara smiled. "Why, there's nothing easier than planting that idea in his head," she said. "I can help you do that."

"You can?" I said, surprised.

"I will invite the colonel to tea. You and Angelica must come too — wear your best uniforms. I will do the rest," she said.

"Really?"

"Yes, really," she continued. "I've not met a man I couldn't … influence…" she paused and took a pull on her cigarette. "Well, I tell a lie — there was one. The one that got away."

She was looking directly at me as she said this. Then the moment was gone.

"I've dealt with men like him before," she said. "It will be a piece of cake."

"All right," I said. I quite believed her. She seemed completely unstoppable.

"I'll arrange the whole thing *tout de suite*, as time is of the essence. I'll let you know when — just be sure to dress up to the nines."

"All right," I said again and looked at Angelica.

"Certainly," she said. "You can count on me and Angus."

"Marvellous," said Barbara. "Anyway, look, I've detained you both long enough. I'm sure you've better things to do than prattle with me all day."

We took this as our cue to leave and stood up.

"See you at the tea," said Barbara.

We left her smoking her cigarette. Silhouetted against the light from the window, she reminded me of a femme fatale from Hollywood — made up to perfection, sitting with elegance and poise, smoking a cigarette.

Angelica and I made our way back to our rooms. As soon as the door was shut, she wrapped her arms around my neck.

"You know," she said, "after that meeting, I've quite forgiven you."

"For what?" I asked suspiciously.

"For Barbara," she said. "I can't imagine anyone withstanding her will, especially you."

"I'm glad you think so highly of my abilities with regards to women," I said.

"Oh, but I do, after all … you got me," she said. Her lips moved closer to mine. "I think you should demonstrate those abilities right now…"

After our meeting with Barbara, I was far more hopeful about getting the Spitfires back than before. One thing I knew about her was that if she set her mind to something, she would get it done. Still, it did not solve the immediate issue of having lost two pilots and having another in the infirmary. Jean was doing well by all accounts, but was not yet ready to return to combat duty.

When we arrived at Banley the next morning, Audrey was waiting for us. As we climbed down from the jeep, I couldn't think why Bentley would want to see me again. However, it turned out that it wasn't Bentley.

"The Marx Brothers —" began Audrey.

"They are here?" I asked in surprise. I had not been expecting them back quite so soon.

"Yes," she replied.

"Then we'd better find out what they want," I said with a sigh, since it invariably involved what Bentley termed a 'hare-brained scheme'.

Angelica and I accompanied Audrey to the mission room, where the Marx Brothers were seated as usual, smoking cigarettes. Harpo gestured for us to take a seat.

"Flight Lieutenant and Section Officer," said Chico when we were seated. "So nice to see you both again."

I ignored this pleasantry, as it was their way of working up to something which probably wasn't very pleasant at all.

"To what do we owe this visit?" I enquired.

"Always to the point," said Harpo.

"Yes, indeed," said Chico. "That's what I like about him."

Beside me, Angelica bristled.

Harpo took a long pull on his cigarette and blew the smoke out, watching it drift up to the ceiling.

"We hear that Operation Wagtail has been going well," he said.

"If you call losing two pilots well, then, I suppose so."

"We're sorry for the loss of your pilots, of course," said Chico.

"Did you come down just to tell me that?" I asked him.

"Not quite, no," Chico continued. "If you remember, we said that we had another mission for you ... something your chaps will find a lot of fun."

I did recall him mentioning that they had something else lined up for the Mavericks but couldn't tell us what it was. I sincerely doubted that it would be fun.

"Which is?"

"Dive-bombing," said Harpo.

I wondered if he had taken leave of his senses, but then I remembered that I was dealing with the Marx Brothers. Their schemes were invariably ridiculous.

"Pardon?"

"Dive-bombing," said Chico. "We want your squadron to train for dive-bombing."

"What? You're being serious?"

"Perfectly."

I immediately thought of an objection to this plan. "But Spitfires are fighters, not dive-bombers," I protested.

"But they could be," said Chico.

It still didn't make any sense, so I probed further. "But why?" I asked him. "What would be the point?"

"The accuracy of dive-bombing against stationary targets has been well proven. It's been tested, and you only have to look at the effectiveness of the Stuka, for example," said Harpo. "Let's just say that the powers that be want to find out if the Spitfire is a suitable plane for carrying out such attacks."

"So another experiment," said Angelica bitterly. "I might have guessed it would be something of that nature."

"Indeed," said Chico. "Your squadron conducts these innovative missions so well that naturally you are the first port of call."

"So, not because we are considered expendable," I said a little caustically.

Chico shook his head at this most emphatically. "Not at all, Flight Lieutenant. I can assure you that the Mavericks are highly regarded in some circles," he replied.

Angelica was not so ready to buy this reassurance. "Which circles might those be?" she asked.

"Well, it's not for us to say," Harpo prevaricated. "But rest assured that the man in charge is very impressed with your mission record."

I gave them the benefit of the doubt and assumed they couldn't name names. He could only mean Churchill, but I presumed he wasn't able to say it. It might be that it wasn't politic to heap accolades on a squadron regarded by some in the Air Force as a dumping ground for unwanted pilots and crew.

"All right," I said, though I wasn't completely convinced. "Tell me more."

The two spies, having finished their cigarettes, immediately lit up another two.

"There is a port in Holland … Den Helder. It's an important naval base for the Kriegsmarine," said Chico. "We want your squadron to carry out a precision dive-bombing attack on the base."

"I see," I said. "Currently, we've only got ten operational Spitfires, and nine pilots fit for combat. At full strength, we'll only have twelve. By my reckoning, that is twelve bombs — surely that's not a very effective number to cause much damage."

Chico smiled. "Ah well, that's not quite true. The Mark IX Spitfire can carry two two-hundred-and-fifty-pound bombs under each wing and a five-hundred pounder under the fuselage. So, in reality, that would be the equivalent of thirty-six planes," he said with a smile.

"Oh, I see," I said. I hadn't known this, but then again, why would I? We'd been a fighter squadron since inception. It was only now that carrying bombs was being suggested.

"Moreover," said Harpo, "a two-hundred-and-fifty-pound bomb has a blast radius of around one hundred and fifteen feet, so it can do a lot of damage."

"Then I assume that a five-hundred-pound bomb has double that?" said Angelica.

"Actually, it's far more," said Chico. "The radius could be up to four hundred and fifty feet or more."

The idea began to make sense. That many bombs dropped on shipping or port facilities could certainly cause a lot more destruction than I had first thought.

"So," I continued, "if that is the case, then these bombs would have to be dropped from a sufficient height to avoid the blowback, I assume. Also, that would limit the number of planes that could drop these at one time."

"All very true," said Harpo. "We'll be bringing in an instructor specifically to train you. However, in essence, the plane needs to climb to between six and eight thousand feet and then dive onto the target at an angle of forty-five to sixty degrees. The bombs must be released at three thousand feet and at the very minimum two thousand, not below that."

"And then?" I asked him.

"You get out of there as fast as you can."

I had become intrigued. This sounded like it required skilful flying. I thought it through for a moment while the Marx Brothers smoked their cigarettes.

"So, we come in low, climb up high, pick our target, dive, drop and go," I summarised. "All the while being exposed to ack-ack fire."

"Well, yes, there is that, but it's only for a very short while," said Chico.

"A short while in which they could be killed," said Angelica caustically.

Chico inclined his head in acknowledgement of this fact.

"Just answer me this," I said. "Is the attack on this port going to be worth it?"

"The German Navy very often have ships of importance there, plus there is a strategic radar station, among other things," said Chico. "We will provide comprehensive intelligence and reconnaissance photographs so that you can pick your targets."

"So, do you want to take it on?" asked Harpo.

Angelica slipped her hand into mine, but we both already knew the answer. In any case, it wasn't really a choice. If we were asked to do it, then we'd just have to do it.

"I'll have to get Bentley's agreement first," I said, which they took to be tacit consent.

"Absolutely," said Harpo.

"Splendid," said Chico.

I was pretty sure Bentley's reaction to any scheme brought by the Marx Brothers wasn't going to be particularly favourable.

"Is there anything else we can help with?" asked Harpo.

"I think you've helped enough for the moment," said Angelica acidly.

I stifled a laugh at this. "Well, I would ask for your help getting our Spitfires back from the Americans, but Barbara has said she'll take care of it," I said.

"Yes, we heard about that," said Chico. "A very unsatisfactory situation."

"Not good for Intelligence cooperation at all," said Harpo.

I took it from these cryptic remarks that there were wheels within wheels. Colonel Todd was increasing his unpopularity in all sorts of quarters.

"If anyone can sort it, Barbara can," said Chico. "A very capable operative."

This spoke volumes. In spite of any irritation they might cause, the Marx Brothers were obviously extremely good at their jobs. They had connections in all sorts of places and managed to pull off some extraordinary things.

"Assuming Bentley agrees, when do you want us to start training?" I asked. "Also, what does this mean for Operation Wagtail?"

"As soon as possible," said Harpo.

"We'll get things going from our end to get your instructor over here," added Chico. "You can suspend Wagtail for the moment while you get this mission underway."

"All right," I said. "We'd best go and see Bentley. I'm sure Section Officer Wilmington will let you know the outcome."

I got up to leave, along with Angelica.

"Toodle pip," said Harpo.

"Chin-chin," said Chico.

We left them smoking their cigarettes as if they hadn't a care in the world.

"I suppose you're going to have to do this," said Angelica as soon as we were in the corridor.

"I don't really have any choice," I replied.

"No, more's the pity."

"Let's go and see Bentley," I said, "as we're already in the building."

It was a short walk to the CO's office. Audrey let us in and then resumed her seat. Bentley was busy shuffling through papers on his desk when we entered. He glanced up at us with interest.

"Ah, back again, I see," he said, picking up his pipe.

We waited for the pipe routine to be completed and for him to be engaged in smoking it.

"What brings you here?" he asked.

"The gentlemen from MI6…" I began.

Bentley's eye immediately began to twitch. He puffed a little faster on his pipe. "Those blasted reprobate clowns were here again?" he said.

"Yes, sir."

"What did they want?" he asked. "As if I didn't know. Some blasted new poppycock scheme, no doubt?"

I hesitated to tell him, since his blood was already up without even knowing what it was.

"Come on, spit it out, Angus. What the bloody hell do those blasted nincompoops want you to do now?"

I took a deep breath. "Dive-bombing, sir," I said.

His right eye twitched alarmingly on hearing this. "What did you say?"

"They want us to do some dive-bombing, sir, in order to —"

I got no further. Bentley catapulted out of his chair with an oath and started pacing his office.

"Dive-bombing? Have they taken leave of their senses? What kind of blasted clown show are they running up there? What on earth gave them the idea that my Spitfire squadron should suddenly become a dive-bomber unit? Of all the ludicrous nonsense they've come up with so far, this is takes the biscuit."

I launched into an explanation as best I could. "It's from the higher-ups, sir. They want to see if Spitfires are capable of dive-bombing. According to them, dive-bombing has a high percentage of accuracy and —"

"I might have known it came from those blasted jumped-up Johnny windbags," he continued, cutting in. "Every bloody hare-brained notion that occurs to those people comes straight down to the Mavericks."

"They said it's because we're highly regarded, sir," said Angelica, "in some very high circles."

"Did they?" said Bentley in disbelieving tones, although he also looked rather pleased at the same time.

Having spent his wrath, he returned to his seat and thoughtfully went about refilling his pipe. Once he'd finished doing that, he lit it once more.

"Go on, tell me what blasted farrago these two have got in mind," he said, a little more calmly.

"They want us to attack Den Helder using dive-bombing," I said. "It's a port in Holland which is important to the Kriegsmarine."

"It's also heavily defended," Angelica put in.

"I see," said Bentley. "And exactly how are you supposed to go about undertaking this exercise? None of you has done this before, I assume."

"Well, sir, they will supply an expert to train us in dive-bombing techniques. Then we'll carry out the mission once proficient. At least that's the theory."

"Theory and practice are two different things. Not that you'd know it with those two bloody charlatans."

Bentley puffed away on his pipe for a while, considering the matter. He didn't like being railroaded into anything.

"Very well," he said at length. "But we're not carrying out any raids until we're back up to full strength, including sufficient planes. I shall be telling them straight."

"Yes, sir," I said.

"I'll get a memo sent to them authorising the mission on that basis," he added. "It's a shame we can't get those Spitfires back from the Americans, but I'm not going to carry on flogging a dead horse. We'll just have to wait until some new ones are delivered."

I glanced at Angelica. We weren't going to tell Bentley of Barbara's plans, particularly as they might come to nothing.

"They also said to suspend Operation Wagtail for the moment," I told him.

"Yes, well, so they should," he replied. "Anyway, you can tell your chaps the good news, and no doubt we'll be expecting this instructor soon enough."

"Yes, sir," I said.

Angelica and I stood up and saluted before leaving the room.

"That went well," she said sardonically, once we were out in the corridor.

"It could have been worse," I replied.

"You mean he could have shouted for a lot longer?" she said, laughing.

"Yes, exactly," I replied, laughing too.

CHAPTER NINE

The dive-bombing news was met with enthusiasm from Jonty in particular, as I might have expected.

"I say, Skipper," he said. "What a jolly wizard idea."

"Yes, Jonty," I replied. "I thought you'd be more than happy to learn how to dive-bomb."

"Rather," he said. "It'll be an absolute blast, I'm sure of it."

"Just don't go getting carried away," said Willie, "like you usually do."

Others, like Arjun, had a more pragmatic view. "Not sure I can really see this catching on, even if it is successful."

"Why's that?" I asked him.

"Too intensive. There are other planes that can carry bigger loads, like the Mosquito, for example. Seems quite a waste of energy," he said.

"The people at the top are always happy to experiment with other people's lives," said Tomas. "That's the way it goes."

"Well, I'm all for it," said Jonty. "It'll make a change from patrols and strafing targets."

I shook my head. Jonty was incorrigible.

"You're hopeless, Jonty," said Angelica with a smile.

I was standing outside the hut thinking about running a patrol that day when an invitation was delivered to me by hand.

"What is that?" asked Angelica. "It looks very posh."

I opened it and read it. It was written on headed notepaper from Lady Barbara Amberly. In the very best handwriting, it invited us to tea with Colonel Todd that afternoon. I handed it over to Angelica to peruse.

"She doesn't hang around," she commented.

Before I could say anything further, we were interrupted by Pilot Officer Harold Jackson.

"Scottish," he said, "can I have a word?"

"Sure, go ahead," I told him.

He glanced at Angelica, who smiled encouragingly.

"Well, it's just that I had this silver cigarette case," he began.

"Yes?" I had a shrewd notion of where this was going, and I wasn't wrong.

"Well, the thing is, Scottish, it's gone missing. I left it in my flying jacket overnight, but now it's not there."

"Right, I see," I said. "Have you mentioned this to anyone else?"

Harold looked concerned. "No, but surely it wouldn't be someone from our unit?"

"I don't think so, no," I told him. "Let's just say we're looking into the matter of other missing items. Write up a report and give it to me. I'm afraid that's all I can do at this juncture."

"Was it very valuable?" Angelica asked him.

"Sentimental value, really. It was my grandfather's," Harold replied.

"Say nothing for the moment," I said, then I had a thought. "Have you seen anyone around our hut recently who isn't part of the unit?"

He considered this and then said, "Only that sergeant who replenishes the supplies of tea and so on."

Angelica shot me a meaningful look.

"Right. Well, leave it with me for a while, if you would?"

"Yes, of course," said Harold.

He returned to the hut and left us on our own once more.

"What are we going to do about Willis?" said Angelica.

"I don't really know," I said. "Perhaps we should talk to Fred, ask how he thinks we could catch him."

Angelica brightened up at this suggestion since it would mean another trip to Annie's Kitchen. "Good idea," she said.

"Not today, though," I said. "I've got to get Tomas to run a patrol, and we've this tea to attend with Colonel Todd."

"Oh, yes," said Angelica, clapping her hands together. "I'm quite looking forward to how that turns out."

I wasn't sure I shared her enthusiasm. However, Barbara was nothing if not devious, so no doubt she had a plan up her sleeve.

After lunch, we repaired to Amberly Manor and went to our rooms. There, I changed into my dress uniform, and Angelica put on hers. Thus attired, we were about to go and find Barbara when there was a knock at the door. I opened it to discover one of the footmen standing outside.

"Her Ladyship requests me to accompany you and your good lady wife to the Green Room, sir," he said. "To partake of tea."

"Thank you," I said. "We're ready."

Angelica and I followed him up and down several flights of stairs and along various corridors to a room I had not seen before. That was not surprising, since Amberly Manor was a very large country mansion.

The footman opened the door to what I assumed was the Green Room. It was lined with dark green wallpaper, while the high ceiling boasted ornate mouldings. The floor-to-ceiling windows looked out onto the formal gardens at the rear. There were majestic-looking paintings and gilded antique statues. The entire room spoke of opulence, and I was certain that was why Barbara had chosen it. Men like Colonel Todd were easily impressed by a show of wealth, particularly ancestral wealth.

Barbara was seated on a settee which was covered in a gold and green filigree pattern. On a rococo-style gilt table stood the tea, which was to be served by a maid standing ready. Colonel Todd was also in evidence in what was sure to be his very best uniform, resplendent with medals. He looked even more florid than when I'd last seen him. He probably thought of visiting Barbara as akin to visiting royalty.

"Ah, Flight Lieutenant and Section Officer Mackennelly," said Barbara, getting up and coming to greet us in a very formal manner. "How good of you to come." She leaned in and whispered, "Let me take the lead." Then, while guiding us to a sofa, she continued, "You know Colonel Todd, of course?"

Todd stood up, and we exchanged salutes. Then we took a seat. The maid began to serve the tea, which consisted of cucumber sandwiches with the crusts cut off, small puffed vol-au-vents and a variety of fairy cakes — the epitome of English aristocratic fare. Barbara was showing off in style. The maid offered the refreshments while Barbara initiated small talk.

"So, Colonel, I hear you've taken over as Base Commander," she said.

"Yes, that's right, I have. It's a very important job and I was asked to do it, you know, because I've done a lot of important things in my life so far. I was the obvious choice to get this very important and strategic base back into shape, which I am doing, and everybody says that I'm doing a good job too," he said.

I glanced at Angelica, but she didn't bat an eyelid at his pomposity.

"Well, I'm sure they are glad to have the benefit of your great experience," Barbara continued.

"Oh yes," said Todd. "I've already made many changes. There were some very bad things going on there, very bad. You know, inefficiencies, waste — so much waste. I've stopped all of that. I run a tight ship."

Todd accepted a cup of coffee, having told the maid that he preferred it to tea. Angelica and I sat listening as Barbara shamelessly drew one boast after another out of Todd.

"I've done a lot of great things in my life, very great things. You wouldn't believe it if I told you…"

For the best part of thirty minutes or more, he regaled us with all of his achievements. We sipped our tea, ate the morsels on offer and listened patiently. It was, after all, a means to an end. Finally, thankfully, he stopped talking about himself.

"So, you two are married," he said, turning to Angelica and I.

"Yes, that's right," I replied.

"And you work together?"

"Yes, we do," Angelica replied.

"In the Mavericks squadron, is that right?"

"Yes."

He took a drink of his coffee. "I've heard some good things about the Mavericks from Captain Booker. A great outfit, he says, a very great outfit."

I stared at him in surprise, considering his attitude the last time we had met him. It appeared that Todd had a chameleon-like character which could change whenever it suited him. However, Barbara saw her opportunity and took it.

"You know, Colonel, the Mavericks, as you say, are such an excellent squadron. They've flown some terribly dangerous missions and along with your chaps, too, by all accounts," she said.

"Yes, yes," Todd agreed, nodding.

"You know, I see a great opportunity for you to become something of a hero with the Mavericks and with the RAF, too," she continued.

Todd's expression perked up at once. "How so?"

"Well, you probably know that the Mavericks, so I've been hearing from Angus here, are short of Spitfires."

"I didn't know that, no. That's a real shame," said Todd.

I glanced at Angelica, who had pursed her lips at such blatant dissembling.

"Well, it's true," said Barbara, ignoring his outright lie. "And I want you to imagine this scene. An official ceremony, with a marching band, a parade where you hand over some of the spare Spitfires you have to the Mavericks. It would be so marvellous. Colonel Todd, the saviour of the Mavericks squadron."

There was a long moment of silence while Todd pictured the scene. I half expected him to demand to know where Barbara had heard about the spare planes. However, she had played him perfectly. That didn't even figure in his thinking.

His face suddenly brightened. He looked as if he'd had an epiphany. "Yes, Lady Barbara," he said. "You are right. This is my moment. I will show everyone just what an excellent leader I am, paving the way to cooperation between the British and American bases."

I could hardly believe my ears. He had swallowed the bait, hook, line and sinker.

"Yes, I can see it now," he continued. "A military parade, a marching band. A handing-over ceremony. What a fantastic idea…"

While he waxed lyrical about the wonderful occasion it was going to be, Barbara turned and surreptitiously winked at us. Todd was too busy painting a picture of his forthcoming role as our saviour to notice.

I thought Barbara had finished, but she hadn't. She had one more ace up her sleeve.

"You know, Colonel," she said, "or might I call you Dougan?" She fluttered her eyelashes at him prettily.

"You may call me Dougan by all means," he said. "It never sounded sweeter than from a woman as beautiful as you."

"Oh, Dougan, you flatter me," said Barbara.

"Believe me, it's not flattery. I've known a lot of women in my time, so many women. You might even call me an expert in that department. I know a beautiful woman when I see one," he said.

"Well, anyway ... Dougan," said Barbara, moving a little closer to him on the sofa, "I really think you are wasted as the base commander of a provincial airbase like this."

I began to catch on to what she was doing. She was trying to rid the American airbase of his presence.

"You do?" he said, looking pleased.

"Yes, I do. A man of your immense talents should be up in London, working at the highest levels, don't you think?"

"Well, I had hoped to get a posting up there, but this is what I got," he said regretfully. "But as I said, I'm doing an excellent job."

Barbara continued to play him like a fish on a hook. "I know people," she said. "I could put in a word if you like, in the right ears. I mean, only if you want me to."

"You'd do that for me?" he said.

"Yes, of course. I'd be more than happy to help you get a leg up the ladder to a place more worthy of your abilities. It seems such a shame for a man of your stature to be running a mere airbase when you could be doing even greater things."

He looked eager now, like a puppy caught under her spell. "If you could, of course, I'd be more than grateful. Do you really think...?"

"Consider it done," she said, smiling.

"I'm really much obliged to you, Barbara," he said. I noticed he had dropped the formality. "I've very much enjoyed this tea. The thing is, I really have to go. I've got to plan this ceremony — it's terribly important."

"It is, of course," said Barbara.

Todd had become effusive, fawning even. Barbara had conquered him like a chess master. I was mightily impressed.

"Well then, I'll take my leave, but if I might see you again sometime..."

"Of course, we'll arrange it soon," said Barbara smoothly.

The colonel stood up, and Barbara went to ring for the footman, who arrived post-haste. Todd took his leave. We watched him exit the room with some relief.

"And that," said Barbara, turning to us when he'd gone, "is how you do it."

"Well, I'm blowed," I said.

"I have to say I'm impressed," Angelica added.

"Darlings," said Barbara, "I've fraternised with Nazi generals in my line of work. This was mere child's play."

"Do you really think you can get him a posting in London?" I asked her.

Barbara smiled knowingly. "MI6 want him gone just as much as you do. Yes, I do have a certain influence, thanks to my late husband ... connections, you know. He'll get a desk job somewhere where he can't cause quite so much damage, but it will, at the same time, appear to be a dreadfully important job with no doubt a medal at the end of it."

She laughed at her own deviousness, and I couldn't help but admire it.

"Anyway, sit down, have some more tea — or something stronger? I think I need it after listening to all that."

Given the momentous nature of what she had achieved, it would have been churlish to refuse.

I had no doubt that the Spitfire handover would come to fruition in fairly short order. However, in the following days, we were distracted by a new arrival. He was piloting a Spitfire and landed on our runway. I was outside the hut at the time with various members of M Flight.

"That's not one of our Spits," said Dylan, indicating the plane as it touched down.

"I wonder who it is?" said Arjun.

The Spitfire came to a standstill, the engine died, and shortly afterwards, the pilot emerged from the cockpit. He jumped down and made his way towards us.

"I'm looking for Flight Lieutenant Mackennelly," he said, stopping in front of me.

"You've found him," I said. "What can I do for you?"

"Flight Lieutenant Kenneth McCracken," he replied, holding out his hand. "I've been ordered here to teach you fellows how to dive-bomb."

He pulled off his flying helmet to reveal an abundance of curly brown hair. He had piercing blue eyes and a rather luxurious moustache which I felt might even rival Bentley's.

I shook his hand and smiled. He had traces of a Scottish accent. I assumed from his name that he might have originally come from that region.

"Welcome to Banley. Let me introduce you to the rest of the crew."

After the niceties were completed, I asked some obvious questions.

"You don't appear to have any luggage," I said. "I am also assuming you'll need some accommodation."

"Anything rough and ready will do," he said. "My luggage is en route by truck, along with some dummy bombs for you chaps to practise with."

"Oh, I see. As for accommodation, I am sure we can do better than that. I'll make some arrangements. The other problem is that we don't have our full complement of pilots. How long are you here for?"

"As long as it takes," he replied.

"Well, I'd better introduce you to our CO, Squadron Leader Bentley," I told him.

"Absolutely," he said. "Lead the way."

I took Kenneth over to Bentley's office. We stood in front of his desk while Bentley diligently studied a memo. Kenneth looked at me, a little puzzled, but remained silent.

"Ah, Angus," said Bentley at length, looking up. "And who's this?"

"This is Flight Lieutenant Kenneth McCracken, sir. He's been sent to instruct us in dive-bombing techniques. I thought I'd bring him to meet you."

Bentley fixed Kenneth with a beady eye. He then began to replenish his pipe, his attention wholly taken up by the ritual. A glance at Kenneth indicated that he found this behaviour rather odd, but then there was no one quite like Bentley.

"Well, take a seat," said Bentley, once he was smoking his pipe contentedly.

We sat down while Bentley puffed away for a moment.

"So, you've got experience with dive-bombing using Spitfires?" Bentley asked Kenneth.

"Yes, sir, I've been leading a team who have been trying out and perfecting the technique," he replied.

"Pity they didn't single your unit out for this blasted mission then, isn't it?" said Bentley, at his most irascible.

"Well, sir, there's only about six of us, so it's probably not enough for a mission," Kenneth told him.

Bentley continued to puff on his pipe while absorbing this information. "Hmm," he said. "Well, make sure you get these chaps well versed in it, so they don't go getting themselves killed."

"I'll do my best, sir," Kenneth answered as diplomatically as he could.

Bentley pointed the stem of his pipe at him, and Kenneth looked rather alarmed.

"You'll do better than your best. I want these people to be expert dive-bombers before they go anywhere near a blasted enemy target, do I make myself clear?"

"Perfectly, sir," said Kenneth. "It will be as you say."

Bentley subsided and then picked up a memo, which he handed to me. "Got you two more pilots, Angus. Should be here any moment."

I took the memo from him and read it. "Pilot Officer Casmir Kaminski — sounds Polish — and Pilot Officer Jules Dubois, apparently from Belgium," I said.

"Yes," said Bentley. "Let's hope they are decent pilots, never mind where they come from."

"Yes, sir," I said.

"Anyway, they can get straight onto the dive-bombing training along with the rest. We should have a couple of Spitfires arriving soon from the factory, too. Nothing like a mission to move some obstacles out of the way."

"I'm glad to hear it," I replied.

"No thanks to the blasted Americans," he added acerbically.

I decided not to mention the prospective handover of several Spitfires, thinking it would be a rather pleasant surprise.

"Right then," Bentley said with an air of finality. "I've things to do, so go and get on with it."

"Sir," I said, taking this to be a dismissal.

Outside the main building, Kenneth turned to me. "Is he always like that?" he asked.

"Depends what kind of mood he's in," I replied.

"Not a good one, by the looks of it," Kenneth remarked.

"Oh, that's not bad for Bentley, but he's an excellent CO. He cares very much about this squadron," I told him.

He raised his eyebrows on hearing this. "Really?"

I laughed. "I know it doesn't seem like it, but yes, really."

The next moment, Angelica arrived and, oblivious to Kenneth's presence, planted a kiss on my lips. We had just become so used to being affectionate around others. Then she noticed the newcomer.

"Oh, who's this?" she said.

"May I present Flight Lieutenant Kenneth McCracken," I said. "Kenneth, this is my wife, Section Officer Angelica Mackennelly."

"Pleased to meet you," said Angelica, furnishing him with a smile. "And what brings you here?"

"I'm here to teach the Mavericks dive-bombing," he said.

"Oh," said Angelica, her smile fading.

"Shall we go and find Fred?" I said, quickly changing the subject. "Ask him to arrange for Kenneth to stay at Amberly?"

"Who is Fred?" asked Kenneth.

"Sergeant Bruce Gordon, our batman," said Angelica.

Kenneth regarded us both with some fascination. I didn't think he'd ever experienced a squadron quite like the Mavericks.

"And you two are married, in the same squadron?" he said.

"Yes, that's right," I confirmed.

"And nobody minds?"

"Mavericks by name, mavericks by nature," said Angelica simply.

Kenneth raised an eyebrow and then evidently decided to go along with it.

"Come on then," I said, starting off to where I thought I would find Gordon. Angelica tucked her arm into mine, and the three of us went together.

We saw Kenneth off to his prospective quarters, with Gordon informing us he'd take care of it. We were about to head back to the hut when we were waylaid by a staff car, which pulled up next to us.

"Hello," said a young man, leaning out of the back window. He had an accent which sounded French. "We're looking for Flight Lieutenant Mackennelly."

"Seems like everyone is looking for me today," I remarked. "Are you the new pilots?"

"Yes, that's right. How did you know?" he asked as he alighted from the car. Another man got out of the other side.

"I heard from the CO about your impending arrival," I told him.

"Ah, well, I'm Pilot Officer Jules Dubois from Belgium, and this is Pilot Officer Casmir Kaminski from Poland, sir, at your service," said Jules.

He was a slight young man in his early twenties with black hair, brown eyes and a small, neat moustache. Casmir was of a similar age but taller, with blond hair and grey eyes. The two men saluted.

"Welcome," I said, returning the salute. "This is Section Officer Angelica Mackennelly. She's the M Flight communicator."

We all shook hands.

"She has also the same name as you," remarked Jules. "She is your sister?"

"I'm his wife," said Angelica, laughing.

"*Ah, bon Dieu*, I am sorry for the mistake," said Jules.

"It's fine," I said. "It's a shame you didn't arrive sooner. I could have had our batman arrange for your accommodation. He's just gone with our new dive-bombing instructor. When he gets back, we'll sort it out."

"Thank you," said Casmir, whose voice had a deep rumble to it.

"*Tres bien*, and in the meantime?" asked Jules.

"Come and meet the rest of the flight," I said.

We walked to the dispersal hut. Jules and Casmir carried their bags, which they had retrieved from the staff car before it drove off.

As we approached the hut, Jonty came up to us.

"What-ho, Skipper," he said. "Look who's here."

I looked past him, and there was Jean.

"He's back and right as rain," said Jonty.

"That's good news," I said, shaking Jean warmly by the hand. "Now we're up to strength."

I made formal introductions and left the newcomers with the others to see them in. I stood outside the hut with Angelica, listening to the laughter within.

"They seem to have settled in all right," she said.

"Yes," I agreed. "They have indeed."

Out on the airfield, Judd's flight was just taking off on a patrol. Bentley had given those duties to them temporarily while we trained for the mission. I looked at Angelica, and she tucked her hand into mine. We both knew that this new mission was dangerous. M Flight would be once more in the firing line.

There was still no word from Colonel Todd, so bright and early the following day we began training. Kenneth, Jules and Casmir had been accommodated at Amberly Manor. Barbara seemed more than happy to oblige the Air Force with the use of her vast number of rooms. Thus, breakfast became a lively affair, as there were more of us partaking in it.

"This is quite a place," said Kenneth. "I never thought I'd get to stay somewhere quite so posh."

"Ah, well," said Jonty, "we've just been lucky."

"The food is also good," said Jules, tucking into the usual fare of eggs, beans, toast and spam. "We did not get such excellent rations before."

We didn't ask where he or Casmir came from before joining the Mavericks. It was an unspoken rule not to ask why other pilots had been sent here. Sometimes they would volunteer the information.

"I'll enjoy this while it lasts," said Kenneth. "I've stayed in some rum places, I can tell you."

He went on to tell us about some of his more amusing exploits while we finished our breakfast. Once we arrived at Banley, I assembled M Flight in the mission room. I had arranged for a large chalkboard to be set up so that Kenneth could use it. I was surprised to see Bentley slip into the back of the room with Audrey and sit down. I assumed he wanted to know what the dive-bombing entailed. He began his pipe routine while Kenneth stood up to speak.

"The first thing I'd like to tell you," said Kenneth, "is that dive-bombing isn't particularly what the Spitfire was designed for. However, it's more than capable of fulfilling that role."

He picked up a piece of chalk and began to sketch.

"In order to carry out a dive-bombing attack, you have to follow this pattern."

He drew a flat line which then rose up in a curve and then down again, whereupon it flattened out once more.

"You have to get your Spitfire to around six thousand feet before you begin the attack," he said, writing that figure at the top of the curve. "In whatever way you approach the target zone, I presume by stealth, you have to climb up in order to drop down. Once there, you turn onto the target and line it up in your gunsight. You need to dive at between forty-five and sixty degrees and keep the aim point in your gunsight."

He followed the line of the curve downwards with the piece of chalk.

"At no less than two thousand feet, you release your bombs, level off, and throttle away as fast as you can."

"Why two thousand feet?" Jonty asked him.

"Because if you go any lower, you'll be dead from the blast," explained Kenneth.

"Oh, right, yes, I see," said Jonty.

I noticed Bentley give him a slightly withering look.

"That, in essence, is how it works," said Kenneth. "You need to watch the G-forces, because they can hit you as you pull out of the dive. It's one reason why you don't climb back up again."

"What's the other reason?" asked Jean.

"The other reason is that you'll be back in the flak zone. That is one of the main hazards of dive-bombing enemy targets. You'll be flying directly into the flak."

Angelica looked at me. I knew what she was thinking, but it couldn't be helped.

"How do we avoid the flak?" said Jules.

"You don't," Kenneth replied. "You just dive and hope that you won't get hit."

This wasn't very reassuring, but it was better for him to tell it as it was. That way, we'd know what to expect.

"The time you'll be exposed to flak is limited. It's just about how long it takes you to get up there, then how long it takes to get down and drop the bombs," Kenneth continued. "The accuracy of dive-bombing has been well tested, and for a trained pilot it is very high, which is why it's a good method for delivering a payload to strategic targets."

Arjun raised his hand. "Once the first bombs have dropped, won't that obscure the target zone for the others?" he said.

"Yes, it will," said Kenneth. "However, it depends on the size of the target zone. For a large target, you could have several Spitfires dive and drop together, attacking different targets. That is probably the way to do it."

"Which presumably requires a fair bit of coordination," I put in.

"Yes, it does. So that's why we'll be practising that approach too."

I realised we had to examine the pictures of the port more closely and work out how many Spitfires could dive-bomb at once. Then we'd have to practise the entire attack operation.

"In order to calculate the angle of descent, you need to coordinate the vertical speed shown on the Vertical Speed Indicator and the Attitude Indicator..."

Kenneth went on to cover the calculation in more detail and explain exactly how to maintain the correct angle. He also explained that the airframe was capable of taking the required forces.

When he had finished, we all were a lot clearer on what was needed.

"The next thing," he said, when nobody had any further queries, "is for me to demonstrate how the dive-bombing works in practice. You will watch from the ground while I make several dummy runs. Then you will all go up and practise it yourselves while I observe from the control tower."

"Sounds like a plan," I said.

"Right then, let's get to it," said Kenneth, putting down the chalk and making for the door.

The others followed him while I hung back with Angelica. Bentley came up to us, along with Audrey.

"Make sure that fool Butterworth doesn't do anything stupid, Angus," he said.

"Yes, sir," I told him.

He didn't look particularly convinced but didn't pursue it any further. "Jolly good, let's see how it all goes. That chap seems to know what he's doing at any rate," he said.

"Yes, he sounds very competent."

"Just as well," said Bentley, before making for the door.

Angelica slipped her hand into mine and we made our way to the airfield. When we arrived, we found the rest of M Flight standing in a group watching Kenneth, who had started up the engine of his kite.

"I say, Skipper," said Jonty. "This looks like a brilliant lark."

"It's not a lark, Jonty," I said in quelling tones. "Make sure you don't do anything silly. Bentley's already spoken to me about it."

"Has he? Oh blast," said Jonty, as if Bentley was the biggest killjoy imaginable.

"Come on, Jonty," said Willie. "Just for once, be sensible."

Jonty didn't answer as we were distracted by the Spitfire taking off. We watched it fly away from the field. Then it returned at quite a lick and suddenly flew upwards in a fairly steep climb. At the top of the climb, the nose dropped abruptly. It came screaming downwards at a tremendous rate. Within seconds, it had pulled off level again and headed away for a circuit.

"By golly, that looks absolutely wizard," said Jonty, who appeared spellbound by the show.

Kenneth went on to perform this feat several times over with what seemed to be considerable ease and precision.

"I suppose it's easy when you've done it enough times," said Dylan.

"Practice," said Tomas. "That is what makes things perfect."

I had to agree. Eventually, Kenneth landed his plane, brought it to a stop and climbed down from the wing. He found an admiring group waiting.

"That was impressive," I said to him.

"Ah, it's easy enough when you know how," said Kenneth, brushing it off.

I looked at my watch and, seeing it was lunchtime, I decided to call a break.

"We'll take lunch, chaps," I said, "and reconvene afterwards."

"Then it will be your turn," said Kenneth.

Jonty looked a little disappointed but fortunately forbore to say anything.

"Let me introduce you to the mess," I said to Kenneth. "I think you'll find it tolerable."

"Lead on," he said. "I'm famished."

CHAPTER TEN

After lunch, it was time for each of us to learn to dive-bomb. As we were still a couple of Spitfires short, we decided to use what we'd got and swap over with the pilots who didn't yet have a plane. I hoped that the new ones would arrive soon or that Colonel Todd would hurry up and hand ours over.

Kenneth repaired to the control tower, where he would be in radio contact with whoever was doing the dive.

"Who's first then?" I asked the others as we all stood ready to go to our kites.

"I think it should be you, no?" said Tomas. "You are the leader."

"All right," I said. "Let's go in sections. Jonty and Kiwi, you can come with me."

"I say," said Jonty. "Good show, Skipper."

I turned to Angelica and dropped a kiss on her lips.

"Take care up there," she said.

"I will."

The three of us headed for our Spitfires. I jumped up onto the wing and got into the cockpit, and Redwood strapped me in.

"Enjoy the ride, sir," he said.

"I'll try," I told him. "By the way, Techie, you will see to Flight Lieutenant McCracken's plane, won't you?"

"Already on it, sir, don't you fret."

He jumped down, and I spun up the prop.

"This is Red Leader," I said to the tower. "I'll be taking up Red Section, Red One and Red Two."

"Roger, Red Leader," said Kenneth. "This is your instructor. Get airborne, then go around one at a time. When the first one has dived and cleared the field, the second goes and so on."

"Wilco," I said, taxiing to the end of the runway.

I opened up the throttle and was soon airborne, followed by Jonty and Willie.

"All right, Red Leader, circle around, then climb to six thousand feet. Drop at sixty degrees if you can to three thousand feet, then flatten out and clear," said Kenneth.

"Roger," I said. "Going around now."

In spite of my experience, I felt my pulse beginning to race. I assumed it was because I wasn't used to this kind of flying.

I took the Spitfire in a circuit around the airfield and out a fair distance. Then I turned back and started climbing quickly, watching the altimeter. I flew at six thousand feet until I was over the airfield, then I let her go.

I dropped the nose and the Spitfire started to dive. I carefully watched the two indicators, VSI and Attitude, to keep the angle at sixty degrees. The ground was rushing up at a tremendous rate. I had one eye on the altimeter, and at three thousand feet, I pulled out of the dive. I felt the G-force hit me, but not enough to cause me to black out.

The whole thing was over in moments.

"Not bad for a first try," said Kenneth. "Go around again and give it another go."

Jonty had been behind me, and as I circled around the field, I watched him take his dive, followed by Willie. Kenneth told them they had done quite well.

The second time I tried the dive, it felt a little easier. The trick was to climb and be above the target if possible, so that you would be less exposed to enemy fire. The third time, it was easier still. We went a couple more times after that, before

Kenneth told us to come in so the next section could have a go.

I landed the Spitfire and taxied to my standing. Angelica was waiting for me, along with Bentley and Audrey.

"Well done, darling," said Angelica. "It didn't look quite as scary as I thought it would."

"It wasn't too bad after all," I said. "Went better than I'd hoped."

"Looked fine to me, Angus," said Bentley, puffing out billows of smoke from his pipe. "Looks like the practice has started off well."

"So far, so good," I said. "We'll be progressing to dummy bombs next."

"Excellent," he said. "On another subject, I would like a word."

"What, here, sir?" I asked him.

"No, we will go to my office along with Section Officer Mackennelly, if you don't mind."

I glanced at Angelica, who mouthed, "Barbara," and then I understood. Perhaps Bentley had received the invitation from Colonel Todd. We accompanied Bentley and Audrey while behind me, I heard the drone of the other Spitfires practising their dives. That would be going on for quite a while.

Once in Bentley's office, he motioned for us to sit while he took his usual place behind his desk. Once there, he began his pipe routine, emptying, scraping and filling the bowl. He lit it and sat back, puffing with some satisfaction.

"I've received a rather odd invitation," he said. "From Colonel Todd."

"Invitation, sir?" I said, assuming a blank expression.

"Yes, an invitation to attend a grand ceremony whereupon the colonel will hand over our Spitfires," he continued.

"Really, sir?" I said in the most innocent tone I could muster.

Bentley was waiting for me to own up. He smoked his pipe for a few moments before brandishing it in my direction. "I'm betting ten to one you had something to do with this, Angus. So, let's have it, how did this come about? Not that I'm objecting to the idea of getting our planes back, you understand."

"No, sir," I said, glancing at Angelica. She gave me a reassuring smile. The only thing to do was tell the truth, and that was probably best where Bentley was concerned.

"Well?"

"Sir," I began, "we happened to mention our predicament to Lady Barbara."

"Go on," he said.

"She works for SOE now," said Angelica, clearly feeling this was important information to impart.

"Does she? Hmm, well, I'm not surprised, but anyway, go on."

"She devised a scheme, sir, to persuade Colonel Todd to relinquish the planes," I began.

Bentley's eyes narrowed. "And how exactly did she do that? Come on, tell me the whole."

Between us, Angelica and I related what had transpired at Barbara's tea party. We explained how Barbara had shamelessly manipulated Todd into thinking that the entire scheme was his idea. Bentley was vastly amused by the end of it.

"The entire thing sounds incredibly devious," he said. "It seems that Lady Barbara has judged Colonel Todd precisely."

"Yes, sir," I said. "It appears so."

"Good," he said with an air of finality. "Good. Well, if Todd wants a show, we'll jolly well give him one. The ceremony is to be in two days' time at the American base. I will brief everyone accordingly so that we turn up there looking as smart as possible. We'll show that blighter what the RAF is all about."

"Yes, sir," I said.

"Jolly good, that will be all. Better get back to your dive-bombing," he said jovially.

The colonel's change of heart had most definitely had a positive effect on the CO's mood, at least for the moment.

We returned to the practice session, which had been going full swing by all accounts. When the other sections had finished, I took Red Section up again for another go. Each time felt a little more natural than the last, which was only to be expected.

When the session was over, Kenneth gathered us all together in the mission room once more.

"That was pretty well done," he said, "for a first try. You all seem to have got the diving part quite well."

"Good show," said Jonty.

"Yes, well, let's not go getting carried away, shall we?" said Kenneth. "The next trick is to drop the bombs on target. In order to do that, your planes will be loaded with dummy bombs. These are the same as the bomb casings but filled with concrete or sand to make up the weight."

I wondered where he was planning to do this, but he appeared to have it all in hand. His truck with the bombs must have arrived, and no doubt Redwood's team had taken care of them.

"In order that we don't make big dents in the airfield," he continued, "I've negotiated that we will place a target — a large red cross — on the adjacent field. You will attempt to drop your bombs on that. The advantage is that with binoculars, I can see it from the tower, and it's not too far for the ground crew to go and retrieve them."

"Doesn't the farmer mind?" asked Arjun.

Most of the fields surrounding the base were farmland.

"It's been sorted," said Kenneth shortly. "Don't worry about it. I've seen to all the details."

He seemed to be remarkably efficient, an obvious boon to the squadron he was currently flying with.

"If there are no more questions, we'll call it a day. We will recommence bright and early tomorrow after breakfast."

As the meeting broke up, I went over to Kenneth to thank him.

"You seemed to have everything in hand," I said to him.

"Oh, I'm used to it," he said. "Bentley's adjutant has been most helpful."

"Has she?" said Angelica, shooting me a sly glance.

"Yes," said Kenneth. "Couldn't have done it without her. Anyway, I've got a couple of things to attend to, if you'll excuse me."

"Of course," I said as he left the room. I turned to Angelica. "I know that look. Are you implying that he and Audrey…?"

"I'm not implying anything," she said with a grin. "But I will be asking her."

The following day, we resumed practice. Angelica came down to watch. Redwood approached as I waited for everyone to gather at the edge of the airfield.

"Sir, we had two Spitfires delivered late yesterday afternoon. I thought you'd like to know," he said. "We've prepped them ready for this morning's exercise."

"That's great news, Techie," I said. "But keep it under your hat. Pretty soon, I think you'll get a whole lot more."

"Really?" he said, looking surprised.

"Mum's the word," I told him.

"I won't tell a soul, except the mechanics."

He went back to carry out last-minute checks on the planes. In the meantime, everyone else in M Flight had gathered, and Kenneth briefed us all.

"As I mentioned yesterday, you're going to be dropping the dummy bombs onto a target. You'll go one at a time. You need to sight the target from a distance so that you can climb up and arrive at the correct height, just as you are on top of it. That will take a bit of practice. After that, you drop down, releasing the bombs at three thousand feet. Any questions?"

Nobody had any, so I gave the flight some final instructions, and then the others headed out to the planes. Kenneth went off towards the control tower.

Angelica and I had a quick embrace.

"Be safe," she said.

"I will."

She held onto me a little longer. "Audrey said she isn't," she said.

"Isn't what?" I asked.

"She isn't doing anything with Kenneth…"

I laughed. We kissed and then I went to my Spitfire. Once I had strapped in and fired up, I taxied to the end of the runway. It had been decided the entire flight would go one after the other, so we took off and went into our usual formation.

I took the flight some distance away from the airbase.

"M Flight, form a line," I said. "Red Section first."

We moved into a long line, one behind the other, rather like a snake.

"All right, let's go," I told them, heading back towards the base.

I deliberately kept at low level since that was how we would approach the port in the real mission, so that we would only be spotted at the last moment. The line spread out, just as I had briefed everyone to do before we left. The large red cross came into view.

"Instructor," I said, "Red Leader going in."

"Roger, Red Leader," said Kenneth.

I took a steep climb up to six thousand feet, at the same time aiming to be over the cross at the end of it. I had managed it in practice, but now found I was off by a margin and had to fly forwards before going into my dive.

"Here goes," I said to the tower as the Spitfire dropped away at high speed.

Once again, the ground rushed towards me while I watched the instruments. At three thousand feet, I hit the bomb release.

"Bombs away," I said, levelling off and, after a few seconds, backing around.

"Not bad, Red Leader," said Kenneth. "That was pretty much on target."

Pleased with my first attempt, I circled the airfield and came in to land. I killed the engine and went over to where Angelica was watching.

"You did it," she said, smiling.

"Yes, although I need to get in the right position quicker," I replied.

"It's actually quite exciting watching it," she said. "And perhaps a bit frightening for the defenders. No wonder people found the Stuka attacks scary."

"If it puts them off their aim," I said, "it's all to the good."

In the meantime, we watched Jonty and Willie drop their bombs. Both of them got pretty close to the cross. The rest of the flight followed suit. All in all, the pilots seemed to have got the hang of it on the first go.

Kenneth came down to talk to us while the ground crew took a truck to gather up all the dummy bombs and bring them back for another round.

"That wasn't bad at all," he said. "I've seen a lot worse."

Everyone laughed at this.

"Anyway, we'll go as many times as we can today and then if it's looking good, we might even go on to multiple plane dives tomorrow. Soon after that, we'll be trying live ordnance. The main thing is to try and get up over the target in one go, if you can. You don't want to be hanging around at six thousand feet in the flak zone; it's very bad for your health."

M Flight repaired to the hut for a cup of tea. Tomas came up to me.

"I hope this is all going to be worth it, Scottish, this diving business," he said.

I shrugged. "Your guess is as good as mine on that score."

"Yes, I know. But for me it's a chance to turn the tables, as you British say. The Germans have terrified my people with their bloody Stukas — now we will give it back to them, eh?"

"We sure will," I replied. "In spades, I hope."

"You and me both, Scottish," he said. "Now, I'm going for tea before we try all this again."

Angelica and I followed him into the hut. Shortly afterwards, we repeated the entire dummy bomb exercise. This time, I really focused on timing, getting up over the target as fast as possible. It was better, but not perfect.

At the right point, I slipped the Spitfire into a dive and released the bombs at three thousand feet, levelling off and throttling away.

"On target, well done, Red Leader," said Kenneth.

After the lunch break, Bentley called a briefing in the hangar. We made our way there and waited for him to arrive.

"What's all this about, Skipper?" asked Jonty.

"You'll find out soon enough," I told him.

"Attention! Senior Officer in the room," barked Judd.

Bentley strode in and got up onto the podium along with Audrey. He stepped forward and surveyed us in his inimitable way.

"In two days' time," he said, "there is to be a ceremony at the American base, convened by the base commander, Colonel Todd."

This intelligence was met with silence. Todd's reputation had become well known on base. There had been a lot of fraternisation going on between the two bases, and this had all but stopped. Rumour had it that there was also frustration from locals who had got used to the GIs spending their money in the hostelries and shops.

"This ceremony is for the purpose of handing us back the Spitfires that we lent them when they first arrived here. It's to be a big show, apparently, which means that every one of you will attend it unless you have vital duties on this base."

If Bentley had thought this would be met with enthusiasm, he was mistaken. However, Bentley in full flow was not a man to be denied.

"Every person going to the parade will turn out in their very best uniforms at parade ground standard. I want shining buckles, boots, the lot, understood? Nobody on this unit will allow the Americans to show us up. We will demonstrate to them that we remain one of the finest units in the RAF, regardless of what anyone says or thinks."

Finally, this got a reaction. A small cheer went up.

"We will put on our own parade, marching in formation and to that end, you will be attending a practice to make sure you haven't forgotten your drill."

There were a few groans, which earned a scowl from Bentley.

"You'd better attend it," he said. "Or I'll have your bloody guts for garters!" This was one of his favourite sayings. "Let me make it clear that if anybody —" he fixed Jonty with a beady eye — "thinks they want to indulge in some kind of tomfoolery on this parade, there will be hell to pay. You'll be on drill for a month, for starters!"

Jonty looked decidedly uncomfortable with this level of scrutiny and started to finger his collar. Having read us the riot act, Bentley calmed down.

"This ceremony is of vital importance," he said in milder tones. "We need those Spitfires, and as inconvenient as you might view this whole farrago, it's crucial for the war effort. So, I need your cooperation, every man and woman on this base, is that understood?"

There was a chorus of assent from the assembled party. Bentley, although irascible, had a knack of appealing to people's better nature.

"All right, well, mind what I said. Make sure your dress uniforms are up to the mark. Wear them proudly; remember we are the RAF. We have fought in the Battle of Britain and beyond, and we have prevailed long before the Americans came on the scene. We will still be here long after they have left, so don't forget it."

The entire hangar erupted with cheers. He had hit the right note. The unpopularity of Colonel Todd was legion by now. If he had achieved one thing, it was that, and in a very short space of time. Bentley smiled, saluted and left the podium.

"He's quite the tartar, your CO," said Kenneth, who had come to listen.

We were wending our way out to undertake more practice.

"He certainly is," I said. "But he would also die for this squadron. He holds this place together, and we're grateful."

"I can see that he's very respected," said Kenneth. "That's important."

By now, we were all back at the field, ready for another attempt at dummy bombing. We would probably manage three more tries before the day was out, depending on how quickly the ground crew could retrieve the bombs and reload them.

"All right," announced Kenneth. "No rest for the wicked. Let's get to it."

He returned to the tower with Angelica while I headed for my plane.

I got into my Spitfire, and the flight took off once more. We completed the same manoeuvre, heading away from the base and then turning back in a line.

I found my judgement had improved as to when to begin the climb, and then I topped out of the curve just right. I dropped down fast and released the bombs.

"On target, Red Leader," said Kenneth.

I was happy enough about that and landed so I could watch the others complete their run. Harold started his dive. I thought perhaps he was going rather fast. Then at three thousand feet, he kept going.

"Pull up, pull up!" I shouted, to no avail, as there was no way he could hear me.

His plane continued to dive and for a heart-stopping moment, I thought he was going to hit the ground. At the last minute, his plane righted itself and screamed out of the dive, just feet from the ground.

"Crikey, that was close," said Jonty, who was standing beside me with Willie.

Harold hadn't dropped his bombs. He circled around and came in to land. In the meantime, the rest of the flight completed their practice.

Harold jumped down from his plane and came up to me.

"What happened?" I asked him.

"I … I blacked out, Scottish," he said. "I'm sorry."

"Don't be sorry," I said, recalling my own blackout experience in a dive.

Kenneth came striding up to us just then. "You came down too fast," he said. "You've got to watch that speed, otherwise the G-forces will be too much. Your angle was all wrong, too. Far too steep."

"Yes, sir," said Harold. "I'll do better next time."

"Don't get blasé about this," said Kenneth. "That's when accidents happen. You've got to be in control at all times. During the mission, you'll be coming in under fire. You've got to keep your cool and focus on what you're doing just the same."

"Yes, sir. I will, sir," said Harold.

"Good lad, you're all right. It happens to the best of us. I'm just glad you pulled out of that dive in time."

"You're not the only one, sir," said Harold. "I got quite a shock when I came to. Instinct took over, though."

"That's the ticket," said Kenneth. "Chalk it up to experience and go again, okay?"

"Yes, sir," said Harold, looking relieved.

Fortunately, no further incidents occurred to mar the practice. On his next run, Harold executed a perfect textbook dive, much to my relief.

When practice was over, Kenneth spoke to us. "What happened today was a salutary lesson for us all. We must stay calm and in control, no matter what. That is what will save your life and make your drop a success. Tomorrow we'll be diving in groups of three, so you'll be acting in unison. It will require coordination. It's likely that this is how you will attack the target, with each Section taking on an area to attack."

"Well done, chaps," I said. "Let's not forget the uniforms and drill practice."

There were good-natured groans all around as we finished up for the day and headed to our billets for dinner.

Although I was sure that Gordon would get my dress uniform ready if asked, I elected to do it myself. He had enough duties to attend to and already looked after us well.

"Are you sure you don't want me to do it, sir?" he asked. "It would really be no trouble."

"No, Fred, you do enough, but if you could obtain an iron and an ironing board, that would help."

He did not argue. I suspected he was quite happy to be relieved of the duty. I had no doubt some of the others would ask him if he could do their uniforms.

"Consider it done, sir," he replied with a smile. "I'm grateful for your consideration."

That evening, after dinner, Angelica and I spent some time ironing our dress uniforms and polishing our boots to a shine. She was very neat and precise about everything, including all the creases being just so. Fortunately, there was very little brass other than buckles and buttons to polish. It wasn't too onerous after all. We soon had it completed.

Our uniforms were then hung up in the wardrobe, with our shiny best boots at the bottom.

"I'm not looking forward to drill tomorrow," said Angelica.

"I don't suppose any of us are," I said. "But Bentley's right. We've got to put on a show."

"For that pompous braggart Todd," she replied acidly.

"It's a means to an end," I said.

"Well, now that we've done our duty," she said, putting her arms around me, "it's time for our reward."

"Is it?"

"Yes, it most certainly is," she murmured, nuzzling my lips with hers.

After which nothing more was said.

The following two days were a hive of activity. In the morning, we had drill. One of the sergeants acted as drill instructor and put us through our paces.

"I thought we'd left all this behind us," grumbled Jonty as we marched up and down the parade ground.

"Stop complaining," said Willie. "It will be over soon enough."

"Not soon enough for me," said Jonty.

"Silence that man, if you please. Keep your mind on the job!" bellowed the sergeant. "Company will turn to the left … *left … turn!*"

So it went on, while alongside us the WAAFs had their own drill instruction, since they would be separate from us on the parade.

As I understood it from the order of events we had been given, the parade would consist of a march-past, saluting Colonel Todd and Squadron Leader Bentley, plus the American base CO. Then there would be the ceremonial handover, which would consist of a speech by Todd. None of us was looking forward to that.

Afterwards, the Spitfires would be handed over. Some of Judd's pilots would take them up and do a flypast, along with the Americans. Following which, apparently, there was to be some kind of celebration lunch. The pilots would return once they'd got the Spitfires safely to our base.

Todd didn't do things by halves. In the end, we'd have quite a number of spare Spitfires, and that was all to the good, although they would have to be repainted with British markings and the Mavericks insignia.

The drill finally came to an end by lunchtime. There would be another drill practice the following morning, and the ceremony was the next day. The weather was holding, and I hoped it would stay fine. I didn't want anything to prevent the handover going ahead.

That afternoon, we practised dive-bombing in sections. The whole flight flew away from the airbase, then returned in groups of three, spaced out behind each other. My section went first. We flew back towards the airfield.

"Red Section, attack formation," I said as we began our dummy run with the target up ahead.

"Roger," said Jonty.

"Roger," said Willie.

We fanned out in a line and kept pace. I would make the decision when to climb, keeping my eye on the target. I flicked a glance left and right to be sure the other two were keeping up. The three of us had flown together so often that doing so wasn't difficult. We reached the point where we needed to start the attack.

"Let's climb now," I said, pulling back on the stick.

Together, we flew upwards, staying in line until we reached the top of the curve at six thousand feet. The target was nicely lined up below us.

"Dive," I said, dropping the nose.

The three of us dived in almost perfect synchronisation, and at three thousand feet, I gave the order.

"Bombs away."

We dropped our bombs and levelled out, throttling up to get clear. The whole thing had gone like clockwork. Whether it would on the day remained to be seen.

"Well done, Red Section," said Kenneth. "You kept it together nicely. Bombs were on target. Blue Section, you're next."

"All right, Red Section, let's go in to land," I said, circling around for an approach. I landed and jumped down from my plane to be joined by Willie and Jonty.

"I say, Skipper, that was a damn good show," said Jonty.

"Yes, though let's not get carried away," I said. "We've got plenty more practising to do."

"Well, I think it's marvellous," he said. "It's like one of those roller coaster rides…"

"Trust you to think of something like that," said Willie with a laugh.

"I'm jolly glad we're doing this mission," said Jonty.

I wondered how glad he was going to be when it happened for real. We'd be doing it under ack-ack fire in the face of the enemy.

Angelica was waiting for us, and I put my arm around her shoulders. We turned to watch the other sections have their go.

"You did well," said Angelica with a smile. "Which is no more than I would expect."

"You see," said Jonty. "Angelica has faith in us."

We couldn't help but laugh. M Flight spent the rest of the afternoon flying practice runs in sections. At the end of the day, Kenneth gathered us all together.

"You've done a good job," he said. "You've learned fast and got up to speed. I'm genuinely impressed."

"We're the Mavericks," said Dylan. "That's what we do."

Kenneth smiled at this. Dylan was proud of his place in the squadron, as were we all.

"Not always easy to tell with a name like that," said Kenneth. "Although I've heard about the squadron's reputation, and what I've heard is good. You've lived up to my expectations."

"Thanks," I replied. "We appreciate it."

"Anyway," Kenneth continued, "don't get too cocky just yet. We've got to try it with live ordnance. So tomorrow afternoon we're going to do just that. We're going to fly out to the range and drop some five-hundred-pound bombs on a target, in single-plane attacks. Let's see how you go with that. In the following days, we'll add the other bombs and then try it with three planes apiece. In the meantime, it won't hurt if you simply practise your dives when you get a chance so that it becomes second nature."

"Absolutely," I said. "Good plan. Don't forget drill tomorrow morning, everyone, and then the day after that it's the big parade."

I think that some had started to look forward to the ceremony, after all. It wasn't often we got to show off our squadron. I was happy that M Flight were not involved in flying the Spitfires back to base, too. If the Americans were going to put on a spread, then I didn't want my chaps to miss the start of it.

The following morning, Angelica and I were up early for drill practice. We got dressed and headed to the dining room for breakfast. Kenneth had been given a room along one of the corridors nearby. As we walked, I was surprised to see the handle of his door turn very slowly. Angelica and I exchanged a curious glance and stopped to see who would come out.

My thoughts were that it might be the sneak thief, although to our knowledge, nothing had gone missing from the manor. The door inched open, and Barbara slid lightly out of the opening, closing the door softly behind her.

She was in a state of déshabillé, wearing only a red silk housecoat, her hair hanging loose down her back. She turned and almost jumped to see us standing there.

"Oh! Gosh, well, Angus and Angelica," she said. "You gave me quite a start."

"Comforting our guest?" asked Angelica in amused tones. It was just like her to be direct.

"Oh, you know, darlings," said Barbara, recovering her composure. "When the opportunity presents itself, why not?"

I was well acquainted with Barbara taking opportunities where she found them.

"Indeed," I said sardonically.

"A woman has needs," said Barbara. "What can I say?"

There wasn't really much *to* say, and given the awkwardness of the situation, she decided to make herself scarce.

"Anyway, I'm off to tidy myself up. If anyone asks, you didn't see me," she continued.

"Mum's the word," said Angelica, stifling a giggle.

Barbara padded barefoot down the corridor in the direction of her own apartments.

"So, it *definitely* wasn't Audrey," said Angelica with a laugh.

"No," I agreed.

We resumed our walk to the dining room.

"Do you think that Barbara has a penchant for Scotsmen?" asked Angelica with a mischievous twinkle in her eye.

"I couldn't possibly comment," I told her, and she laughed.

Then she stopped and turned to face me. "How do you feel about Barbara? Now you've seen her again?" she asked seriously.

I could tell from her expression that she was a little anxious.

"I love you, you silly goose. I never did love her, darling, I've told you that," I said.

"All right," she said, smiling. She kissed me lightly on the lips. "But I'm not a goose."

"You're my very best goose," I teased.

"Oh, you!" she said in mock exasperation. "Anyway, come on, I'm famished."

She tucked her arm into mine and we continued down to breakfast in perfect harmony. The morning was taken up by drill once more. We practised a march-past, and Bentley came to see how it was all proceeding. He stood and smoked his pipe, then left without comment. I assumed this meant that he approved.

After lunch, it was time to practise with the live ordnance. Kenneth gathered us around once more.

"This time, you're going to dive over the target that has been marked out on the range. Your job is to drop the bomb within the designated area. Since you're going in one by one, you will, of course, find that the smoke might obscure things, but no matter. I just want you to get the feel of what it's really going to be like. I'll be in a Spitfire circling around, watching. Any questions?"

There were none, and everyone was keen to get to it.

"Take care," said Angelica, winding her arms around my neck and giving me a kiss.

"I will," I replied.

"I say, Skipper," said Jonty. "Isn't this the business? I've been looking forward to it!"

"No doubt you have," I said. "Just keep it tight and stick to what you've learned."

"He means don't do anything bloody stupid," said Willie, translating for me.

"As if I would," said Jonty, sounding outraged.

We couldn't help but laugh at this. Jonty bore it with good humour.

"Well, I'm not going to fool around with live ordnance," he said.

"I certainly hope not," I told him.

Moments later, I was strapped into the cockpit of my Spitfire and fired up the engine. I taxied to the end of the runway, and then we were airborne.

"M Flight, single file, low-level approach," I said as I took a bearing towards the target zone.

The range wasn't too far away, and soon enough I could see a large white square marked out in a flat field. My pulse quickened with the thought of dropping an actual bomb.

"I'm going in," I said.

The procedure was to wait until the plane dropping the bomb was clear, and then the next plane would follow on. This was simply for safety. In a real mission, we'd be attacking quickly all together so that we could get in and out very fast.

I began my climb to six thousand feet and hit the top of the curve. I dropped the nose and headed down, keeping an eye on the airspeed and other indicators. I made sure I wasn't going too fast. I had become accustomed to the ground racing up towards me, and it didn't faze me. Then at three thousand feet, I released the bomb.

"Bombs away," I said, levelling off and throttling up.

Checking my mirror, I caught sight of the tremendous explosion as the five-hundred pounder went off.

"Good shot, Red Leader," said Kenneth. "Next one go."

"I say, that was spectacular," said Jonty, whose turn it was now.

"Keep your mind on the job, will you?" said Kenneth, admonishing him.

"Wilco," said Jonty.

I circled around to watch him. He executed a nice curve up and then dropped down fast.

"Whoopie!" cried Jonty, unable to resist the excitement of it all. "Bombs away."

His bomb released at three thousand feet and dropped into the target zone while he levelled off and cleared the area. The explosion was impressive.

"Well done," said Kenneth. "Next."

This continued until all twelve of us had dropped our bombs. Thankfully, it went without a hitch.

"Return to base, M Flight," I said. "Form up on me."

We resumed normal formation and headed back to Banley. We landed and I brought the Spitfire to a standstill, killed the engine and jumped down from the wing.

"That was a damn fine show, Skipper," said Jonty as he caught up with me. "Never thought dropping bombs would be so much fun."

"You could always transfer to be a bomber pilot," said Willie.

"Not on your nelly," Jonty shot back. "I'm not giving up my Spitfire for anyone. Besides, who would you play chess with?"

"Someone who doesn't cheat," responded Willie.

"I do not cheat," said Jonty hotly. "You're the one playing with New Zealand rules…"

I left them engaged in yet another argument as I was distracted by Angelica. She came up to me and wrapped her arms around my neck.

"How was that?" she asked me.

"Explosive," I quipped.

"I'll show you explosive," she said, placing her lips on mine.

CHAPTER ELEVEN

Kenneth had been pleased with the result of our first live bombing practice. We'd take a break for the big ceremony, then resume the day after, when we would be dropping three bombs each. We'd then progress onto dropping a set of bombs in sections of three planes at a time. This would simulate a real attack.

Given the importance which had been placed on the handover ceremony by Bentley, we all dispersed to our billets to make final preparations. Kenneth told me he could do with the break, and since he had not brought a dress uniform, he wouldn't be attending the handover.

The day of the ceremony dawned misty at first, but the sun was shining through, and it would soon burn off. Angelica and I got dressed and went down to breakfast. All the others were there looking very smart, I was pleased to see.

"What-ho, Skipper," said Jonty. "Looking forward to the big parade?"

"As much as anyone else," I replied, accepting a plate of scrambled eggs on toast with some bacon and baked beans on the side. When Barbara was in residence, I noticed that the food, which was already very good, rose to an even higher standard. She must have had words with the kitchen or pulled a few strings to get items like bacon.

"I think it will be lots of fun," said Angelica, tucking into her plate of food.

After breakfast, Gordon drove me and Angelica to the American base. He was also looking very smart and would be taking part. The others made their own way.

At the American base, it was all very organised. The cars were shown to a parking area, and then we were guided to an assembly point for the RAF. Next to us, the American contingent was getting ready.

Sandford spotted us and came over. "This is quite an unexpected turn of events," he said with a grin.

"Very much so," I replied. I felt this wasn't the time to let him in on the secret. We would see what transpired first.

We chatted amicably, and then it was time to assemble.

"See you later," he said.

"Yes indeed."

Angelica went to join the WAAFs, while out of the corner of my eye, I spotted Barbara's Rolls-Royce arriving. Naturally, she would be one of the guests of honour. In fact, there seemed to be a number of local civilians in evidence too. I assumed that Todd wanted to put on a show for the general populace as well as all of us. He loved an audience.

It was soon time for us to assemble. We formed up in ranks. The American contingent would lead the parade, followed by the RAF and then the WAAFs.

The Americans had a military band which struck up 'Yankee Doodle Dandy' for starters, much to Jonty's delight.

"Don't you dare whistle," hissed Willie, who was standing next to him in the ranks.

"I wasn't going to."

"Quiet on parade!" yelled the parade sergeant.

Then came the order to start.

"Parade ... forward ... march!"

We followed the band out onto a wide area in front of the hangars, which served for the occasion as the parade ground. A big stand had been erected where all the guests were seated, and in front of that was a podium. On the podium was Colonel

Todd with the CO of the American base and Bentley, plus various other senior officers. Todd had obviously put the base to a huge amount of trouble on account of his parade.

Over on the field were twelve Spitfires bedecked in red, white and blue ribbons. There were balloons, American flags, the whole nine yards. It was pomp and circumstance, and then some. I dreaded to think how much it had all cost.

As we passed the podium, the parade sergeant called out, "Eyes right!" I could see Colonel Todd smiling benignly upon us, as if all of this was just for him. He saluted and waved as we passed. Bentley, on the other hand, held a salute for the entire time.

Part of me wished we hadn't had to resort to this level of deviousness to get what we wanted. However, it couldn't be helped.

The band played a variety of marching tunes while we completed a circuit of the parade area, then they fell silent.

"Parade ... halt!" came the order, and we all came to a stop.

"Parade, right turn!" shouted the sergeant.

We all turned to face the podium.

"Stand at ... ease!"

We stood in the easy position and waited. It was now time for Colonel Todd's speech. Even though I had not yet heard it, I could imagine exactly how it was going to go. I wasn't disappointed.

A public address system had been set up for Todd to use so that everyone could hear him. Representatives of the local press were also there. It would be widely reported. He stepped up to the mic and then held up his hands for silence, even though there was already silence on the parade ground.

"Thank you, thank you all," he said, "for coming to this very great and momentous parade. This is a very special occasion. I hope you're enjoying it so far?"

He waited, and there was a smattering of muted applause at this. It was only to be expected from a predominantly reserved British audience.

"I hope you like my great parade, because as far as parades go, it's one of the best. I know how to put on a parade, believe you me… Anyway, the point is that when I heard my British friends next door were running short of planes, I was shocked," he continued.

I glanced at Bentley, who was staring straight ahead, stony-faced. I wondered what was going through his mind. I couldn't imagine it was anything particularly benign towards Todd.

"So I said to my adjutant, I said, 'These guys need planes, and we need to do something about it.' I did, yes, I did. And of course I *could* do something about it, because we had some Spitfires. They were just sitting there, not being used because now we've got these P-47 Thunderbolts."

He paused for a moment, looking around to make sure everyone was listening.

"I don't know if you've heard of the Thunderbolt. It's an American plane, a very advanced fighter plane that can do many incredible things. The Spitfire is very good, but the Thunderbolt, well, the name says it all. We're bringing the thunder to the Germans, that's for sure."

There were one or two stifled sniggers from our ranks at this. We all knew that the P-47 was pretty much evenly matched with the Spitfire. We also knew that McClusky's view of the planes was widely shared by the other pilots who had to fly them.

"So I immediately said to my adjutant, 'You know what? The British need these Spitfires and we're going to give them to them.' I said it just like that. That's really why we're here today — to hand over these planes to the RAF. I had no hesitation in doing so once I knew how much they were needed."

I couldn't imagine how Bentley was containing himself on hearing this blatant dissembling, but he did so remarkably well. It was pretty outrageous, even for Todd.

"So," said Todd, "we're going to be handing them over in a few moments, but before we do that, I also have some great news."

I waited because this was surely the punchline.

"Yes, the boys upstairs, you know, they've told me that I've been doing an incredible job here on the base, getting it shipshape and so on. They said, 'Dougan, we need you upstairs. We need your talents, which are being wasted on that airbase. You've done a good job, but now it's time for you to move on.' So, sadly, I'll be leaving very soon for a new position. The CO will take over once more, as it's been decided that they don't need a base commander after all now that I've got it all running smoothly."

Barbara had come through with her promise. Sandford and many others would be overjoyed at the news, I was sure.

"So," Todd continued, "it's a sad but also a happy occasion for you all on this base. I'm sorry to be leaving, but I'm sure that you'll keep on doing a good job without me, as you must."

He paused, and this time there was more applause. I suspected it was because he would be leaving.

"So, before we hand over the Spitfires, I'll ask Squadron Leader Bentley, Commanding Officer of the Mavericks, to say a few words."

Todd stepped back to further applause, and Bentley stepped forward. I wondered if he was missing his pipe since he hadn't been able to smoke it.

"Thank you, Colonel Todd, for your generous support of our squadron and for returning the planes to the RAF," said Bentley in clipped tones. "We are really *very* grateful. Thanks again."

He stepped back after this very brief speech. It spoke volumes regarding his disapproval of the entire event.

Todd stepped forward again. "So now it is my great pleasure to declare the Spitfires officially handed over to the Mavericks squadron!"

This time, there were cheers from everyone. That part, at least, we could show a lot of appreciation for.

Judd and his pilots marched forward and saluted the podium. Then they set off at a run for the Spitfires. The ribbons were removed, then we watched while they were helped into the planes. The twelve Merlins starting up was a stirring sound.

In short order, they taxied to the end of the runway and then took off. Judd formed them up as they circled the airfield.

"Parade … attention!" ordered the parade sergeant.

As Judd's squadron executed a low flypast over us, we all saluted. The audience cheered like mad. It brought a smile to my face. The Spitfire held a special place in our hearts because we all knew how the plane had helped save the day during the Battle of Britain.

Judd brought them for a flypast once more with that familiar whine as they passed over, then they banked away and were gone, heading for Banley Airfield.

Todd stepped up to the mic again. "What a great occasion, ladies, gentlemen, members of the armed forces of America and Britain. A great plane, the Spitfire, a very great plane.

Anyway, that brings the formal proceedings to an end. I invite you to take refreshments in the hangar, listen to the band, and celebrate the great achievement that I have brought about. So, thank you all for coming to *my* parade!"

There were plenty of cheers at the prospect of American hospitality, which was known to be very generous. On this occasion, Todd had pulled out all the stops.

"Parade ... fall out!" shouted the parade sergeant.

We immediately dispersed. Most people headed for the hangar while the band struck up some jazzy tunes.

Angelica came up to me. "Come on," she said. "Let's get in the queue!"

There were tables laden with food and a bar serving drinks. On one side of the hangar was a makeshift stage, ready for a band. We made our way over to where the food was being served. The queue moved quite quickly and we were soon seated at one of the many tables which had been set around the edge of the vast hangar. A table had been set up for Todd and the other senior officers, including Bentley. They were being served by some of the American ordinary ranks.

"I say, Skipper, this is a damn good show," said Jonty, joining us.

"It certainly is," I agreed.

"I would have liked to have flown one of the Spitfires back, though," Jonty continued.

"Well, I imagine Bentley didn't want you doing the flypast," said Willie, "in case you pulled some kind of stupid stunt."

"I say!" said Jonty, protesting.

"Jonty," said Angelica kindly, "you know you very well might."

"I suppose that's true," Jonty acknowledged ruefully.

"What did you make of the speech, Scottish?" said Tomas, who had also joined us at our table.

"He had a lot to say ... mainly about himself," I said, smiling.

"In my country, we have a saying," said Tomas. "Speaking is silver, silence is gold."

"I guess Todd hasn't heard that proverb then," observed Willie.

We all laughed and tucked into the excellent American fare. There were hamburgers, hotdogs, French fries and fried chicken, along with a number of other interesting culinary dishes, including apple pie. The bar was serving Coca-Cola, fresh lemonade and other soft drinks. There was a limited amount of cold American beer too.

While we were eating, a band took to the stage. They started knocking out some dance numbers, and a few people started dancing. Naturally, Angelica wanted to join in, so I obliged her. Then I let Willie take over, since he wasn't able to dance with Olga. She and Maria were unable to attend on account of Maria's security; it didn't do for her to be seen outside of the base.

While I was watching my wife on the dance floor, Sandford sat down beside me.

"So, tell me," he said, "how did you manage it?"

"Why do you think it was me?" I asked innocently.

"Because I don't know anyone else who could pull it off," he said with a laugh.

"It's not me you have to thank," I told him. "It's Lady Barbara over there."

She was on the dance floor with Todd, who appeared to be enjoying himself tremendously.

"Oh?" he said.

"I'll tell you the whole when it's a little more private," I told him.

He smiled. "I'll look forward to hearing that story. And Todd's going," he said. "That's something to celebrate anyway."

"You must be glad."

"Me and the whole goddamn base," he said. "Maybe things can get back to normal. We can restore the relationship he ruined with you guys."

"It's easily mended," I told him. "Don't fret."

The dance number finished. Angelica came breathless off the floor. She took a long drink of her Coca-Cola. I knew she wasn't through with dancing by a long chalk. I was just about to offer to take her for another twirl when Sandford asked first.

"Mind if I borrow your wife?" he said as the band struck up another number.

"Of course he doesn't," said Angelica.

"Be my guest," I told him.

I watched them jiving with great admiration for Angelica's *joie de vivre*. I hoped that she would never lose that spirit, which had so captivated my heart.

The party continued late into the afternoon before breaking up. Eventually we said our goodbyes, found Gordon, and returned to Banley.

"That was quite a shindig, sir," said Gordon.

"It was splendid," said Angelica, her eyes still shining. "I loved the dancing so much."

"Yes, I suppose we should thank Todd for giving himself a good send-off," I said sardonically.

"And for giving our planes back," Angelica pointed out. "Even if it was Barbara who persuaded him."

"That too."

"Perhaps things can calm down a little at Banley now, sir," said Gordon.

Unfortunately, as we soon found out, Gordon's optimism was sadly misplaced.

I arrived at the dispersal hut along with Angelica to find it in uproar. There were loud arguments and exclamations from the members of M Flight.

"Skipper," said Jonty as soon as he saw me, "it's happened again!"

"What's happened, Jonty?" I asked him.

"Things going missing," he replied.

"Pardon?" I could hardly hear him above the row.

Tomas banged loudly on the table with a tin mug and the place fell silent.

"Now," I said to the hut in general, "what's going on?"

"Scottish, my silver pen, it's been stolen," said Dylan.

"And my lucky Roman coin," put in Stanley. "It was my talisman."

"I had a pocket watch," said Casmir.

"My St Christopher medal," chimed in Jules.

I held up my hand for silence. It seemed as if the thief had taken advantage of our absence. I decided to confirm this assumption.

"Did you have them before the parade today?" I asked.

There were nods all round.

"So, someone has taken them while we were all off the base," I surmised.

"That's it," said Jonty. "So, we just find out who was here, question them and —"

"I'll deal with this, Jonty," I said, cutting in. As much as I liked his enthusiasm, the last thing I needed was for people to take matters into their own hands. "First of all, I'm going to take the issue to Bentley. It's highly likely that the thief covered their tracks."

"If you say so, Skipper," said Jonty, looking dejected.

"Can one of you write a list of all the items that have gone missing," I said. "I'll take it to Bentley and discuss what to do next."

"I'll do it," offered Dylan.

The others crowded around while he cast about for a pencil and paper.

"Let's go," I said to Angelica, once we had the list.

As we left the hut, I heard Tomas call out behind us.

"Scottish, wait," he said, hurrying to catch up.

"Tomas?" I said, turning round.

"You know who this is, no?" he said. "You know who did this?"

As usual, not much got past him. I exchanged a glance with Angelica. There was no point in dissembling.

"We don't know for sure," I said. "We have a suspect."

"Come on, Scottish, come on, it's me, Tomas. Who is this thief, eh?"

"Suspected thief," I replied firmly.

Tomas laughed scornfully at my caveat. "If you suspect him, then it's likely he is the one," he said.

I sighed. He wasn't going to take no for an answer.

"Fine. This is the situation," I began. I told him what had transpired up to now and our suspicions about Sergeant Willis.

Tomas listened patiently until I had finished.

"Well," he said, "the answer is simple. You and I will find him ... we take him around the back of his hut ... I punch him many times ... and then he will talk."

I shook my head. I had been expecting some such suggestion from him.

"We're not doing anything of the sort," I told him severely. "We're doing this by the book."

"Ah, these books. Always it's the books with you British!" Tomas said in disgust.

"Innocent until proven guilty," I told him. "Regardless of our suspicions."

"Come on, Scottish, come on," said Tomas, undeterred. "He is guilty. I know ... I know."

Angelica giggled and I shot her a quelling look. Her eyes were dancing with merriment.

"Look," I said, "I am going to talk to Bentley and then perhaps come up with a plan which will not involve punching people to make them talk!"

Tomas held up his hands in a gesture of innocence. "Okay, Scottish, I am getting the picture. I was just trying to help. We can do it your way," he said.

"If and when we have a plan, then I'll tell you about it," I informed him in no uncertain terms.

Tomas nodded. "All right. You can count on me. I will help you catch this Sergeant Thief. Just tell me the word. Now, I'm going for tea."

We watched him head back to the hut. He and I had been in a few scrapes before, so I was now obliged to include him in any plans. However, I didn't have any idea what those plans might be.

"Shall we go?" said Angelica, an amused smile still playing on her lips.

"Yes," I said. "By all means, and it's not funny."

"Oh, but it is," she said, letting out a peal of laughter.

Bentley was in his office when we arrived. He was smoking his pipe and leaning back in his chair, staring at the ceiling. As soon as he saw us, he brandished the stem of his pipe in our direction. I was rather taken aback, but wasn't able to get a word in edgeways.

"That blasted jumped-up Johhny nincompoop!" he bellowed furiously. "Standing up there like he's our bloody saviour. What a bare-faced bloody cheek!"

We both knew he was talking about Todd. He'd obviously been stewing about it since the parade. Angelica and I elected to remain silent while the storm continued.

"I could not believe my ears," he said, jumping from his chair and pacing the room. "He said, 'The British need these Spitfires and we're going to give them to them' — just as if he hadn't told us several days earlier there was no way on this earth he would hand them over!"

He puffed furiously on his pipe before letting fly a few more choice words.

"What a charlatan. An absolute tommy-rot talker. A bloody clown in a uniform. Never in my life have I heard such a load of poppycock as I heard today. The gall of the man. The absolute unmitigated effrontery. His audacity is beyond the pale, Angus, I don't mind telling you. I was frankly flabbergasted at the impudence of it all... *His* parade indeed. Harrumph!"

Having sufficiently vented his ire, he resumed his seat. He indicated we should also sit and then proceeded to go through his entire pipe ritual. As this had a calming effect on his temper, neither of us interrupted the process. He relit it and started to puff on it more contentedly.

"Anyway, we've got twelve more Spitfires and I'm keeping those, mark you. The Ministry is not bloody well having them back. I didn't endure that blasted clown show only to give them up again." Bentley fell silent for a few moments, and then elected to mitigate his scorn. "You all did well, though, an excellent display," he went on. "We showed our mettle all right. Anyway, I am assuming you didn't come here to discuss the failings of our friend across the way there."

I wasn't sure whether, following the recent outburst, I was particularly happy to deliver more bad news. However, there was no other way. He had to be informed.

"Sir," I said, "while we were off the base, a number of items went missing from our hut."

"What?" Bentley exclaimed, his eye starting to twitch alarmingly.

"Some items we think ... were stolen."

"What items?" he asked in a voice of icy calm.

"So far, the ones I've been told about are..." I read through the list while Bentley puffed on his pipe at an increasingly alarming rate.

"For God's sake!" he said, erupting from his chair once more. "Is nothing sacred? Isn't it sufficient that we've had to suffer the biggest charade this side of London? And now we've got a bloody kleptomaniac on the loose at Banley! It's outside of enough!"

"I thought you should be made aware, sir," I said. "You told me not to pursue it."

He turned to me. "Did I? Well, I want you to bloody well pursue it with vigour. Can't have this sort of thing going on. I will call a briefing of the whole base tomorrow and read the riot act."

"Understood," I said, although I could not really see how doing that would help. "In the meantime, sir, I'll try to think of some way we can trap the thief into revealing themselves."

"Yes, you do that," said Bentley. "And keep me up to date. Naturally, you will also need to continue with the dive-bombing training. I'm sure those blasted spies will turn up any day now and tell us when they want this damned mission to take place. So you need to be ready for that."

"Yes, sir," I said.

"Jolly good," he said with a nod.

We left him smoking his pipe and shuffling through the papers on his desk. I didn't feel his heart was quite in it. He'd probably had more than he could stomach for one day.

"What are we going to do now?" said Angelica, once we were outside.

"We're going home," I said. "Then, tomorrow, we'll go for tea with Fred after practice and see if he can help us come up with a plan."

"How very splendid," said Angelica.

"I thought you'd like it," I replied.

On which note, we headed for the jeep.

CHAPTER TWELVE

The following morning, we resumed our practice. As usual, we gathered in a group while Kenneth explained the order of the day.

"You will drop three bombs each, singly, on the target zone, then return to base. After the planes are rearmed, you will go again, and this time drop in sections of three. So that means coordinating as before and dropping together on the command of the Section Leader."

"How far apart should we be?" asked Arjun.

It was an important question. I still had to consider the actual tactics for the port and how we would attack it.

"It all depends on the breadth of the target you're attacking," said Kenneth. "No more than a wingspan apart for the purposes of this exercise. However, on the real mission, you may well be further apart than that."

There were no more questions, so I turned to Angelica and kissed her.

"Take care, darling," she said.

"I will," I replied.

I left her standing there and went over to my plane. After I took off, she would go to her post on comms. I climbed aboard, and Redwood strapped me in.

"All three bombs are ready," he said.

"Thanks, Techie," I replied. Then a thought struck me. "How are the Spitfires we got from the Americans?"

He smiled. "Well maintained, thankfully, and so we don't have to do much except paint them," he said.

I felt Sandford would have made sure his planes were kept in order — I was pleased to hear that I was right on that score.

"Where are you putting them all?" I asked Redwood.

I knew that as big as the hangar was, there was limited space inside it. Twelve Spitfires would take up a lot of room.

"We're camouflaging them outside, on Bentley's orders," he said.

Bentley was a wise old owl for sure. He didn't want anyone visiting the base and seeing all those planes. He knew how to hang on to his assets once he had acquired them.

"Good idea," I said.

Redwood jumped down from the wing, and I spun up the prop. The Merlin fired to life, and then I gave Angelica a wave before taxiing down to the end of the runway.

We were airborne shortly afterwards.

"M Flight, single-file formation on me," I said, leading them away from the airfield at low level.

Kenneth had taken off in his Spitfire and would be circling the target area, keeping an eye on us from a distance.

Once we reached the designated spot, I turned towards the firing range.

"M Flight, attack in single file by sections. I'll go first," I said, throttling up.

I headed towards the target zone at speed. As it came into view, I climbed to six thousand feet. At the peak, I dipped the nose downwards. The ground came screaming towards me. I kept my eye on the gunsight and the instruments at the same time. Then, as I hit three thousand feet, I released the bombs.

"Bombs away," I said, levelling out fast and flying quickly out of the target zone. Behind me came three explosions. I banked around to see smoke pouring from the target area.

"Well done, Red Leader," said Kenneth. "Next one please."

I circled around as the others carried out their bombing runs.

When it came to Dylan, he hit three thousand feet, ready to release.

"Bombs away," he said, but the bombs didn't drop. "Oh blast. It's not working. They're not releasing."

Dylan was not paying attention, but Kenneth was on the ball.

"Abort. Abort now!" he barked. "Leave it and get out of there."

Even I could see that Dylan was well under two thousand feet as he pulled out.

"Sorry about that," said Dylan. "Can I give it another go?"

"Return to base," Kenneth told him. "Get it checked out."

"Wilco." I could hear the disappointment in his voice.

Shortly afterwards, everyone had completed their bombing run, and I took the flight back to Banley. After landing, I walked over to where Dylan was talking to Redwood.

"What happened?" I asked Dylan as I came up to them.

"I don't know, Scottish," he replied. "The bombs just wouldn't go. It worked fine yesterday."

"We'll look into it, sir," said Redwood. "And we'll check all the other planes too."

This was worrying, as we couldn't have the bomb releases failing on the mission. Before I could think about it any further, Kenneth arrived.

"You should have pulled out at two thousand maximum," he admonished Dylan.

"Sorry, sir, it was just the bomb release — I was distracted," said Dylan.

"You can't afford to be distracted. That's how people die. Things go wrong and you have to deal with that accordingly," said Kenneth firmly.

"But the bombs —" Dylan began.

"The bombs can go hang," said Kenneth, cutting in. "One pilot can drop many bombs, but we can't replace that pilot quite so easily, get it?"

"Yes, sir, sorry. I'll remember next time," said Dylan.

"See that you do," said Kenneth. "All the time you were dithering, you could have been shot to pieces by flak, or you could have smashed into the ground. Either way, you would not come home to tell the tale."

He looked around. The rest of M Flight had joined us by now.

"This is a lesson to you all. Follow the damned rules. Pull out at two thousand feet maximum, no matter what, and then get the hell out," he said.

"I second that," I added. "It's my job to bring you all back home in one piece."

We all repaired to the hut while the Spitfires were rearmed and Redwood checked over Dylan's plane.

We hadn't been in the hut long when Audrey appeared.

"Bentley has called a general meeting in the hangar, no exceptions," she told us.

"Let's get to it, chaps," I said.

"What does old Bentley want now?" groaned Jonty.

"It's probably something you've done," Willie replied.

"I haven't done anything!" came the immediate retort.

Angelica and I glanced at each other, knowing full well why Bentley had called the meeting. When we reached the hangar, we saw that pretty much everybody on the base, apart from the sentries, had gathered. Angelica nudged me. I looked in the direction she indicated, and there was Sergeant Willis. This could be interesting.

"Senior officer in the room!" barked Judd, and the hangar came to attention.

Bentley strode up to the front in his usual brisk fashion. He stood on the podium and surveyed the assembled company coolly before addressing us.

"It has come to my attention," he began, "that a number of personal items belonging to people on this base have gone missing."

This was greeted with silence, although looks were exchanged, particularly between members of M Flight who had had some things taken. I glanced at Willis, who showed no visible reaction.

"I can only conclude," Bentley continued, "that these things were not misplaced or lost somehow. No, there is only one possibility."

He paused for dramatic effect. Then suddenly, in typical Bentley fashion, he brandished the stem of his pipe at his audience.

"There appears to be a thief on this base. I'm absolutely appalled to discover this. I'm shocked, frankly, that a member of this squadron would stoop so low as to take belongings from other members of the Mavericks."

There were murmurs at this. I also noticed that the pipe was pointing, seemingly by chance, directly at Willis. Willis was staring straight ahead as if he were unaware of it. If he was the guilty party, he was doing a good job of keeping a straight face.

"Anyway," said Bentley, "before I take further action, which, sadly, I will have to do, I'm going to give the thief a chance to redeem themselves. If they return everything that has gone missing by o-nine-hundred tomorrow morning, then I will say no more. If not, then I will have to begin a formal investigation, much as it pains me, to find the culprit. And when I do, I will throw the bloody book at them!"

This was a classic move which was often used on errant schoolboys. However, in my experience, it never worked, though I couldn't blame Bentley for trying.

"All right. That's all I have to say for now. But mark my words, if those items do not reappear, then tomorrow is going to be a different story."

He left the podium without another word and strode out of the hangar, Audrey by his side.

The hangar erupted into animated chatter.

"Let's get out of here," I said to Angelica, not wanting to listen to it.

As we left the hangar, Jonty and Willie caught up with us.

"I say, Skipper," said Jonty. "That reminded me of Old Bagshot, my housemaster, whose prize rowing trophy went missing — he did much the same thing."

"And did it work?" I asked.

"Good Lord, no," said Jonty. "The next morning, the entire trophy cabinet was empty. He went off like a firecracker. The place was in uproar for days until the trophies reappeared on the chapel roof."

"That was you, Jonty, wasn't it?" said Angelica, laughing.

"Oh, blast!" said Jonty. "How did you guess?"

"It couldn't have been anyone else," said Willie, shaking his head.

We all laughed at this. Jonty had a fount of stories regarding his rather wayward life at public school.

"Let's hope it does work," I said. "Anyway, we've got some more practice to do."

We all made our way back to the airfield. While we waited for Kenneth, Redwood approached.

"We've checked the bomb release on that Spitfire, sir," he said. "We found a small glitch, which we've sorted. It shouldn't happen again. Just to be safe, we've also checked all the others. I'm certain we've cured the problem."

"Thank you, Techie," I told him.

"All in a day's work," he said. "Anyway, I'll get back to it, as we're making final checks before you go up for your practice."

He saluted before returning to the waiting planes on the field. Kenneth had arrived by this time.

"All's right and tight," I told him. "The bomb release problem is fixed."

"Right then," he said. "If we can tear ourselves away from the devilish deeds of highway robbers for the moment, we've got the next stage of the practice to do, which is bombing in sections. Are we ready?"

There was a chorus of affirmation in response.

"Then let's get to it."

I said goodbye to Angelica and made my way to my Spitfire. Shortly afterwards I was airborne, along with the rest of M Flight.

"M Flight, form up," I said as we took our usual formation and flew in the opposite direction to the target. When we hit the waypoint, I turned the flight around.

"Low-level approach to target, attack in sections," I said.

I continued to run the practice along the lines of the real mission. We would be coming in fast over the sea, then pop up and dive-bomb the port, hopefully before the Germans realised it.

"Let's go," I said, opening up the throttle.

I felt a slight surge of adrenaline, imagining this was the real thing. The ground flashed by beneath us as I kept my attention firmly on the terrain ahead. The target would be visible any moment, then there it was. The approach was thankfully flat, rather as it would be crossing the Channel.

"Red Section attack, followed by Blue, Yellow and Green," I said.

Jonty and Willie stayed on my wings, but now we fanned out in a line, a wingspan apart as Kenneth had told us.

"Climbing now, Red Section," I said, climbing swiftly upwards to six thousand feet.

It was starting to feel quite natural, as if I'd been doing it for a long time. That was the benefit of practice. We hit the top of the curve.

"Red Section, dive," I said, dropping the nose.

The three of us dropped at high speed, keeping in line and at the correct angle. It was harder work for the other two keeping pace with me. I watched the altimeter going down while keeping the target in the gunsight.

At three thousand feet, I released my bomb load. "Bombs away and flatten out. Let's get out of here."

We came out of the dive and flattened off, throttling up. We sped away from the scene as the nine bombs exploded behind us. I banked around to see smoke pouring off the target while Blue Section made their attack run.

"Well done, Red Leader," said Kenneth. "You can return to base."

On the mission, I wouldn't be hanging around, but at the same time, I would need to be sure that the others could catch me up. It needed careful planning. That was something I was going to have to tackle next.

We landed and waited for the rest of the flight to return. They did so shortly afterwards, followed by Kenneth.

Kenneth strode over to us, smiling broadly. "Well, gentlemen," he said, "I think you've got it. Give yourselves a big hand."

We all clapped, and there were a few whoops.

"That's pretty much it for the training," he said. "You know what to do, you know how to do it, and now you just need to keep practising. I'm going to hand all of that over to Scottish here."

"Thanks," I said sardonically.

"What will you do now?" Jean asked him. "Are you leaving us?"

"I will be sticking around until the mission is over — those are my orders — but I'll be in the background. It's your show now. I've done my bit, although I'm here to give advice and help if needed," Kenneth replied.

"When do you think the mission will take place?" Arjun asked me.

"I don't know," I said. "Whenever the Marx Brothers come and tell us."

Kenneth cocked his head in enquiry at this and the nickname had to be explained. He naturally found this rather amusing.

"I'll be informing the powers that be and, of course, your CO, that the training is complete," he said. "That will probably initiate some kind of action on their part."

The rest of M Flight dispersed, leaving me, Angelica and Kenneth alone.

"So, what will you be doing with all this leisure time?" I asked him.

"Oh, the manor has its … attractions," he said cryptically.

I knew exactly what those were.

"Anyway," he continued, "I'm going to head off and see Bentley. I'm around if you need me."

"Thanks," I said. "I might run my attack plan by you once I've worked it out."

"By all means," he said, clapping me lightly on the shoulder.

He strolled away, heading for the main building. I turned to Angelica, who had joined me by this time.

"I think it's time to pick Fred's brains," I said.

"Annie's Kitchen?" Angelica asked with a smile.

"Absolutely," I replied.

We found Gordon and before long we were once more seated in what had become, for us, a hallowed establishment. The stuff of legend, as far as the hot crumpets were concerned. These were now sitting on a plate beside some jam and butter. A steaming pot of tea completed the spread.

Angelica picked up the pot and poured the tea, handing a cup to each of us. She then seized a crumpet, ladled butter and jam onto it, and took a bite, savouring it with an expression of excessive enjoyment.

"Well, sir?" said Gordon when we had followed Angelica's example. "What did you want to talk to me about?"

"This ultimatum of Bentley's," I said. "Do you think it will work?"

Gordon stirred his tea and took a sip. "In a word, sir, no. I've never heard of such a ploy having a satisfactory outcome," he replied. "If the thief is indeed who we think it is, then I don't believe it's going to have any effect at all on that individual."

We all knew he was talking about Willis.

"Those are our thoughts too," said Angelica, "aren't they, darling?"

"Yes, they are," I said, smiling at the endearment. "So, we were wondering if you have any ideas about how to catch him."

Gordon took another bite of his crumpet. "Well, sir, much as we did with the Ace Raider, you've got to supply some bait and then hope that he takes you up on it," he said.

"Lie in wait for him, you mean?"

"In a nutshell."

We all had another round of crumpets before continuing the conversation.

"What kind of bait would lure him out?" I eventually asked.

"It has to be something substantial and at the same time, attractive," he said. "What items have gone missing so far?"

"A lot of them seem to be silver or hold some kind of sentimental value," I told him.

He laughed. "Rather like a magpie then, sir, fond of shiny things."

"Yes, I suppose that's true. I wonder what he's doing with them?"

"Usually, a thief will get rid of the goods, as it were, through a fence. Someone who will take them and sell them on. However, I've not heard any such rumours recently…" He trailed off.

I got the picture. Gordon was a man of many parts. He knew all kinds of people, and had his ear to the ground. If someone were selling such items on, he would have heard about it.

"Anyway, if he's not fencing these items off, then perhaps he's just collecting them," Gordon went on.

"Collecting them?" I said in surprise.

"Some people cannot help it, sir. It's a compulsion … a bad one, but a compulsion nevertheless."

"Are you insinuating that Willis is a kleptomaniac?" asked Angelica.

"Could be," Gordon replied noncommittally.

The conversation was interrupted by the arrival of a fresh pot of tea and more crumpets. We set about these with a will.

"Then we will just have to find something shiny as a lure," I said at length. "And then someone to put the word out there so we can set the trap."

The thought occurred to me and Angelica at the same time.

"Jonty," we said in unison.

We all burst out laughing.

"He's perfect for the job," said Angelica. "Now we just need a suitable piece of silver to tempt the thief into our trap."

"We'll have to run this by Bentley," I said. "He'll be furious if he finds out another way."

"Yes," Angelica agreed.

Having come to a conclusion on setting the trap, the conversation moved on to other things. Afterwards, we made our way back to Amberly Manor. I needed time to think about the port attack plan because I had a shrewd notion that the Marx Brothers would descend upon us in short order.

Later that night, as I lay in bed with Angelica, she turned to me.

"You're never to take Barbara to Annie's," she said suddenly.

I looked at her in the half-light. "What? I've no intention of taking her anywhere," I said.

"Well, I'm just saying. I have limits. That's our place, mine and yours ... and Fred's."

"Have you been thinking about this all afternoon?" I asked her, wondering if the spectre of my past would ever quite go away.

"Maybe," she said softly.

I turned to her and whispered, "Silly thing."

"I'm not a thing," she said with a chuckle while pulling me closer. "I'm your loving wife."

I kissed her then, because it seemed like the best answer I could give her.

I went to see Bentley the following morning to tell him about the trap. I was let into his office by Audrey, who looked decidedly less than her cheerful self.

The reason was soon revealed when I stood in front of Bentley's desk. He motioned for me to sit in a rather brusque manner.

"Ah, Angus," he said without preamble. "Would you believe it, that blasted bounder of a thief has stolen my pipe!"

"Your pipe, sir?" I said, puzzled, since he was currently engaged in smoking a pipe at that very moment.

"Yes, my pipe," he said irritably, then seeing my expression, he went on, "Not this one — this is my spare. I am talking about my favourite bloody pipe. The cheek of it! The absolute effrontery! How dare he? I'll have his bloody guts for garters!"

"Sir, we don't know for sure —" I began, but was cut short.

"I know we don't know for certain who it is!" he barked. "But I know who I think it bloody well is. That blasted popinjay of a sergeant, coming in here like he owns the place, and now this!"

It appeared that Bentley had firmly settled on Sergeant Willis being the culprit. There was a point which occurred to me, and I put it to him as mildly as I could.

"But how could he have stolen your pipe, sir?" I asked. It seemed a reasonable question, since the pipe was never far from his person.

"I don't know," he said hotly. "Sleight of hand, God knows — all I *do* know is that it's missing, and you will turn this base inside out until it's found!"

The significance of the pipe to Bentley was almost the same as a religious icon. It was like a boon companion. I couldn't quite understand it, not being a smoker myself. However, I could see that Bentley meant business. I thought it best to pose an alternative to ransacking the entire base, looking for his pipe.

"Sir, we've conceived a plan to try and catch the thief red-handed," I said.

"Who's we?" he asked suspiciously.

"Sergeant Gordon and Section Officer Mackennelly," I replied.

He puffed on his replacement pipe for a moment and then seemed to be satisfied that our collective inspiration might be worth listening to. "All right, go on."

"This is what we propose..." I said, laying out the whole to him.

He listened patiently enough and puffed away meditatively for a while afterwards. "And you think this is going to work, do you?" he asked with a note of scepticism in his tone.

"I think it has a good chance, sir, yes," I said.

"And what artefact do you propose to use as bait?" he enquired.

"Something valuable — we haven't thought about that," I admitted.

"Then I suggest you do, forthwith," he said, still in an irascible mood. "All right, I will sanction this scheme. I jolly well hope that it works."

"Thank you, sir," I said.

"Don't thank me — just catch that blasted thief. It's the outside of enough! This thieving has to stop. Stealing people's pipes left, right and centre — I won't have it!" he snapped.

Realising he wasn't going to be so easily mollified, I beat a hasty retreat. Naturally, I was waylaid by Angelica before I got too many steps from Bentley's office.

"Well?" she said, tucking her arm into mine.

"Step into our office," I replied with a smile.

"With pleasure."

Once seated on our favourite bench, I enlightened her as to the latest occurrence.

"Bentley's pipe has been stolen," I said.

"What? His pipe?" she said, suppressing a laugh.

"Yes, and it's no laughing matter," I told her with mock severity. "He's extremely cut up over it."

She couldn't help but find the idea of someone stealing Bentley's pipe inordinately funny and was overcome with mirth. "I'm sorry," she said. "It's just…"

"Anyway," I replied, ignoring this less than sympathetic response to Bentley's plight, "we've got the go-ahead to lay the trap."

"Oh, good," she said, finally recovering her composure. "Now all we need is the bait."

We didn't have time to ponder what we could use for bait because shortly afterwards, Audrey came to find me.

"Is it Bentley again?" I asked her, wondering what he wanted this time.

"No," she said. "It's the…"

"Marx Brothers," said Angelica, finishing for her.

It was inevitable that they would arrive now that our training was complete. I assumed that this signalled the urgency of the mission.

"I suppose we'd better go and see them," I said, getting up from the bench.

The three of us made our way to the main building.

"Is Bentley very upset about his pipe?" Angelica asked Audrey as we walked.

"He was beside himself when he discovered it was missing," Audrey replied. "He turned the air rather blue, I'm afraid."

"Oh dear," said Angelica. "Well, we're going to put the thief plan into action as soon as we have something to use as bait."

Audrey stopped for a moment, and so did we.

"What sort of thing do you need?" she asked.

"Something shiny, preferably silver … valuable," I said. "The thief seems to like shiny things."

Audrey thought for a moment. "Maybe I can help," she said. "I have a teapot; it's a legacy from my aunt. It's actually gold-plated on top of silver, very ornate, so I think it's quite valuable. Would that do?"

"It would be perfect," said Angelica. "But are you sure?"

"As long as you'll take care of it," Audrey said. "I'm rather fond of it, and it's kind of a nest egg in case I need the money one day."

"It will be in our sight the whole time," I told her.

"Excellent. I'll polish it up and bring it in," she replied.

We resumed walking and shortly afterwards, Audrey showed us into the mission room.

The Marx Brothers were sitting at ease, smoking cigarettes. Their hats and trench coats were laid carelessly on a table nearby.

"Ah, Flight Lieutenant and Section Officer," said Harpo, indicating a couple of chairs.

"How nice to see you," said Chico, taking a drag on his cigarette.

"I'm assuming you're here about the proposed attack on Den Helder," I said, once we had sat down.

"He's got it," said Harpo.

"Yes indeed," said Chico.

They continued to smoke without saying anything for a few moments, in a most annoying fashion. Since it was their way, I held my peace.

"When is the mission to take place?" asked Angelica, fed up with the silence.

"All in good time," said Harpo, exasperatingly insouciant as always. "What are your plans of attack first?"

I had been pondering this and had discussed it with Angelica, so I was able to answer. "My thoughts were to approach the port on the left side of the sandbar, flying at low level, then turning down for a direct attack from the seaward side. We'll attack in four sections at the same time, but different areas of the port — I think it's big enough for that. The advantage is that we get in and get out as fast as possible."

"An excellent plan," said Chico. "We would like you to focus your attacks on any German ships that are in the harbour, with the port facilities being secondary."

"All right," I said. "We'll have to make that decision just before the attack begins, then."

Harpo took another drag on his cigarette. "Precisely," he replied.

"So, when is the attack to take place?" Angelica repeated, not to be deterred.

"She's impatient," said Harpo.

"She is," said Chico.

I could tell Angelica was becoming infuriated by this, although we both knew that the spies couldn't do anything without a measure of theatrics.

Chico blew smoke into the air, watching it curl towards the ceiling before speaking. "The attack should take place in one week's time, preferably. We'll provide up-to-date reconnaissance, which will include positions of flak batteries and so forth."

I knew the port was heavily defended. It was going to be dangerous. We'd be flying in at dawn to give ourselves the best chance. The good thing was that we'd still have a full load of ammo to defend ourselves in case we were attacked by fighters on the way out. This was a distinct possibility.

"You set the date," said Harpo. "Let us know. We'll come down for some moral support, that sort of thing."

"All right," I said. "If there's nothing else?"

"No, no," said Chico. "That's all for now. We'll be off shortly to visit our American friends next door."

I assumed this meant that friendly relations had resumed with Todd's impending departure.

"Are they really going to give Colonel Todd an important job in London?" Angelica asked.

"He will believe it to be important," said Harpo. "The reality might be somewhat different."

"Couldn't they just send him back to America?" I asked him.

"Ah," said Chico. "Wheels within wheels."

He didn't give a further explanation to this cryptic utterance. Not that I particularly cared, as long as Todd was out of our hair. I stood up, and Angelica followed suit.

"We'll be going then," I said.

"Toodle pip," said Harpo.

"Chin-chin," said Chico.

We left the room and made our way to the dispersal hut.

"The mission is really going to happen now," said Angelica.

"Yes," I replied.

She clutched my arm a little tighter as we walked. I couldn't say anything to mitigate her worry. Duty called, and both of us knew that duty had to be done.

When we arrived at the hut, I decided I might as well alert everyone to the imminence of the mission. I called for silence.

"What-ho, Skipper," said Jonty when I had everyone's attention. "What's it all about?"

"Let the man speak," said Willie.

"What it's all about, Jonty, is the mission we've all been training for. We've been given the go-ahead. The mission will take place in approximately a week's time. I will hold a briefing very shortly; however, we need to make sure that we practise dive-bombing every day," I said.

"Does that mean with ordnance?" asked Arjun.

"No," I replied. "I don't think we need to keep dropping bombs to prove we can. What I mean is keeping sharp on the diving part. Go up each day and just do a few dives. Then, just before the mission, we'll run a rehearsal to make sure everyone knows what they need to do for the real thing. Got it?"

I felt confident I could trust the rest of the squadron to undertake what I asked without arranging any more formal practice sessions.

"You've got it, Skipper. Wilco loud and clear," said Jonty.

"When shall we start, Scottish?" asked Dylan.

"As soon as you like. In fact, now is as good a time as any," I told him, thinking that if the rest of them went to practise, I could have a quick chat with Jonty about the role we wanted him to play.

"Right then, I'm going up. Who's with me?" said Dylan, making for the door.

The others followed him out, but I stopped Jonty with a light touch on the arm. Willie naturally stopped too, since the two of them were practically inseparable in spite of their constant bickering.

"I want to talk to you, Jonty," I said.

"Really?" he replied, taking on a slightly hunted look.

This was hardly surprising considering the number of run-ins he'd had with Bentley over the years. I hastened to reassure him.

"You haven't done anything wrong, Jonty. I just need you to do something important."

The hut was empty apart from myself, Angelica, Jonty and Willie. Outside, I could hear the sound of Merlin engines roaring to life. It was the ideal time to put our plan into action.

"Let's sit down," I suggested. M Flight started to take off on the airfield, and I was glad that it would give us a few moments of privacy. "Jonty," I went on when we were all seated, "would you like to help us catch the thief?"

Jonty's face lit up at once. "Yes, Skipper, of course."

"So, let's say, for the sake of argument, that you've come into a legacy, a very special legacy," I began.

Jonty's face became incredulous at once. "No, really? Have I?" he said. "I didn't know. Was it my aunt Agatha? She was very old."

Willie rolled his eyes.

"No, listen, you haven't come into a legacy, Jonty," I said patiently.

"But I thought you said I had," Jonty protested.

I sighed, and Willie shook his head.

"Not for real. Let's start again. Suppose you had come into a legacy," I said.

Jonty frowned on hearing this. "You just said I hadn't, and now you're saying I have. I wish you'd make up your mind, Skipper," said Jonty.

"Let me try," said Angelica, interrupting what was descending rapidly into a farce.

"Be my guest," I told her, hoping she might fare better than I had so far.

"Jonty, listen carefully. We're going to play pretend — you remember doing that when you were young?" said Angelica.

Jonty nodded at once. "Yes, certainly. I used to do it all the time. Got into a lot of trouble, particularly that one…"

Angelica put a hand on his arm to stop his reminiscences. "Jonty, listen," she said. "We are going to pretend that you have come into a legacy, all right? Do you see?"

The penny dropped. Jonty finally seemed to put two and two together. "Oh! I see, ah! Just pretending. Well, why didn't you say so?"

"We did, you nincom…" began Willie, who had evidently been keeping quiet with some difficulty.

Angelica motioned for him to shush, so he subsided somewhat reluctantly. She nodded to me and I then continued with the explanation.

"We're going to pretend that your aunt has left you a gold-plated teapot which is very valuable."

"I think my Aunt Marigold probably did have a teapot like that," said Jonty.

"Whichever aunt you like," I said. "Now, when we tell you, we want you to go and blab it around the base as loudly as you can, so that everyone knows. Then you'll say that you're keeping it in the hut as you're using it for your tea because it's so special. Can you do that?"

"What?" Jonty exclaimed. "I wouldn't do that, certainly not with a valuable teapot. Best to keep it on the QT, otherwise someone might try to steal it."

"This is never going to work," groaned Willie, who had cottoned on to our intention right away. Exasperated, he turned to his friend. "Listen, Jonty, you need to blab it around so we can set a trap for the thief. He'll come to get it, and we'll get him, all right?"

Jonty nodded. "Oh, I see. That makes sense. So, when do I do this pretending lark?"

"We'll tell you," I said. "In the meantime, don't say anything — got it?"

"Right," said Jonty. "Though perhaps we need a codeword, so I know when it's time to say it."

Angelica came to the rescue. "We'll call it Operation Teapot, okay? When we tell you that Operation Teapot is a go, then you'll know it's time to start spreading the rumour about your legacy. In fact, we'll even lend you a teapot so that you can show it around."

"I thought you said it was a pretend teapot," Jonty objected.

"God preserve us," said Willie.

"We're borrowing one from Audrey," Angelica explained, "so that we can trap the thief. Now do you understand?"

"Oh well, I get it, of course," said Jonty. "If only you'd explained it properly in the first place!"

"Why, *why* did I get posted to the Mavericks?" said Willie dramatically.

Angelica and I looked at each other and burst out laughing.

"Oh, Jonty," she said. "You are just impossible."

CHAPTER THIRTEEN

A couple of days after the conversation with Jonty, Angelica and I had yet to decide when to set the trap. I still had to practise too and went up with Jonty and Willie to go through some dives.

It was all going pretty well. I found it easier and easier to mark my target, fly upwards to the requisite height and then drop at exactly the right angle. Pulling out of the dive wasn't too bad either.

We were just completing our final dive of the morning. I went first, climbing to six thousand feet, dropping down and pulling out at three thousand feet. Before the practice, Jonty had been telling us how easy the whole thing had become.

"It's a piece of cake now, Skipper," he said. "In fact, I'm sure I could dive lower."

"Well, you won't," I said firmly. "Stick to three thousand feet."

"If you say so, Skipper."

I should have taken that as a warning that Jonty would try something foolish. We were no longer diving on a big red cross in the field next to our airfield, but had picked various other targets like a bush or a tree to dive at instead. This was far more realistic, and we'd need to be spotting our targets on the actual mission.

I had just levelled off and was banking around to watch the other two, when to my horror I saw Jonty start his dive.

"Here I go, Skipper," he said. "Watch me!"

He'd picked a target: General Grimthorne's house. My heart sank as I watched his Spitfire dropping like a stone towards the general's residence. The general was sitting in his garden, reading a newspaper. Beside him was a table with what looked like a tea tray on it. The general was in the act of taking a sip of tea when he must have looked up. He stared at the plane bearing down on him as if he were transfixed.

"Jonty," I said helplessly. "Jonty, pull up, for God's sake."

But Jonty, being Jonty, wasn't listening.

"It's all right, Skipper. I've got it all under control," he said airily.

"Jonty!" I shouted, but it was to no avail.

He dropped well below the threshold and kept going before finally levelling off at what I considered a foolhardy altitude for anyone, including an experienced pilot.

As he did so, the general gave a start. His cup and the table went flying. I banked around again to see him shaking his fist at Jonty's plane as he hightailed it off into the distance.

"Now we really are in the bloody basket," remarked Willie.

"Do your dive, Kiwi, and let's go home. That means you too, Jonty," I said, turning back for the airfield.

"Wilco, Skipper. That was quite a wheeze," said Jonty, completely unabashed.

I had no doubt that Bentley would appear very shortly, if not as soon as we landed. It was all we needed with a mission to fly.

Shortly afterwards, I brought my Spitfire to a stop at my usual standing. I jumped down from the wing to see Angelica coming towards me.

"What's Jonty done now?" she asked me, having heard something of what had happened on the comms.

"He's only gone and dive-bombed the bloody general's house," said Willie, catching me up.

"Oh, Jonty," said Angelica when the miscreant appeared. "You are such a very silly boy."

I felt it incumbent upon me to remonstrate with Jonty, even though I knew that Bentley's wrath would not be long in following.

"Jonty," I said, "what on earth possessed you to dive-bomb General Grimthorne?"

"Well, you said pick a target, Skipper, so I did," Jonty informed me.

"Not that bloody target, you idiot," said Willie. "How many times have we been told it's off limits?"

"Ah," said Jonty. "We were told not to buzz his house. Nobody said anything about dive-bombing it."

I sighed, and Willie put his hand over his face in a gesture of resignation. "I give up," he said. "I really do."

"Anyway," I continued, "it looks like you're going to have to face the music."

I had clocked Audrey heading our way with purpose. I was pretty sure I knew what that purpose was.

"Oh blast, really?" said Jonty.

Audrey arrived in front of us, looking somewhat apologetic. "Bentley wants to see Pilot Officer Butterworth," she said, "and also his Flight Leader."

She meant me, of course.

"Nothing I wasn't expecting," I said with resignation. "Come on, Jonty. Don't say I didn't tell you this would happen."

The four of us accompanied Audrey to Bentley's office. He would not be surprised to see all of us, as we'd made several appearances on Jonty's account of late.

"I don't understand why you keep doing things like this," Willie said to him.

"Old Bagshot said much the same thing," Jonty replied.

I shook my head. Jonty was incorrigible, and that was all there was to it.

In short order, we were standing in front of Bentley's desk while he began his pipe routine with what looked like a brand new pipe. He left us standing, which was always a bad sign.

"You know the trouble with new pipes," he said conversationally, as he puffed out smoke.

"No, sir," I replied.

"They need breaking in, getting used to and all that," he continued. "This can be a bit irritating to start with. However, once they are smoked a few times, they cease to be any trouble at all. In fact, they become like an old friend, do you see?"

I didn't really see at all, though I wasn't about to tell Bentley that. I assumed it to be some kind of analogy.

He got up out of his seat and came around to our side of the desk. "How long is it that you've served with this squadron, Butterworth?" he said.

"Since the war started, sir," said Jonty, keeping his gaze straight ahead.

"Since the war started. And refresh my memory as to why you were sent to the Mavericks?"

"Insubordination, pranks, that kind of thing. Conduct unbecoming, I think they said," Jonty told him.

"Yes, exactly." Bentley's voice had taken on a dangerous edge. "However, unlike this new pipe, which will get into the right habits, you evidently haven't."

"No, sir," said Jonty, since he had no alternative but to agree.

"Well, I've had enough of it, do you hear? Enough!" Bentley thundered. "I am sick and tired of getting phone calls from General bloody Grimthorne on account of you! Do you think I haven't got enough to do apart from dealing with your blasted tomfoolery?"

Jonty, realising that he'd once more crossed the line, attempted to redress. "Sir, I apologise —" he began.

Bentley cut him off. "Oh, you do, do you? Well, I've heard all that before. You need to stop acting the giddy goat in this squadron. I'm not going to ask what idiotic notion prompted you to dive-bomb the general's house, because I'm sure it won't make any blasted sense at all."

"No, sir," said Jonty.

Bentley stared at him for a while longer, puffing on his pipe before once more resuming his seat. "Well, you can apologise to the general, Butterworth," he said. "In fact, the lot of you will accompany me to his residence this afternoon, where Butterworth will give a heartfelt apology in person. You will vow never to do it again, even if I have to make you swear it on the Bible."

"Yes, sir," said Jonty. "I'll give the best apology I've ever given, sir, I can assure you of that."

"You damn well better," said Bentley. "Now, get out of my office. You are all dismissed."

Once away from the main building, Jonty heaved a sigh of relief. "I think that went rather well, all things considered," he said.

"All things considered, perhaps you might not have done it in the first place," I told him.

"There is that, Skipper. But on the positive side, we'll get to see the general's house close up, which should be rather fun."

I wasn't sure that I was particularly enamoured of the idea of being confronted with an irate general, but I forbore to say so. Jonty was irrepressible and would undoubtedly remain so for the rest of the war.

"Don't disappear anywhere in the meantime," I told him.

"I shall be playing chess, Skipper," he replied. "I can't get into trouble doing that."

Considering the arguments he and Willie had over their chess games, I didn't agree with his assessment. However, I watched them proceed into the hut, after which Angelica and I went to our bench.

"Poor Jonty," said Angelica, leaning into me. "He never seems to be able to stay in Bentley's good books."

I put my arm around her. "Perhaps he might redeem himself by helping us catch the thief," I said without much optimism.

"I wonder what the general is like," she mused.

We were soon to discover what General Grimthorne was like as we presented ourselves outside his front door at four o'clock that afternoon. I glanced around at the well-kept lawns and the picket fence with neat hedges. To the side of his rather large residence was an expanse of lawn. We all knew that he grew vegetables at the back of his house and seemed to be enjoying his retirement in spite of the war. Jonty's antics were probably the only thing to disturb his peaceful existence.

Bentley rapped smartly on the door, which was opened by a young woman who I assumed was a housemaid.

"Ah, sirs," she said. "The general is expecting you. Please come in."

We filed into a large square hallway, which was lined with dark wood. On the walls hung various paintings and antique-looking weapons, the sort of décor one might expect a military man to have. There was a large staircase in the centre.

"Come this way, please," said the maid, leading us through a door and into an inordinately large living room with a sizeable fireplace. The room extended out into a conservatory that looked out onto the lawns.

General Grimthorne was seated in one of the easy chairs. He was well into his fifties with a very large handlebar moustache that rivalled Bentley's by a good margin. He had a ruddy complexion and grey hair. Even though he was retired, he was still wearing his uniform. I imagined this was on account of the war, although it seemed unlikely he would be called up if he had not been so far.

The general stood up to greet us.

"Ah, good afternoon, sir," said Bentley, saluting him.

We all followed suit.

"Hello, hello," said the general, who seemed in quite an affable mood. "Thank you for coming. I've taken the liberty of arranging for some tea."

He gestured towards a table on one side where there were plates of sandwiches and cakes, plus a pot of tea with several cups, a milk jug and sugar bowl. I wasn't quite expecting this, and it seemed that neither was Bentley from his look of surprise. Bentley was naturally far too polite to demur.

"Please," said the general, "have a seat."

We arranged ourselves on various sofas and armchairs. I sat next to Angelica, Bentley next to Audrey. Jonty and Willie took an armchair each, along with Gordon, who had driven us to the general's house. Bentley had insisted on Gordon joining us inside. Audrey had driven Bentley in a staff car.

"You wanted to see me, I gather," said the general once we were all seated.

"Yes, sir, we did. Pilot Officer Butterworth here has something he'd like to say," said Bentley, gesturing for Jonty to stand up.

Jonty did so while the general regarded him with interest.

"General Grimthorne," he said, "I just wanted to say that…" He hesitated.

Jonty's attention had been taken by something at the far end of the living room. I followed his gaze. I had not noticed it before, but there was a very large model train set laid out on a table. It was well landscaped with hills, trees, little figures and trains among other things.

"Ahem."

Bentley glared at Jonty and indicated that he should continue. Jonty tore his gaze away from the trainset and started again.

"General, I just wanted to give you a heartfelt apology for … for…" The trainset caught his eye yet again. "I say, is that a Hornby Dublo, sir, with a steam engine?" he blurted out.

"Butterworth!" barked Bentley as Jonty went completely off-script.

However, the general was instantly diverted. "Why yes, it is," he said. "Do you know it?"

"I had one myself, sir, though nothing on the scale of this. It looks magnificent."

Much to Bentley's visible annoyance, the general got out of his chair.

"Would you like a closer look?" he asked Jonty.

"Rather! It looks absolutely spiffing," came the reply.

"Come over and I'll show you," said Grimthorne. He turned to the maid, who was standing ready. "Hannah, serve the tea to my guests while I show this young enthusiast my railway."

"Well, if that don't beat all," said Willie under his breath, watching Jonty and Grimthorne walk over to the railway set.

Hannah offered us refreshments and cups of tea. The general and Jonty were soon engaged in animated conversation about what appeared to be Grimthorne's favourite hobby, the purpose of our visit completely forgotten.

In the meantime, we consumed the rather excellent fare and sipped our tea. Bentley, resigned to the unexpected turn of events, took out his pipe. He lit it and puffed away, listening to Jonty singing the praises of General Grimthorne's model railway.

Eventually, the general seemed to remember that we were also present. "Oh, I say," he said. "How very remiss of me. I was quite carried away. Has Hannah been taking care of you?"

"Admirably, sir," I said, stepping into the breach.

"Well, I'll take a cup of tea," said Grimthorne. "And you must have one too … Butterworth, is it?"

"Yes, sir, thank you," said Jonty.

Hannah served them tea while Bentley decided that, in spite of things not going quite to plan, he would see to it that Jonty made his apology.

"Now then, Butterworth," he said. "What were you saying to the general before?"

"Ah," said Jonty. He placed his teacup down on the table and stood up. "General," he said with far more confidence than he had evinced at the beginning of the visit, "I am extremely sorry about the dive-bombing incident this morning and on a number of other occasions."

"So that was you, was it?" said Grimthorne.

"Yes, sir, I'm afraid so, sir, and —"

"Oh, stuff and nonsense," the general continued. "Nothing wrong with a bit of high jinks. God knows I got up to some when I was your age. The scourge of my commanding officer, he used to say, but now look at me."

"He really *ought* to apologise, sir," said Bentley, looking somewhat aggrieved that the purpose of us being there had been thwarted.

"Oh, never mind it. It's all forgotten about," said the general dismissively. "I won't hear another word about it."

With that, we finished our tea while the general regaled us with a few stories about the Great War. He was pleased to hear that Gordon had also served, and the two of them had quite a conversation about it.

Finally, Bentley decided enough was enough and called a halt to the proceedings. "Thank you, sir, for your kind hospitality," he said. "But duty calls."

"Going so soon?" said the general. "Butterworth, you must come and visit me again. We'll have a play with my trains, eh?"

"I would like that excessively, sir," said Jonty.

"I'll hold you to it, young whippersnapper," said Grimthorne as we all stood up.

We saluted and took our leave. I was left with the impression that the general had enjoyed our social call after all. Perhaps he was quite lonely. I decided that I would encourage Jonty to take him up on his offer.

Hannah saw us out and we walked down the path to the cars.

"Don't think this absolves you of anything, Butterworth," said Bentley. "Do not even think of buzzing the general's house again."

"No, sir," said Jonty.

"Stuff and nonsense," said Bentley bitterly to no one in particular. "I'll give him stuff and nonsense the next time he phones up to complain. Audrey, let's get back to Banley. I've got plenty to catch up on after kicking my heels in there for the best part of an hour."

"Yes, sir," said Audrey, opening the car door for him.

"Well," said Angelica as we watched the staff car pull away, "looks like fortune was smiling on you, Jonty."

"Yes, indeed," he agreed. "That was a stroke of luck, him having a train set."

"You'll never grow up, will you?" said Willie as we climbed into the jeep.

"Perhaps he shouldn't after all," mused Angelica. "He wouldn't be the same old Jonty if he did."

"Let's go home, Fred," I said, though privately I thought perhaps Angelica was right.

The following afternoon I held a formal briefing. M Flight were assembled, along with Bentley, Audrey, Kenneth and the Marx Brothers. I was up at the front with the Marx Brothers.

"The mission — which we are going to call Operation Thunder Flash — is to attack the Dutch port of Den Helder," I said. "This is a significant base for the Kriegsmarine, but it's also heavily defended by ack-ack batteries. This means we will be dive-bombing while facing flak. Flight Lieutenant McCracken will give us some tips on that in a moment."

I paused, but the others looked impassive. Bentley was smoking his pipe, happy to take a back seat.

"As with the other missions," I continued, "we will stage a dawn attack, since that's the best chance we've got of taking Jerry by surprise. That means that we will leave Banley as soon as it starts to get light. We will fly up to Great Yarmouth and then directly across the water to Den Helder. We will be flying at low level to try and keep under the radar."

On the wall was an enlarged map of the port and surroundings.

"Den Helder is on the northern end of a peninsula and effectively opens onto an inland sea," I said, pointing it out on the map. "There is a sandbar at the entrance to the inland sea, and we will fly to the left of it."

I indicated the route that we would be taking.

"The port will be on our right-hand side, and we will attack the port from the north. We will fan out in an attack line in our sections. You will pick a target on approach, concentrating on any ships that are docked in the harbour. Then we will execute a dive-bombing attack in unison, drop the ordnance and get out over the water the same way we came in."

"Are we expecting any defence by the Luftwaffe?" asked Arjun when I'd finished speaking.

"I can't say for sure," I replied. "But what I can say is that we will be fully armed so that we can defend ourselves should the need arise. However, our primary objective is to drop the bombs regardless."

"What if they come after us, Skipper?" said Jonty.

"We'll decide whether to fight or not if that happens," I said.

It would be impossible to say in advance, since these situations could develop without warning. That was the hazard of going in over enemy territory.

"I'll now ask the Flight Lieutenant to give us the benefit of his advice."

Kenneth stood up. "I can't tell you much, except try not to get shot," he said to a ripple of laughter. "But joking aside, your time in the flak zone will be limited. Once you are in that dive, you can't do much about it except keep diving and hope it doesn't hit you. You are a moving target and dropping at the same time, so that makes it harder for the gunners. Don't be deflected from your course — just drop the bombs and then go."

"I'll now ask my colleagues from MI6 if they want to say anything," I said, indicating the Marx Brothers, who had up until now been smoking while they listened. The two of them put their cigarettes out simultaneously and stepped forward.

"I can't stress the importance of this mission enough," said Harpo. "From the perspective of Den Helder being a strategic port, any damage we can do is beneficial to the war effort."

"However," said Chico, "we also want to prove that Spitfires can take up the role of fighter bombers and, in this case, dive-bombers. This is something the War Office is keen to find out."

"The Mavericks have been picked because of your excellent track record of carrying out missions. It needs fearless and skilled pilots," said Harpo. "And you are *it*. We wish you the best of luck."

The two of them, having had their say, sat back down. I looked over to where Bentley was sitting, still smoking his pipe. He stood up after giving me a quick nod.

"I've not much to add," he said, "except do your duty, as I know you will. As I always say, make sure you come back and bring those bloody planes back in one piece. Just because we've got a whole lot of spares doesn't mean we need to use them."

This raised a few smiles. Bentley sat down and I wrapped things up.

"I encourage you to study the photographs of the port and get an idea of the layout. We're not designating targets, as I said. We will pick them when we get there. Are there any questions?"

Dylan raised his hand. "When exactly are we going?"

"In a few days' time," I said. "I will let you know the day before, but, in the meantime, keep up the practice. We'll also be doing a rehearsal of the mission tomorrow."

There were no further questions, so I ended the briefing. Tomas came up to me as the others were leaving.

"So, Scottish," he said, "we are the guinea pigs once again…"

I smiled. "The Marx Brothers say it's because we're so good at the missions," I replied wryly.

"Ah, and you believe this?" he scoffed.

"I'd rather believe that than we're an experimental squadron," I told him.

"Maybe you're right, Scottish, maybe you're right."

When he had gone, Angelica wound her arms around my neck. I pulled her close and held her tight. I knew she was feeling anxious. Sometimes words were not enough.

"What now?" she said.

"Perhaps we should put Operation Teapot into action," I replied with a smile. If nothing else, it would be a diversion from the impending mission.

"All right," she smiled. "Let's go and see Jonty."

Jonty was conveniently standing outside the hut talking to Willie when we arrived. I beckoned them over.

"Jonty," I said, "it's time for Operation Teapot."

He stared at me blankly, and I thought we were going to have to explain it all over again. Then realisation hit him.

"Ah!" he said. "Right you are, Skipper."

"Make sure you tell everyone," I said.

"And in the pub tonight," Angelica added.

"We'll rendezvous after closing time and lie in wait," I told him.

I decided that the thief would wait until he was sure everyone had safely gone home to their beds before striking.

"Wilco," said Jonty.

He was as good as his word. He went inside and announced his pretended legacy. He was so voluble on the subject that I was sure that the word would spread pretty rapidly around the base.

Shortly after this, Tomas collared me again. "Scottish," he said, "what is this teapot business?"

"What do you mean?" I asked him, trying to play innocent.

It didn't work.

"Come on, Scottish, come on. I know that something is going on. You are setting some bait, no?"

Nothing got past Tomas, so I told him the plan.

"Ah, well, how do you know that the thief is going to wait until closing time?" he said.

"I just thought he might," I replied.

"I will stay when the others have gone, just in case, then you can come later," he replied.

I was forced to admit this was a better idea. "All right, but if he turns up before we get there, I don't want to arrive and find a dead body," I said in admonishing tones.

"Ah, not dead no, but he might have a bump on his head."

I sincerely hoped the thief wouldn't come earlier. The chances were he might not come at all, but I felt that the lurid descriptions of the teapot were enough to tempt anyone. Besides, Angelica had obtained the actual artefact from Audrey, and Jonty was able to show it around, so several people had now seen it. If Willis was indeed the thief, it would be bound to reach his ears.

Later that night Angelica, Jonty, Willie, Gordon and I returned to the hut. It was in darkness, and we approached it cautiously. I knocked on the door. It was opened by Tomas.

"He hasn't been yet," he hissed in a stage whisper. "You'd better come inside."

We entered the hut and arranged ourselves near the back to wait, hiding behind the furniture. The teapot had been placed on a table in the middle of the room.

The minutes ticked by, and closing time came and went. After another half an hour, Jonty whispered, "I don't think he's coming, Skipper."

"Quiet," said Willie.

"We will wait a little longer," I told him.

I remembered all the times on patrol that Jonty had vowed we wouldn't see any Germans, only for them to suddenly appear. I wondered if the same might occur now.

A few minutes later, in the gloom, I saw Tomas hold a finger to his lips. The door handle to the hut was slowly turning. I stiffened and drew my pistol. The others did likewise. Jonty's jinx had struck again.

The door opened, and a torch came on. It was extremely bright. We stayed crouched down, stock-still. The torch did a cursory sweep of the room while we kept our heads below the furniture. Then the beam lit up the table, where the teapot sat in all its glory.

The figure holding the torch entered the room. It was impossible to see who it was behind the beam of the torch. The figure began to advance towards the table. It was moments like these when the unexpected usually happened.

Percy, who had been quietly sleeping on his perch, suddenly erupted into loud squawking. "Aaaark," he cawed. "Aaaark, look out, look out, aaark!"

The thief shone the torch on the bird, who started repeating, "Put that light out, put that light out," over and over again.

Tomas decided it was time to act and stood up, pointing his revolver. "Stop or I will shoot!" he shouted at the intruder.

Now he'd blown our cover, the rest of us stood up too. The tableau remained frozen for only a second before the torch went out and the thief bolted for the door. He slammed it behind him as he ran.

"After him!" said Tomas as he rushed towards the door, followed by the rest of us.

"Can you see anything?" I said, once we were outside. I peered around the base, but there was no sign of anybody.

"The thief must have run like the wind," said Tomas.

"That's torn it," said Willie to Jonty. "Your bloody parrot!"

"Percy couldn't help it. He was scared," said Jonty, jumping to the defence of his precious pet.

"Better lock up the hut," I said. "Then let's look around the base and see if we can find any trace of the thief."

"I don't think we'll find him," said Tomas gloomily.

"Nevertheless, we can look," I said firmly, reluctant to give up quite so easily.

We took a tour around all of the buildings to no avail until we arrived at the Nissen hut, which was usually occupied by Willis. There were no lights on and no sign of occupation.

"Why don't we try the door?" suggested Gordon.

I couldn't imagine that the place would be left open, but I thought perhaps it was worth a shot. "Go on then," I agreed.

Gordon turned the handle, and to my surprise, the door opened. It swung inward. He looked at me as if seeking permission to enter. We had the perfect excuse to take a look inside.

"Let's go in," I told him.

We entered the hut, which was in darkness. There was nothing untoward among the stacked shelves. I could just make out the desk at the end. Suddenly, a door opened. There was the click of a switch, and the place was flooded with light.

Willis was standing in his pyjamas, holding a pistol. He took in our sudden appearance with what appeared to be surprise mixed with irritation.

"What do you want?" he demanded.

"We're just checking on security," said Gordon smoothly.

"In here? At this time of night?" said Willis with some belligerence.

I decided to take a hand in the proceedings, watching for his reaction.

"There was a prowler on the base, and your door was open. Did you see anyone?" I asked him.

He didn't seem fazed by the question. "No, I've been asleep."

"Weren't you at the pub a while back?" Jonty put in.

"What of it?" Willis shot back.

"When did you leave?" asked Willie.

Willis began to look a little discomposed. "Are you accusing me of something?"

"Just asking questions," I said. "Do you always leave your door unlocked at night?"

It was something one might forget if a person was in a hurry to conceal themselves. Willis didn't look as if he'd been running, but then it had taken us a while to reach the Nissen hut.

Willis erupted unexpectedly. "You *are* accusing me! You're saying I'm the thief, aren't you?"

We all exchanged glances, since none of us had implied he was involved.

"Of course not," I said soothingly, but Willis was now full of bluster and fury.

"I won't stand for it! I'm here to do my job, just the same as the rest of you, and you barge in here with all sorts of accusations."

"We haven't made any accusations," said Gordon evenly. "All we said was that we were looking for a prowler."

"You may as well have," Willis continued. "Do you want to search my room too? Go on then. Maybe you'll find all the stolen goods in there."

It was a double bluff. He knew that we couldn't take him up on the offer. We had no choice but to stage a tactical withdrawal.

"It's fine. We're leaving — sorry to bother you," I said.

"You should think first before accusing people of doing things they haven't done, sir," he said, putting on an aggrieved tone.

"Goodnight, Sergeant," I said ushering the others outside.

As we walked away, I heard the door being locked. It confirmed my suspicions that he had forgotten to do so.

"What did you make of that?" said Willie once we were out of earshot.

"A guilty man often gives himself away," said Gordon.

We all knew what he meant.

"Ah, you should have let me search his room," said Tomas.

"And what if we didn't find anything?" I replied. "Then we'd have to explain ourselves to Bentley. I couldn't take the risk."

"He's guilty," said Tomas. "We didn't catch him this time, but we will."

"I think we've done enough for one night," I said. "We'd best collect the teapot and go home."

It didn't seem wise to leave it in the hut overnight. It might occur to the thief to try again.

CHAPTER FOURTEEN

The following morning, it was no surprise that I found myself in Bentley's office. I had to report to him anyway, but true to form, Audrey was there to meet me as the jeep pulled up.

"No need to tell me," I said. "Bentley wants to see me."

She laughed. "Yes, sir."

I took Angelica with me but elected not to go mob-handed by including the others, as it probably wouldn't help Bentley's temper.

Once we arrived and were seated, Bentley went through his pipe routine. After his initial annoyance at losing his old pipe, he now seemed quite resigned to it.

"I've just had a call from Sergeant Willis's senior officer," he said, "who demanded to know why we're accusing his sergeant of thievery. I assume you have a good explanation?"

His manner was quite calm, but I chose my words carefully so as not to set him off.

"We put Operation Teapot into action last night, sir," I said.

"And what in the blue blazes is Operation Teapot?" he demanded in irascible tones.

"It was the bait, sir, for the trap I told you about that we set to catch the thief," I told him.

He puffed on his pipe for a moment. "A teapot?" he said, sounding incredulous. "You used a teapot as bait?"

"Well, it's a rather special one, sir," I began, realising that unless I got on and told him the whole, we might be there all morning.

When I had finished and Audrey had shown him the teapot in question, he was somewhat mollified.

"So, the plan failed," he said flatly.

"We might have caught him if —"

"If it hadn't been for that blasted parrot of Butterworth's," he said, cutting in.

"That was rather unfortunate, yes, sir," I replied.

He pointed the stem of the pipe in our direction. "I knew it was a mistake letting that bloody parrot onto this airbase," he said crossly.

"You can hardly blame the parrot, sir," I said, trying to defend poor Percy's honour. "It was probably a natural reaction ... if you're a parrot."

Bentley wasn't in the mood to hear it. "I most certainly *can* blame it. Wretched bird has caused enough trouble ... going up in Spitfires, for one thing."

"To be fair, sir, it was Butterworth who took him up," I replied at the risk of reminding Bentley of another of Jonty's follies.

"Yes," he said. "Another of that bloody fool's addlepated pranks. Well, all right, but just tell Butterworth to keep his bloody parrot under control in future."

I glanced at Angelica, who was suppressing a smirk. Hopefully, Bentley didn't see it.

"Yes, sir, I will," I said.

"Anyway, as much as it pains me to say it, you'd better leave off any further action looking for the thief for the moment. Needless to say, nothing got returned after that meeting. We're just going to have to let it go for now," he said. "For one thing, I can't abide any more complaints from Willis or his superior."

"We'll concentrate on the mission from now on, sir," I assured him, discretion being the better part of valour.

"See that you do. We can discuss the thievery question after that," he replied.

It seemed that he was somewhat reluctant to let the issue drop altogether. I didn't see how we were going to catch Willis in any case, if it really was him.

"Very well," he continued. "Carry on."

We took this as a dismissal. Once we were outside the building, Angelica started laughing.

"I'm sorry," she said and then, by way of explanation, "Jonty's parrot."

I soon saw the funny side too and we both laughed.

"What are we going to do now?" she asked me as she caught her breath.

"Nothing much we can do," I said. "Willis seems to have got us stymied for the moment, so unless he makes a wrong move, we're at a stalemate."

"Then I sincerely hope he does," said Angelica firmly.

I had to agree with her on that score. The mission would now become our main focus.

We took off after lunch and flew in formation quite some distance from the range, where a target from the previous practice was still set out. I decided that we didn't need to drop any further ordnance until the actual mission. We knew that part of it worked. It was simply the logistics of dive-bombing as a single group.

Once we reached the waypoint that I had set, I took the flight back towards the target zone at speed and at low level.

"Target in sight," I said. "Attack!"

Each pilot was to pick a spot and then keep it in their gunsight when they dived. I climbed to six thousand feet along with the rest of the flight, who kept pace. Then I tilted the nose down and began to dive. Eleven other Spitfires dived with me.

At three thousand feet, I said, "Bombs away."

This was the cue to flatten out of the dive and bank away as fast as possible from the drop zone. I turned to the left, and everyone else followed suit. It seemed to have been a successful rehearsal. I was just contemplating whether we should go again for good measure, when Dylan let out a cry.

"Bandits, three o'clock and coming in fast," he said.

I could hardly believe my ears, but there they were, Focke-Wulfs coming in on the attack.

"Break, break, pick a mark and engage," I said, there being nothing else to do. "Control, we're under attack. Our position is over the firing range."

The tower would probably scramble Judd's squadron if they were available to help. I didn't have time to think about where the Germans had come from or why.

I flew towards one of the Wulfs, while the rest of the flight engaged the others. I sighed. It was the last thing we needed.

The radio was filled with chatter.

"I'm on his tail. I've got him in my sights."

"Fire, fire!"

"He's behind you."

"Watch out — turn, turn now!"

The Wulf I had picked out opened fire, and I had to execute a sharp turn. Tracers flew past me, just missing my plane. He was angling to get behind me, but I turned again to come at him from the side. He banked away sharply.

Now I was chasing him while he started weaving. He tried to loop and roll so I would become a target, but I was wise to this and evaded the manoeuvre.

"I've got him! I've got him!" said Dylan triumphantly.

Out of the corner of my eye, I saw a smoking Wulf dive to earth. That was one down. However, the Wulf I was battling with was wily and fast.

I fired off a couple of bursts, which missed, then I heard Jonty in full war cry.

"Tally-ho, Skipper," he said gleefully as he opened fire on my Wulf from the side.

The German hadn't seen him. Jonty had managed to shake off his pursuer to come to my aid. The Jerry's canopy shattered, and the plane dove downwards.

"Thanks, Jonty," I said.

In spite of his wayward antics, he could always be relied on in a dogfight.

I saw one more German get hit before they broke off contact just as suddenly as they had arrived. Over in the distance, I saw the reason. Judd's flight was coming to our rescue.

"Here comes the cavalry," said Arjun.

Judd's squadron went off in hot pursuit of the fleeing Jerries.

"Thanks, Blue Leader," I said to him over the radio.

"Don't mention it," he replied.

"M Flight, let's return to base," I said. "Form up."

We took up our usual formation and headed back to Banley, landing in short order. As soon as my kite was at the standing, Angelica came running over to me.

I caught her in an embrace, and she kissed me.

"Oh God," she said. "I couldn't believe it when those Wulfs turned up."

"Join the club," I remarked wryly.

There was a discreet cough beside us, which could only be Bentley. Angelica detached herself and stood next to me.

"What happened, Angus?" said Bentley, looking concerned. He took out his pipe and began to light it.

"We got jumped by Jerry, sir," I replied. "Came out of nowhere while we were practising our mission."

"Hmm," he said, looking serious. "Coincidence or something else?"

"I don't know, sir," I said.

It did seem odd that they had turned up like that, although it could have been a random attack. We'd had similar events happen before, which had turned out to be due to a spy.

"Is it likely anyone knows about your mission target?" asked Bentley.

"No, sir," I said. "But they would have seen us practising for something, if that's what you mean."

We both knew what he meant. Could there be yet another spy in our midst? Bentley puffed on his pipe for a moment.

"What do you want to do?" he said at length.

"Regarding what, sir?" I replied.

"The mission."

Did I want to abort the mission? That was what he was asking. On the one hand, it might be wise, but on the other hand, moving swiftly might negate anything a spy, if there was one, might have told the Germans. I didn't think the Germans were aware of our target; the Marx Brothers would have discovered that if so. The mission room was kept under lock and key and also guarded once the mission orders released.

"We'll go tomorrow morning, sir," I told him. "That's the only sensible thing to do."

Now we'd worked so hard for this mission, I wanted to see it through.

"All right," said Bentley. "Tell nobody except your ground crew and M Flight. It's your mission, but I support your decision."

He turned on his heel and walked away with Audrey.

"I'm sorry," I said, turning to Angelica. "You know that —"

She put a finger to my lips. "I know," she said. "It's okay. You've got to do it. Just come back, all right?"

Now that Bentley had gone, the rest of the flight crowded around me.

"That was quite a to-do," said Arjun.

"Damn Jerries, always turning up where they're not wanted," said Jean.

We all laughed.

"Come into the hut," I said to the rest of the flight. "I have something to say."

That night, Angelica and I had eaten dinner early and gone to bed. We'd be leaving at the crack of dawn on the raid.

As we lay in bed, she sighed a little theatrically. "You know, I should really be quite cross with you," she said softly.

I turned to her and pulled her close. "Because I'm going on a mission?"

"No, you have to do that. But we could have gone to our hotel for the night, if it wasn't so soon."

Angelica liked to spend a night away sometimes as a treat. We'd got used to doing it before important events. This time it couldn't be helped.

"We can go when I come back," I said.

"I'll hold you to that," she whispered.

We kissed, and the mission was temporarily forgotten.

All too soon, the alarm went off for our early start. We got dressed and headed downstairs to the dining room. As usual,

Gordon had arranged for those of us going on the mission to be given an early meal.

Jonty, Willie and the others were there, tucking into eggs, beans, toast and some ham on the side.

I accepted my plate of food from one of the maids and started eating. Angelica sat down beside me and did likewise.

"What-ho, Skipper," said Jonty. "Ready for the fray?"

"As I'll ever be," I said.

"Well, I am," said Dylan, who was always up for action.

There was an undercurrent of excitement in the room. I could feel it. Perhaps Angelica felt it too. She reached out, touched my arm and smiled.

All too soon, we were on our way to Banley Airfield. I sat in the back of the jeep with Angelica, holding her close. Gordon, who was normally quite talkative, let us have our moment.

We both knew this wasn't an easy mission. The dive-bombing put us in pole position to get hit by enemy fire. We'd studied the photographs. There were plenty of flak batteries on and around the port. The Germans were known to be very good at their air defences. I tried not to think about it. It was easier to play the cards once they were dealt. In spite of all the intelligence we'd had, there were too many unknowns about this mission.

We arrived at Banley and jumped down from the jeep.

"Good luck, sir," said Gordon. "Godspeed."

"Thanks, Fred," I replied with a smile.

As we walked away, he lit up a cigarette. The light from his match flared briefly, and then all that was left was a small glow in the darkness.

Angelica tucked her arm into mine, and shortly afterwards we arrived at the hut. The rest of the flight was there, waiting for the off.

"Do whatever you need to do," I told them. "We'll be leaving as soon as it starts to get light."

While we were waiting, Bentley and Audrey arrived at the hut unexpectedly.

"At ease," he said, before we could all snap to attention. "I just came to see you all off and to say good luck. I know you will all do your duty and do it well. Come back safely and preferably in one piece."

"Thank you, sir," I said.

Outside, the sky was beginning to turn grey. It was time to go.

"All right, chaps," I said. "Let's get to it and get this done."

Bentley moved discreetly to one side while the rest of the pilots made for their planes. I turned to Angelica and pulled her into an embrace.

"Come back safe, darling," she said.

"I will. I love you."

"I love you too."

In the pale dawning light, I saw her eyes were a little moist.

"I *will* be back," I told her firmly, to ease her fears.

As our fingers parted, I flicked a salute to Bentley, who was standing smoking his pipe. Then I went to my Spitfire and climbed up onto the wing.

Redwood helped me into the cockpit and to strap in.

"The bombs are all loaded, sir, releases checked, guns all primed and ready with full ammo," he said.

"Thanks, Techie," I replied.

"Fly safe," he said, before jumping down. "The boys painted a few messages on the bombs for Jerry."

I laughed. I could imagine what they were. I'd heard tales of ground crews writing, 'This one's for Adolf' and suchlike on the bombs before they were loaded.

I spun up the prop, and the Merlin roared to life. It joined the dawn chorus of the other eleven Spitfires. I waved to Angelica, and she blew me a kiss. I could see Bentley saluting us as we taxied to the end of the runway.

In moments we were airborne in the stillness of the early morning sky. I set a bearing which would take us up to Great Yarmouth, past Ipswich, Stowmarket, Framlingham and Lowestoft. I elected to fly overland and close to the ground to avoid detection by the Germans.

"Nighthawks," I said. "Low-level flying, formation on me, here we go."

I had chosen Nighthawks as the codename. It seemed appropriate. We were going to fly in and swoop down on Jerry from on high, just like a hawk.

The ground flashed by beneath us as we flew over fields, farms, trees and hedges. It wasn't a long trip to Den Helder and we would hopefully have the advantage of surprise. We were flying as fast as I dared, time being of the essence.

The landscape began to turn from monochrome into weak, washed-out colours. The full glory would not be seen until sunup. I hoped that by then we'd be on our way home.

For the most part, we kept radio silence. Secrecy was vital. The Germans listened in on many frequencies, which meant the less said, the better when heading into enemy territory.

At length, the seaside town of Great Yarmouth loomed up before us. The white sand of the beach stretched out along the shoreline. I took us on a course just south of the town, and within moments we were over the water.

The Channel was grey and slightly choppy, an endless vista of water. We were flying just above wave height, which took most of my attention. I had fixed a bearing that was intended to bring us to the sandbar at the entrance to Den Helder harbour.

"Keep your eyes peeled, Nighthawks," I said.

I didn't expect to encounter a Jerry patrol, but if we did, then that could ruin the mission altogether.

Fortunately, nothing untoward occurred, and before long, the large teardrop-shaped sandbank appeared, signifying the mouth of the inland sea. My pulse began to quicken as we got closer.

I set a course to bring us around to the left of the sandbar and then head directly down the middle of the passage between the sandbar on our right and the land on our left.

I flicked an anxious glance toward the shoreline, but there was no sign of movement or any indication that we had been spotted. So far, so good.

As we cleared the inlet, I could see the peninsula in front of us. At the end of it was the port of Den Helder. The buildings, grey hulks of ships and bunkers were clear enough. I turned and took the flight parallel to the shore until we were lined up with the port. This was it. The culmination of all of our training. All of the practice would come down to just a few minutes of intense action. My heart began to thump in my chest.

"Nighthawks, attack formation," I said. "Target is on our three o'clock."

This was the signal. We turned and fanned out into a line but remained together in our sections. We were now approaching the port at speed. I could see some of the larger ships in the harbour. We were lucky; the German Navy was in port.

"Pick your targets," I said, fixing my attention on a large vessel in front of me. Without really thinking, I knew it was time. "Nighthawks climb."

I pulled up on the stick and watched the altimeter going up. For a long moment, there was no response from the port, and then all hell broke loose.

Bursts of flame spewed out from the ack-ack below, and flak was starting to fill the air. Puffs of black smoke with deadly metal shards began exploding all around.

There was no time to think. My heart was racing and the adrenaline coursed through my veins.

The altimeter hit six thousand. It was the moment of truth.

"Dive," I said.

Twelve Spitfires plummeted to earth.

"Jesus Christ Almighty," said Dylan as the flak began bursting around us.

It was akin to diving into Dante's *Inferno*, trying not to get killed while at the same time keeping an eye on all the instruments and the proposed target in the gunsight.

There was a burst of flak near my cockpit. I heard a couple of pings as if some metal had hit my plane. I kept diving, hoping it wasn't something vital. If it was, then it was too late anyway. I would deliver the payload regardless.

"That was bloody close," said Jonty on my wing.

The altimeter showed three thousand feet.

"Bombs away," I said, releasing them onto the ship below.

"Bombs away..." the cry echoed through the squadron.

Thirty-six bombs whistled to earth. Flak burst all around us. My one purpose now was to get out with all speed. I flattened off and banked sharply away from the port.

"Get out! Get the hell out, Nighthawks!" I yelled down the radio.

The bombs hit and exploded one after the other. A huge fireball filled the air. We didn't have the luxury of checking the target; that would be for the reconnaissance planes to do later.

Then came a shout I had been dreading.

"I'm hit, I've been hit," said Casmir. "My engine."

I glanced quickly in his direction. Smoke was pouring from his kite. He must have taken a direct hit from a flak barrage.

"Bail," I said frantically, knowing there was nothing I could do to help him. "Bail out."

We turned away from the port, making for the sandbar. In the periphery of my vision, I saw a parachute. Casmir had made it, although the war would now be over for him.

The rest of us were remarkably still intact. Ack-ack batteries opened up from the shoreline, now they knew we were there. Tracers started hurtling towards us, but we just had to keep going.

I set a course for home, flying directly over the sandbar. There was no point in returning to low level; we were well and truly in the Jerries' sights.

Tracers spewed up into the air and flak continued to explode around us. Then it was behind us, and the worst of it was over.

"Is everyone okay?" I asked as the sandbar eased away below us. In moments, we were out over the open water.

"Took a few pings, Skipper, I think," said Jonty.

The answers came back affirmative from the others as the flight formed up on me, minus one aircraft. We'd been lucky, but I wondered if we would continue to be so. I eased the safety off my guns, anticipating retaliation from the Luftwaffe.

Halfway across the Channel, it arrived.

"Bandits on our nine o'clock," said Arjun. "They're coming in fast."

I looked over to see some Focke-Wulfs heading our way. A quick mental calculation told me we probably would not outrun them. In any case, I decided, what the hell? My blood was up.

"Break, Nighthawks, break. Let's take them," I said.

"You want a fight, Jerry?" said Tomas belligerently. "Now you will get a fight."

In moments, we engaged with the German planes. We were all hyped up on adrenaline from the bombing raid, and our reactions seemed to be faster than usual.

I picked a mark and flew towards him. He started to flick his plane away from me, but I had him in my sights and fired.

The bullets hit home, shredding his wing. The Wulf went into a flat spin, diving into the water. I turned my attention to finding the next one.

The Mavericks were diving and weaving in and out of the German planes.

"Yes, I got him," said Jules as another German headed downwards, with smoke pouring from his engine.

"Take that, you Jerry!" It was Harold, who peppered the tail of a Wulf, which turned and started for home.

I saw my chance with another German who was chasing Willie. I got behind him and fired. The bullets struck his wings. He dropped down abruptly towards the sea. Then I saw him recover and start to make for the Dutch coast.

All of a sudden, the Wulfs broke off their engagement. They started to hightail it back to friendlier skies. In the distance, I saw a patrol of British Hurricanes flying in our direction. The Germans didn't like the odds.

"Just in the nick of time," said Stanley.

Although we were getting the better of the Jerries, it was probably just as well.

"All right, Nighthawks, let's go home," I said.

We formed up while the Hurricanes flew on past us, giving us a wave. The Germans were long gone.

Great Yarmouth passed below. It seemed only a few moments ago that we'd left it. The speed and intensity of the action had made the minutes seem to flash by. In no time at all, we were over Banley, and then we landed.

I taxied my Spitfire to the standing and killed the engine with some relief. As I jumped down from the wing, I saw Angelica hurtling towards me. I braced for the inevitable impact.

"Oof!" I said as she landed in my arms.

"Thank God you are safe," she said, kissing me with all the fervour she could muster.

"I'm glad to be home," I told her as soon as I could speak.

"Was it very bad?" she asked.

"It was something I'd prefer not to keep doing, if I'm honest," I said with a smile. "It was fraught but over in a jiffy."

I spied Bentley and Audrey walking towards us. Angelica let me go and stood beside me to await their arrival.

"You made it back ... bar one," said Bentley, taking his pipe from his pocket.

"Yes, sir. I'm afraid Casmir was hit, but as far as I could tell, he bailed," I said.

Bentley lit his pipe and smoked it for a few moments. "Yes," he said. "A damn shame ... though you're lucky it wasn't more."

He gestured with the stem of his pipe to our planes. I hadn't really paid much attention to them when we landed, but looking at them in full daylight, I could see that several had sustained some flak damage, including my own.

"Holes everywhere," said Bentley.

"There was a lot of flak, sir," I told him.

"So, I can see."

He puffed on his pipe a little longer. I wondered if he was going to complain about it, but instead, to my surprise, he said,

"Oh well, can't be helped. Redwood's team is going to have a lot of repairs to do. Anyway, well done, Angus."

With that, he walked away to inspect the damage.

"I say, Skipper," said Jonty. "That was a damn fine show. It was so much fun. When can we do it again?"

"You have got to be bloody well joking," said Willie.

"No, I might even write a song about it," said Jonty, unperturbed.

"God help us all," said Willie, making a face.

"As much as you might have enjoyed it, Jonty, I sincerely hope we won't be doing it again any time soon," I told him.

"Really, Skipper? Oh blast!"

He looked so disappointed that the rest of us couldn't help but burst out laughing.

I expected that there would be a debrief soon enough, but in the meantime, Angelica and I joined the rest of the crew in the hut. Bentley had sorted out some refreshments for our return. We partook of these gratefully while the chatter was all about the mission.

I was just about to take a sip of my tea when the door to the hut opened. To my surprise, it was Sergeant Willis. In his hands, he had some packets of tea and sugar. I didn't think he was expecting to find us all in there either. However, only the slightest flicker of annoyance appeared on his face, and then it was gone.

"I've just come to replenish the supplies, sir," Willis informed me, moving into the hut.

He was no doubt conscious of a few hostile stares from the likes of Jonty and Tomas, but Willis was made of sterner stuff. He elected to brazen it out.

"Yes, fine, Sergeant," I said. "Just put it down on the table..."

The words had hardly left my mouth when Percy interrupted me.

"There he is, there he is," he squawked suddenly.

"What are you talking about, Percy?" said Jonty.

"That man ... that man ... that man," Percy went on. He clung to the bars of his cage and angled his head so that he was looking directly at Willis.

"What an odd bird," said Willis, now slightly more perturbed.

Angelica nudged me, and I noticed that Willis was sidling back to the door.

"What man, Percy?" said Jonty, sounding a little exasperated.

"Chess piece, he took it, he took it, heeee took it!" sang the parrot gleefully.

I stared at Percy and then at Willis. The alarm on his face was plain enough.

Before any of us could do anything sensible, Willis was out of the door.

"Let's get after him!" I shouted to the others, following suit.

Outside, I saw Willis hurtling across the grass at a tremendous rate. By now, the rest of the flight was outside too. I started to follow, but Willis disappeared behind a building, and then he was gone.

"So, it *was* him!" said Jonty. "He took the chess piece!"

"And my cigarette case!" said Harold.

Several others added to the clamour that Willis must be the thief who had taken their belongings. The only problem was that Willis was nowhere to be seen.

"Split up," I said. "We'll search the base."

"I'll come with you," said Tomas.

The others formed groups and headed off in different directions. I went with Tomas and Angelica in the direction of the mess. It seemed highly unlikely he was there, but then again, it might be somewhere he could hide.

Arjun, Jean and Dylan made for the main gate to alert the sentries. Others went to the hangars and outbuildings, as well as the main building.

"I don't think he will be in here," said Tomas as I started to push open the mess hall door.

Just then, a shot rang out from within. We entered the mess to discover Willis with a gun trained on Maria. Olga was lying on the floor some distance from where Maria was sitting, clutching her shoulder. A bloodstain was spreading over her blouse from a bullet wound.

"This," Willis was saying, "is for the glorious Reich."

Our intrusion onto the scene caused him to look up.

"What are you doing?" I said to him, conscious that none of us had drawn our pistols.

In the time it would take to do so, he would have fired. Keeping him talking was the only option while I tried to find a way out.

"I'm taking revenge for the Reich against this filthy traitorous harlot," he informed us.

I couldn't quite fathom how Sergeant Willis was suddenly a German spy, but there wasn't any time to ponder it.

"Why do you need to do that?" I replied. "It won't make any difference now."

"It will please the Führer, and that is all that matters. I have been given orders, and I will carry them out," he said.

We were starting to move slowly towards him as his attention shifted between us and Maria. He couldn't keep the gun trained on all of us at the same time, and he knew it.

"You can rush me, but she will die before you can reach me," he said in order to forestall any action on our part.

I was forced to acknowledge that this was true. The distance between us and him was still too great to make the attempt.

"How could you betray your king and country like this?" I demanded. "You, a respected sergeant in the forces?"

"This is not my country," he sneered. "It never was. Now it's time for her to die!"

He steadied his aim while Maria sat seemingly in passive acceptance of her fate. It was an impossible situation. I wondered fleetingly if by flinging myself on him I could close the gap and spoil his shot. Beside me, Tomas was no doubt thinking the same thing.

Before either of us could try it, Charlie the chef came out of the door to the kitchens. He took in the scene with one glance.

"Oi! What are you lot playing at?" he shouted. "No guns in my mess hall!"

Willis shifted his aim and fired at Charlie, who dived for cover. It was a calculated diversion, but just enough to give me time to intervene. Then fate took a hand.

I was about to dive at Willis when Olga suddenly said, "Now!"

Maria flung herself sideways as Willis turned back towards her. He fired at her empty seat. At the same time, Olga had slid her own gun over to Maria.

In one fluid movement Maria snatched up the gun, went up on one knee, and fired. The shot hit Willis in the chest. His body jerked, flinging his pistol away from him. But Maria didn't stop. She stood up and fired again. Willis stared at her in surprise as another bullet struck him.

Walking towards him, she fired once more. Willis went down onto his back, flung by the force of the bullet. Maria kept walking until she stood over him. Then she methodically emptied the clip.

Shot after shot rang out.

"That is for me, my people and all those your Führer has murdered in cold blood," she said as she pulled the trigger again and again until the gun was empty, and it started to click.

Angelica went up to her and gently took the pistol from her hand. "It's over," she said. "It's all over…"

Maria collapsed into her arms and started to sob violently. "I hate them, I hate them so much," she said, her voice coming out in a harsh rasp.

"Of course you do, of course. Hush now, it's over," said Angelica soothingly.

The shooting had brought everyone into the mess. There was a cry of anguish as Willie rushed over to Olga.

"Olga! Oh my God, Olga!" he said, kneeling down beside her and cradling her close. "Help, she needs help."

"Get a stretcher, someone," I said. "Get her to the medical unit, and somebody fetch Bentley."

"No need," said a voice behind me. It was Bentley. "Now then, what's all this about?"

The aftermath of the shooting took some time to sort out. Olga was ably cared for by Dr Ramachandran, who removed the bullet without too much trouble. She refused to stay in the medical unit, saying that she belonged by Maria's side.

Some of us went to check Willis's room, where a transmitting radio was discovered under his bed, as well as a German passport and other accoutrements for spying. In addition, we found a suitcase full of stolen goods.

Bentley's pipe was returned to him. His face lit up when he saw it.

"A pipe is like an old friend," he informed me. "It will never let you down…"

The following day, I was seated along with Angelica, Bentley, Audrey, Maria, Olga and Willie in the mission room with the Marx Brothers. Bentley had demanded a proper debrief.

He lit his old pipe with some satisfaction while the Marx Brothers sat smoking their cigarettes.

"That was quite a turn-up for the books," said Harpo at length.

"That's what you call it, is it?" demanded Bentley. "Another blasted spy, and an assassination attempt … yet again … on my airbase. In addition, the man was a raving kleptomaniac. I'd say it was bordering on farcical."

"We must admit that we didn't see it coming," said Chico.

"Who was Willis really?" I asked the Marx Brothers, since otherwise Bentley was bound to get exceedingly irate, goaded by their insouciance.

"Ah," said Harpo, blowing out smoke. "He's what you might call a sleeper agent for the Nazis."

"A sleeper agent?" said Bentley.

"Yes, he would have been embedded into our society quite some time ago. Then he worked his way into the RAF using logistics as a way of gaining access to all kinds of places and possibly secrets."

"Yet he wouldn't have done anything until he was activated," added Chico.

"He was activated to kill me," said Maria.

"That was quite some shooting, from what we hear," said Harpo. "You are to be congratulated."

"Olga has been teaching me," said Maria. "She said you never know when it might come in handy."

"The official story will be that Willis went rogue after he was discovered to be a thief," said Harpo. "He sustained the fatal bullet wounds while trying to escape custody."

I glanced at Angelica. She raised her eyebrows. It was only to be expected from the Marx Brothers.

"I suppose that blasted parrot has redeemed itself," said Bentley.

"Well, he did rather nail the culprit," I replied with a smile.

The discussion continued around whether Maria needed more security. It was decided that she would also be supplied with a firearm. Bentley wouldn't hear of her being removed from the base. Shortly afterwards, the meeting broke up. The Marx Brothers, Bentley and Audrey left.

"Could you maybe think about marrying me?" Willie said to Olga. "Before you get shot again?"

Olga laughed. It had been a bone of contention between them in the past.

"Well, maybe I will," she said. "Why don't we discuss it over a cup of tea at my place?"

Angelica and I watched them leave, then we were alone.

"Well, husband," she said.

"Well, wife?" I replied with a smile.

"I think there's only one way to celebrate this happy ending," she whispered, wrapping her arms around my neck.

"Oh, and what's that?" I whispered back.

"Let me show you…"

A NOTE TO THE READER

Dear Reader,

I hope that you have enjoyed this seventh volume of the Mavericks' adventures. As always, the missions are fictional but based loosely upon the types of missions that were the order of the day. The idea of attacking targets of opportunity was something which came to the fore much more strongly after D-Day when the RAF was in Europe once more, but I felt that it was nevertheless plausible that these missions would precede it, particularly after Germany's defeat in Russia.

The Spitfire was not initially used as a dive-bomber, as it was primarily designed as a fighter interceptor. However, as the war continued, new ideas and uses for the plane took hold. It was easily convertible to be a fighter bomber, even though that wasn't first envisaged as its role. Dive-bombing came to the fore in 1944 for attacking V1 rocket sites and other ground attack missions. There is a specific way that dive-bombing was to be carried out and it's written up in the *Spitfire Manual.* I tried to keep this as authentic as possible in terms of its operation.

I conceived the idea that a squadron like the Mavericks would have been used to try out the dive-bombing techniques before they became widely used, thus it became the basis for part of this particular story. The port of Den Helder was attacked many times by the allies, as it was of strategic importance to the Germans. Therefore, it's conceivable that a dive-bombing attack would have been all too likely.

Apart from that, as always I like to preserve the ready sense of humour and Jonty's predilection for pranks. Although war is a serious business, I feel that the banter and humour in my books reflects the British Blitz spirit which stayed strong throughout the war. The British always have been resourceful and readily turn to humour in the face of adversity.

I'm certain there will be more Mavericks' adventures to come, so watch this space.

I would be very grateful if you could spare the time to write a review on **Amazon** and **Goodreads**. As an author, these reviews are hugely important, and always appreciated.

You can connect with me in other ways too, via my **website**, **Facebook**, **Twitter**, **Instagram**, and a special **Spitfire Mavericks Page**.

I very much hope you were entertained enough to read the next book in the Spitfire Mavericks series.

Warmest regards,

D. R. Bailey

Sapere Books is an exciting new publisher of brilliant fiction and popular history.

To find out more about our latest releases and our monthly bargain books visit our website:
saperebooks.com